BADASS

A STEPBOTHER SEAL ROMANCE

LINDA BARLOW
& ALANA ALBERTSON

Bolero Books, LLC
POWAY, CALIFORNIA

Badass
A Stepbrother Seal Romance
Copyright © 2015 by Alana Albertson & Linda Barlow

Bolero Books, LLC
11956 Bernardo Plaza Dr. #510
San Diego, CA 92128
www.buybolerobooks.com

Publisher's Note: This is a work of fiction. Names, characters, places, and incidents are a product of the author's imagination. Locales and public names are sometimes used for atmospheric purposes. Any resemblance to actual people, living or dead, or to businesses, companies, events, institutions, or locales is completely coincidental.

Book Layout & Design – JT Formatting
Cover Design by Regina Wamba – Mae I Design

Ordering Information:
Quantity sales. Special discounts are available on quantity purchases by corporations, associations, and others. For details, contact the "Special Sales Department" at the address above.

BADASS / Alana Albertson & Linda Barlow – 1st ed.
ISBN 978-1-941665-99-2

PART ONE

CHAPTER 1

Cassie

THE FIRST TIME I SAW him, I knew he was one arrogant badass.

He had a way of standing, with his hips cocked as if he was about to drive his dick right into you. Purely for his own pleasure, with no care for yours.

I knew the type. Tall, square-jawed, body fit and honed and sculpted. He was handsome and he knew it. He *used* it. His cool, assessing blue eyes lit on me briefly as he hauled his gear off his Harley—of course he rode a Harley. He didn't look at me for long. This was a dude with a purpose, and at the moment, his purpose was diving out at the reef in La Jolla near the Children's Pool.

It was nearing sunset, but people did dive at night. Was he going in without a partner? That would be reckless, but it didn't surprise me. Mr. Bad Boy Harley-driving Asshole didn't mind taking risks. Probably an adrenaline junkie.

I couldn't seem to stop watching as he pulled off his clothes down to his swim trunks and squeezed his muscled physique into a black, shiny wetsuit. At one point, as if he sensed me, his head swiveled around and he shot me a long, silent glance. I tried to tell myself that he was looking at someone else, but I felt as if my shorts and top had been stripped away under his gaze. As if he could see me naked.

Even worse, heat shot through my belly at the thought. I *wanted* to be naked with him.

I should have known right then that he was trouble.

He donned his tank and mask and headed into the surf, holding his flippers. Just before he was swallowed up by the sea, he raised a hand, as if in salute. I looked around self-consciously. I was the only person nearby. Yup. The arrogant jerk was waving to me.

I reminded myself that I wasn't here to ogle hot divers. I often walked down to the seashore at sunset. It was a great way to relax during a stressful time. It was my first year at a new school—University of California, San Diego. Even though it was grad school, I felt like a freshman in college again. Could I do the work? Make the grade? Was I good enough, or had my admission to the program been a crazy mistake?

I'd done well in the fall quarter, but I didn't feel settled in. I'd grown up on the east coast, and I was still adjusting to the California lifestyle. Like going to the beach in February.

I'd come to watch the La Jolla sea lions and harbor seals that hung out here in large numbers, particularly during the summer breeding season. At this time of year, the animals would mostly be foraging in the water. The females would be raising their growing pups—nursing them and teaching them to hunt.

I wasn't going to get too close, because I didn't want to startle any sea lions who might be on the beach. I sat under the awning listening for their distinctive calls. I wasn't just idly curious. I was planning to do some research on the vocalizations of sea mammals. I wanted to come to a better understanding of the communication systems the animals used with each other, and I also hoped to study their cognitive abilities.

The barks and growls of the sea lions combining with the lapping of the waves soothed me, and I settled into a relaxed, almost meditative state. I'm not sure how much time went by before I was jolted into sharper awareness by what I recognized as a pup's distress call.

Shit. There was still enough light in the sky for me to see the sea lion who was agitated. I thought I recognized him as one of the pups who had been born last summer when I'd moved to La Jolla. He was the right size—about six months old. He was in the water a few yards offshore, twisting and moving his neck in a manner that I knew was unusual. I didn't see his mom around. She was probably out in deeper water, hunting.

There wasn't anything I could do. I hoped his mother would be back soon to help him. He might be sick or injured. Not all pups survived. That was the way of nature, and even though it hurt my heart to hear his distress, humans weren't supposed to intervene. There was a law against it, in fact.

Since there were no other sea lions on the beach, I crossed the rope barrier and went down to the surf. I moved slowly and quietly, not wanting to add to the animal's troubles by frightening him. He saw me and went still. So did I.

Then, to my amazement, he came closer to me. A chill went over me as his soft eyes met mine. It was the strangest thing— like looking into the trusting eyes of a faithful dog. But this was a wild creature. I must have been imagining things.

I should have left the area. His mother might show up at any time, and she would not be happy about a human interacting with her pup. He lowered his head and made another soft sound of distress. He was looking right at me.

Was he asking me for help? Whoa. Some of the sea lions had gotten quite used to people. There were always tourists coming down to the cove, trying to swim with them or teach them tricks. Usually this caused them all to scatter, but a young pup who had seen humans hanging around for all of his short life might be less frightened of us than other wild creatures.

He moved his neck again, and I realized what was wrong with him. Somehow he had gotten a twist of bright red plastic wrapped around his throat. Oh no. A surge of anger stiffened my entire body.

I wasn't sure what the plastic thing was. Probably some piece of human refuse that had been carelessly disposed of in the sea. But it looked strong and tight. If it stayed in place as he grew, it would slowly slice into his hide and cause horrific, painful wounds. He would either die of those wounds or strangle to death as his neck grew too thick for the tough plastic.

I cast a quick look around. I was alone on the beach. There was no one to see me or report me for breaking the law if I tried to help the poor creature. Normally I wouldn't do it. I'd walk away. If the pup was sick or if he'd been the victim of a predator attack, I'd accept it. Baby sea lions died. Survival of the fittest and all that.

But this was going to lead to an agonizing death because of some careless or stupid humans. And that pissed me off.

I approached the pup slowly. When he still didn't flee, I slid off my shoes and waded into the water. I was wearing shorts and a tank top. It didn't matter if my clothes got wet.

The pup gave another soft sound of distress and arched his neck. The plastic was looped around his throat and the end of it was trailing along his side. All I had to do was grab the thing and lift it over his head. It looked tight, but it wasn't cutting into his flesh. Yet. If I could get it off, he ought to be fine.

Such a little thing. I made up my mind. His eyes continued to gaze at me trustingly. I knew I couldn't turn away. I took a couple more steps into the surf. He thrashed around, as if he wasn't too sure this was a great idea.

"I know how you feel, boy," I said softly. "You and I are not supposed to interact, but hey, if some human did this to you, some human can damn well try to fix it."

I was up to my thighs in the water now, and a bit unsteady because of the incoming waves. The water wasn't exactly balmy, either. I envied that diver for his wetsuit.

I cooed to the pup, moving with infinite slowness, getting nearer and nearer, reaching out for the plastic.

It was slimy and slipped out of my hand. The sea lion bucked and made a louder noise of distress, but he didn't swim away. I got a firmer grip, steeling myself not to flinch as he thrashed. He was scared and I was breathing hard now, determined to do this before he fled in terror and was stuck with the damn thing until it killed him.

"It's okay, one more try, boy. Hang on for just another minute, okay?"

I grabbed the plastic with both hands and lifted it as quickly and smoothly as I could. The pup cringed and tossed his head and pulled me off balance. I lost my footing, but I hung on. I felt the force as he lunged away in panic, but the plastic stayed caught between my fingers. One more shake of his head and he was free.

I practically wept with relief as I saw, before he dived back into the water, that I'd removed it all. There was a mark around his neck where the damn stuff had been, but I was pretty sure his injuries would heal.

In the distance, I heard an adult sea lion bark. It was probably the pup's mother, and she sounded upset.

And then I heard a human voice, as a diver heaved up, his wetsuit gleaming, just a couple a yards away from me. "What the fuck do you think you're doing?" asked the same hell-hot biker who had tossed me that mocking salute. "You fool around with the baby and now the mother is coming for you."

And before I could say a word in my defense, the big oaf grabbed me up in his arms and carried me out of the water.

CHAPTER 2

Shane

I GRABBED MY EQUIPMENT AND headed to the water. Gorgeous sunset as usual in La Jolla, though nothing compared to the sunsets back in my home state of Montana. I missed the cool mountain breeze, the peaceful silence from the lack of tourists.

Well, at least the Southern California women were the sexiest, bar none. Tanned, incredible bodies, dressed year round in bikinis and skimpy sundresses. Most liked to party as much as I did, so I never had problems finding a hookup who wanted what I wanted—nothing but a good time.

As I took off my clothes, I saw some chick staring at me from the awning over Children's Pool. She was pretty far away but I could see her red hair, white tank, and jean shorts. I gave her a friendly wave. Maybe if she stuck around until I finished my dive, she'd be lucky enough to go home with me tonight.

The water was calm and dark. I was usually the only one out diving here at this time of the evening. But after a rough day sleeping off a "balls-to-dawn" shift busting the balls of wannabe

Navy SEALs candidates on base, I could think of no better way to relax and spend my last day in the States than a sunset dive in the La Jolla Cove. The nocturnal creatures and predators appeared, their colors that looked dull in the daytime shone vibrantly with a diving light.

Most people always dove with a buddy, but I didn't need a goddam babysitter checking my equipment for me. I had enough fucking oxygen, and if I ran out I could hold my breath for five minutes—a useful skill for stalking pirates. Also came in handy when eating pussy.

I descended into the waters, slowly swimming through my favorite cave. Saw a beautiful ray, a horn shark, a few sheep crabs, and some spiny lobsters. A yellow eel saw my light and dug itself into the sand. I spent so much time in the ocean for work, it was nice to come down here and just be able to appreciate the beauty of the marine life without having to worry about catching a terrorist.

I began my ascent, bidding goodbye to my hobby for at least nine months or quite possibly forever—I was set to deploy to the Middle East tomorrow night.

As the waves buckled under the wind and closer to the shore I saw what looked like a flame. A few strokes closer and I realized that the flame was a flash of red hair, attached to the head of a beautiful woman. The girl who'd been staring at me earlier.

I swam over to her and saw her hands touching the pup's neck. What the fuck was this bitch doing? No one was allowed down at Children's Pool, the La Jolla beach area where all the seals and sea lions reside. There was a reason the place was roped off. A fucking tourist no doubt, probably taking one of those goddam selfies with a sea lion.

She released the pup who scampered into the water. I noticed a mother sea lion rolling toward this woman.

I grabbed the girl from behind, took a moment to gaze at her plump ass. "What the fuck do you think you're doing?" My cock pressed against her soft curves, the heat from her body warmed mine up instantly. "You fool around with the baby and now the mother is coming for you."

I threw her on my back and carried her out of the water. She didn't protest, and I wouldn't have given a fuck if she had.

Now she owed me.

I placed her on the warm sand and checked her out. Curvy, tan, flat belly. Definitely fuckable.

I released her and she jumped back on the sand. Her nipple buds poked through her wet tank top and I wanted to suck on them.

"The pup had plastic wrapped around his neck. I removed it—otherwise he would have died."

"Well he will die anyway. That's the cycle of life. And due to your dumbass rescue attempt, you probably killed a bunch of other sea lions in the flush to get away from you."

Her head tipped back and her lips turned up. I couldn't wait to see those same lips sucking my cock.

"There were no other sea lions on the shore. I'm a marine biologist. I know the risks. Now he at least has a chance."

Marine biologist? This bitch was probably one of those dumb-ass SeaWorld trainers who exploited animals by making them dance around to music and retrieve cola cans. "Okay, Dr. Doolittle. Leave the sea lions alone. If I hadn't gotten you out of there, the mom would've attacked you—or you could've been arrested."

"Well, thanks, I guess." She didn't sound too grateful. "Nice meeting you," she added, sounding snarky now. She blinked back at the moonlight, and though she tried to look away, her green eyes glossed over and softened when she glanced at me.

Yup, she wanted me. I'd make it easy for her. "No, you aren't getting away that easy, babe. You broke a law. There's something call the Marine Mammal Act. I'm sure you know all about it, since you're a marine biologist."

"I'm aware of it, yes. You won't tell anyone, will you?"

Bitch looked up at me through her eyelashes and gave me a sweet smile. I laughed. She must've mistaken me for a man who fell for that kind of crap, the kind of guy who wanted a girlfriend and cared about making a woman happy. I was not that man.

I walked up closer to her, right in her space. "No, I won't. My lips are sealed. But I'm gonna have to fuck you first."

Her pupils dilated at my request. I'd throw in some incentive. I removed my equipment and peeled off my wet suit, revealing my tattoos and rock-hard body. There, that should do the trick.

CHAPTER 3

Cassie

WHOA. HAD THIS JERK REALLY just *said* that?

He had. He was standing there in the sand, with sparkling droplets of sea water cruising slowly down some of the sweetest muscles I had ever seen, cocky as hell, demanding that I buy him off with sex? What a jackass!

Did he seriously think I might consider it? Did other women lie down for this asshat and spread their legs?

Damn, they probably did. It wasn't just his gorgeous pecs... and abs...and quads... It was the whole package. He had that "I'm so bad, babe. Nobody can fuck you like I can" thing going for him. The wicked grin, the jutting chin, the way he'd swooped down and carried me out of the water, the "I dare you" glint in his blinding blue eyes.

I was a total sucker for bad boys. I know. It's a weakness. It had never brought me anything but heartache.

I ramped myself up to resist. I had to forget the hot flash that shot through me when he'd bumped his body up against mine in the water. That totally hadn't happened. No way.

He was hot, but so what? There were gorgeous, super well-built guys aplenty in the San Diego area. Marines, Navy guys. SEALS, even. But I didn't usually hit the bars where the military types hung out. What with keeping up with my courses and working part time at the Birch Aquarium, which was associated with my grad program at the Scripps Institution of Oceanography, I didn't have time for a social life. I didn't want to get mixed up with those guys, anyway. Not that this creep looked all that military, especially with his longish hair. But how did he get that buff bod?

Stop staring at his body, Cassie! God, I could swear the boy was preening—showing off what he had to offer, jutting out his pelvis to show off what I could see was a big, hard dick. Dude was seriously packing.

His hair was long and he had scruffy whiskers that were not quite a beard—as if he only shaved once or twice a week. I would *not* think about how those rough whiskers would feel against my bare breasts. Between my thighs…

Stop it, girl! Get a grip!

Maybe he was some kind of surfer dude, hanging out day after day on the beach, waiting for the perfect wave. And the horny chicks.

"You're thinking about it, aren't you?" His voice was deep and had some kind of sexy Western drawl. "How it would feel to have me inside you. How you'd writhe and pant and clench your pussy around me. How you'd scream out my name as you came hard around my cock."

Whew! I wanted to fan myself. "I don't even know your name."

Um, why had I said that? I needed to distract myself from the absurd feelings of lust his stupid words inspired. What was wrong with me? Had it been that long since I'd last gotten laid?'

Yeah, sadly it had. What with finishing college, settling in at UCSD, and fretting that I was in over my head with grad school and a job, I hadn't gone looking for hookups.

"Name's Shane," the big jerk said. "Can't wait to hear you scream it out loud."

"Asshole suits you better." I turned my back and stalked away. But stalking on a sandy beach isn't that easy to do. I was just trying to keep my dignity, not that I had much left.

The worst of it was, I knew he'd been right to call me out over the baby sea lion. I was a serious ocean wildlife researcher, and I knew better than to interfere with the natural order of things. Rescuing injured sea mammals was not my job, and it could do more harm than good. Only the strong survive. In the wild, whether on land or in the sea, fitness was everything—that was how nature worked.

I couldn't regret it, though. Not when I thought of the way those big, soft eyes of the sea lion had looked into mine. Now that the foreign material was off his neck, he would do fine. I had probably saved a life today.

My tormenter came after me. Of course. He wasn't the type to give up easily.

"You don't think I'm letting you walk away, do you? Think about the trouble you could get into if I told someone."

"Yeah, right. Who're you gonna tell? Anyway, your word against mine." But I stopped. Was it because I really thought he could cause trouble for me?

I don't think so. I think I stopped for other reasons altogether. I remembered the sweet sensation I'd felt when his body had pressed up against mine in the water. Damn! I wanted to feel that again.

"Okay." He gave me a thousand watt smile. "Forget the sea lion. Forget getting in trouble." He took a step closer so he was in my space, blotting out the beach and the sea and the moon. There were crystals of sand dusting his tan skin. Tats—beautiful whirls of ink. Marble-hard flesh, muscle, and bone. "Forget everything but this."

I felt his hands grip my hair and my shoulder just before his mouth captured mine.

When his lips smashed into mine, it was hotter than, I don't know, just about anything. Crazy. Wild. There I was, out on a beach at night, pressing myself into the rock-hard body of some stranger who had grabbed me and hauled me to shore without even asking permission to touch me. And now he was doing it again. Touching me. And, wow, it felt so incredibly good.

It was as if I'd been given a hit of a powerful drug. As soon as he pulled me into the cradle of his thighs, where I could feel his cock jutting into my belly and jerking as if it were already inside me, I turned into some kind of wild woman. I'd seen marine animals go into a mating frenzy—sharks went nuts sometimes—violent fucking that left blood in the water. If he—what did he say his name was, Shane?—if Shane was a shark, then I was a goner, because I needed that fat, hard dick inside me in the worst way.

I was kissing him back, grabbing his hair, his shoulders, his ass, and digging my nails into his hard butt as we ground our bodies together. "Not here," I said, with my last trace of rationality. I wasn't going to screw in the sand like a couple of sea lions, was I?

"Come with me," he ordered, looping a strong arm around my shoulders and leading me up the steps away from the water.

I went. It was crazy, I know. I'd probably regret it, but I was going to fuck a cocky, arrogant bad-boy jerk.

I should have been ashamed of myself. But something deep inside me was fizzing with the thrill of my own wildness, my own daring. I never did stuff like this. But, dammit, I was doing it tonight.

CHAPTER 4

Shane

WELL, THAT WAS EVEN EASIER than I thought it would be. She didn't even put up a fight. Just hopped on the back of my bike, wrapped her tight body around mine, and let me take her back to my place.

The cool ocean air blew around us, and I savored this peaceful drive. My last few hours of freedom were always the ones that remained ingrained in my mind during my deployment.

Our ride along the coast had us leaving pretentious La Jolla for rowdy Pacific Beach. I pulled up to my apartment. It was small, had bars on the windows, and was a short walk to one of my favorite watering holes.

She removed the spare helmet I'd given her and her hair cascaded over her face. Her red locks were wild, wet, and sandy. I couldn't wait to see her naked, her hair brushing her nipples as she rode my cock.

I led her inside and she sat on my couch, rubbing her hands on her thighs. No matter how sexy she was, I could tell she was nervous. I wanted to put her at ease, at the very least assure her that I wasn't a serial killer.

"You want a glass of water? All that salt water dehydrates you."

She nodded yes and I poured two glasses and sat down next to her. I tried staring deep into her green eyes, but she was avoiding eye contact.

After she gulped down her water, she looked up at me. "So, what do you do? Besides diving solo at night."

That was what I did. Though I was usually wearing night vision goggles and jumping out of a zodiac boat. "I'm a diver. Working for a boating company. Maintenance on the ships, scraping barnacles off the bottom." I didn't flinch. Navy SEALs never told people what they did for a living. Unless we wanted to get laid. She was already in my apartment after only knowing me for less than an hour, so I decided impressing her wasn't worth the effort.

"That's cool. I've done some diving, too, but I don't do it much unless it's for research. I love the ocean. We have a sailboat—my dad, that is. He loves to sail and to fish."

"Yeah?"

"That's how I got interested in marine biology. I started out in biochemistry, but I was also interested in environmental science, so marine bio seemed like a natural fit. Did you go to college?"

I took a sip of my own water and studied this girl. She was smart, smarter than my average lay. "I'm self taught."

Her eyes focused on the door, probably trying to plan an escape route if she deemed I was a psycho. "Really? That's cool. School's not for everyone. I love it, but sometimes you learn even more by just observing. That's why I was out there tonight. Watching the sea lions in their natural environment, listening to their vocalizations, you learn so much more than you ever would by reading a book."

I didn't react to her, but I was impressed by her accomplishments. She'd never want to get serious with a guy like me. Not that I was looking for anything more than a one-night stand. Girls like her always wanted to be fucked by a SEAL. Just the same way that rich banker guys wanted to bang hot supermodels. But once these pretentious types of both sexes enjoyed their time fucking in the slums, they'd run off and marry respectable partners to appease their families.

"So what's your name, smarty pants?"

She bit her lip. "It's Cassandra, well, Cassie. My parents both majored in Classics. My dad actually wanted to get his doctorate in Classics, but most universities closed their programs, so he's an economics professor."

Yup, way out of my league. She was going to be a Ph.D., and came from an academic family. I was a fuck-up in high school, joined the navy the day I turned eighteen, and left for boot camp the week after I graduated. But I wasn't a dumbass—I was a Navy SEAL corpsman, a trained medic. I saved lives. I even had it in the back of my head that one day after I retired, I'd go to med school. But that dream was far away for now.

Her eyes were now staring at a sketch I'd drawn of a lake near my home in Montana.

"That's really cool. Who's the artist?"

"No clue. Just something I picked up at the flea market."

Her head tilted as if she was trying to get a closer look at the drawing. I needed to distract her before she started asking more questions. "Let me show you something." I took off my shirt, and pointed to my upper shoulder blade.

Her pupils widened. "You have a tattoo of Sammy the Seal? That was my favorite book as a kid."

"Mine too. My mom used to read it to me every night."

She smiled and shifted her position on the sofa so her hips pointed toward me.

Enough small talk. I'd given her a personal anecdote, a glimpse into the emotional connection that women craved. Now it was time to hear her scream my name.

CHAPTER 5

Cassie

THE MOTORCYCLE RIDE TO SHANE'S place had been exhilarating, and I'd focused on how good it felt to be pressed against his back with the powerful Harley engine roaring and pulsing between my thighs. It felt as if we were flying.

But once we got off the bike and he ushered me into his small apartment, I started getting nervous. What the hell was I doing here? I didn't know this guy. He'd helped me out on the beach, yes—that female sea lion had been enraged by what she'd perceived as my threat to her pup. She hadn't been zooming in from the deeper water to thank me. Sea lions were smart, but not that smart.

But just because this diver had done me a good turn in the sea—and been a total ass about it—didn't mean he was trustworthy.

He'd demanded I pay him back with sex. Was I really going to? Now that I was here, did I have any choice?

I could just turn around and leave. If he tried to stop me, I'd scream my lungs out. Someone would come running to my aid, right?

If you were going to do that, why did you climb on the back of his bike?

Okay, my mind was doing somersaults. I wanted this tall, buff, grinning sex god. I just didn't want anything bad to happen.

He must have realized that I was on the verge of losing it, because he changed his aggressive attitude a bit. Asked me a couple questions about myself. I made a feeble attempt at conversation, too. Meanwhile I was looking about the place surreptitiously, trying to get a better read on him.

The first thing I noticed was that his apartment was neat and sparkling clean, which was unusual in a guy living alone. There wasn't a speck of dust on the floor or on any of the surfaces and the carpet had obviously been vacuumed recently. Through an open door that led from the living room to his bedroom, I could see a double bed that was tightly and precisely made. Wow. Maybe he had a cleaning service come in once a week? Seemed unlikely, since the apartment was modest. When I asked what he did for a living, he said he cleaned barnacles off the bottom of boats. Seriously? Was that even a real job? If so, it probably didn't pay much.

He was a diver, though, and divers could probably get hired to do all sorts of things. Could you make a career of being a diver? Maybe he did tourist dives? Or maybe he worked for some big shipping company where cleaning off their barnacles was a really important job?

There was some nice art work on his walls, I noticed. Mostly drawings and sketches, carefully framed. He didn't seem like the type of guy who would invest in art, so I wondered if he had drawn them himself. He'd been quick to turn aside my one question on the subject. He obviously wasn't too into talking.

He could be a serial killer, for all I knew.

Just when I was once again beginning to plot my escape, he ripped off his shirt (oh my god!) and showed me his tattoo. Well, one of his tattoos. It was Sammy the Seal—one of my favorite childhood characters. I'd loved that book! This big, strong dude with the laughing eyes and the big-ass grin that melted me all the way down to his toes had gone into a tattoo parlor and asked for Sammy the Seal ink?

That took balls. And maybe a sense of humor, too? Playfulness at least. That tattoo would stay with him forever.

I felt myself relax. Now that his chest was bare, I was remembering what I'd come here for. And why I'd agreed. And suddenly I didn't want to wait.

"I have a tattoo, too," I told him. And, as he had done, I pulled my top over my head. Thank God I was wearing good underwear. I don't know why I had put on the black bra and its matching thong. I didn't usually wear man-killer undies. Just luck, I guess. Of course, my clothes were still wet and I was a bit sandy, but I guess the same was true of him.

He slid right up next to me on the sofa, looking at the spot I pointed to on the upper slope of my right breast. I had a small dolphin there, spine arching in a joyful dive. It was tiny, but artfully inked.

"That's nice," he said, touching my dolphin with the tip of one finger. His voice was low and husky and I knew it wasn't just the tattoo he was talking about.

I arched my spine too, pushing my breast into the palm of his hand. He made a small sound and then his fingers clamped down on me. He kneaded and caressed while pulses of arousal beat between my legs. His other hand slipped into my hair and tilted my head back. He kissed my mouth—gently at first, then more insistently. I opened to him, enjoying his taste, his faintly salty smell, the pressure of his lips.

I kissed him harder, engaging his tongue. His beautiful body was right there, so I stroked my hands over his shoulders and his back, marveling at the ridges of muscle shifting under his smooth skin, like marble under silk.

His fingers compressed one of my nipples, making me gasp. Some kind of special heat enveloped me and I wanted more, wanted it faster, harder. I reached for the waistband of his pants and his cock was there, just under the surface, trying to burst through the fabric. I slid my hand along it, squeezed, grasped, and heard him groan. Then he was tearing at my clothes and I at his.

Somehow we exchanged the needed information, yes I was on the pill but of course he had to use condoms. He had plenty, he assured me, as he coaxed my lust-crazed body from the sofa to the bedroom to that perfectly-made bed.

He didn't bother to unmake it. He tossed me down on the coverlet, stripped off his pants and his shoes and pulled my shorts over my hips. He growled when he saw the thong. Then he laughed and flipped me over onto my belly. "I need to admire your ass. Yeah. It's definitely worthy of admiration."

I giggled too. "I'll say the same for your cock." I pushed my hair away from my eyes and looked back over my shoulder to get a better look. It was one awesome-looking cock—huge and hard and jutting. My pussy was drenched at the thought of having that inside me.

He crawled onto the bed with me and I felt him straddling my legs from behind. My bra had vanished; I think it was still in the living room. He tugged on the thong between my ass cheeks, making me ride the taut fabric in front. My clit just about had a heart attack.

His face came down near the back of my neck and he said softly in my ear, "So how we gonna do this, doll? Quick and dirty? Or slow and smooth?"

His voice practically caused me to come. Damn, he was hot. "Both?"

He laughed and brought one hand down hard across my ass cheeks. I yelped, but not really in protest. "Anything for the greedy lady. Let's start with quick and dirty, then."

I squirmed and tried to roll over. He allowed it. I lifted my hips so he could remove the thong. His hand slid in where it had been. "So hot and wet for me," he whispered. A finger stabbed into me and I arched in pleasure. "I knew you wanted to fuck me the moment I saw you."

Well, that was a bit much, but I was too far gone to take offense. So what if he was a cocky asshole? He had magic fingers—he knew just where to put them and what to do with them. Right now that was good enough for me.

It was quick and it was dirty. He wasted no time before he pulled on a condom, and then he started giving me sexy orders:

"Spread those gorgeous thighs for me, babe. I hope you like it hard, 'cause you are gonna get fucked like you've never been fucked before. Arch your back. I want those breasts pushed up where I can see them, hon. Those tits are too fine to be ignored."

As he drew back his pelvis and thrust into me, he dipped his head and tongued my nipple. Oh god oh god, it felt so good.

"Raise your hips a bit, doll. That's it. Grind your muff against me now. You want it quick and dirty...well give me dirty. You like this? Tell me."

"I love it," I gasped. I didn't usually talk dirty during sex, but right now I'd do just about anything he asked.

"Yeah?" He slid ever so slowly in and out, then quickened his pace. "Tell me. Tell me what you want."

"I want you to fuck me. Harder. Faster." I lifted and ground against him, just as he had told me to do. I did some thrusts and added a few circles for variation. I was going to give as good as I got.

I could tell by the sound of his voice that I was getting to him, whether or not he wanted to admit it. "Okay, princess. Here we go, then. Hang on."

I hung on, my fingers digging into his back and ass as he slammed into me. With the way he'd told me to arch my hips and the position he was holding, my clit was getting direct stimulation. That was fine with me! He had an awesome way of grinding against me with every entry that sent me soaring. I tried to reciprocate by clenching my inner muscles on his dick every time it sank in deep and I was rewarded by his shudders of pleasure. "Yeah, babe, give it to me," he muttered. "Give me everything you've got."

I did. I felt crazy-wild and almost out of control. He filled me up and I absolutely loved it. Quick and dirty, yeah.

The sweet tension locked and loaded faster than I'd ever dreamed it could happen. Pleasure ricocheted down my spine and out into my limbs as I felt myself explode into climax. I keened softly as my muscles convulsed around his cock. His movements sped up and he stiffened and erupted, too, holding himself up on his powerful biceps as his last few thrusts speared me.

We ended up panting in each other's arms, hearts slamming and breathing in gasps. One of us started to laugh after a few moments...I'm not even sure if it was him or me. But soon we were both laughing, because wow, that was intense.

As we both tried to regain some small measure of rationality, I rolled onto my side and Shane rolled with me and cuddled me from behind, his arms around me and his pelvis tucked against my ass. One of his hands stroked my hair. Neither of us spoke, but it felt cozy and good. My eyes drifted shut and I think I may have drowsed for a few minutes. Perhaps he did, too.

But then I felt him shift, which jolted me back to wakefulness. He got up from the bed and disappeared through a door that was, I realized, the bathroom. When he came back a couple of minutes later, I had climbed out of bed and was looking for my clothes.

Shane was still naked. And beautiful. "Hey. Whatcha doing? If you need the bathroom, it's through there."

"Getting my clothes back on," I said. I was feeling a mild panic. I'd really liked what had just happened between us. Too much. I had to get out of here before I started wanting it to happen again. Because that would be insane. I didn't even know this guy. I had just fucked some guy I'd met about an hour ago. I'd never done that before in my life.

He caught one of my wrists in his big hand. "No clothes. I like you naked. Well, I like you in the thong, too, but right now naked is fine." His other hand cruised down my front from my collarbone to one of my breasts. His thumb rubbed my nipple. "That was quick and dirty. We still got slow and smooth coming up. And maybe a few other variations."

It didn't take more than a few caresses from him before I was ready to forget about leaving. While he stroked my breasts and paid special attention to my super-sensitive nipples, I couldn't help staring at his hard, lean body—those muscles, those tats, all that youthful energy. The tight curve of his ass fascinated me. The way his cock rose right back up when he touched me, even though he'd come not that long before.

I reached out for that prime cock and slid my hand up and down the shaft. He grinned as he thickened even more, until my fingers could barely contain his circumference. I ran my thumb over the rim and pressed the underside with just a hint of my nail. His spine arched. "Damn. That's good. You have great hands." Then his hands were on my shoulders, pressing me down. "Show me how good your mouth is."

I dropped to my knees, both willing and excited. He had a bit of a dominant sexual thing going, and I liked it. I took his balls in one hand and his cock in the other and brought him toward my lips. I teased him by taking him in slowly—just the tip of my tongue at first on the head and a couple of circles around the rim. I felt him grip my hair and shove my face harder against his pelvis. Again, his roughness made my pussy weep. I liked this game. I liked that he was arrogant and a pain in the ass. I don't know why, but it just crazy turned me on.

I took his length deep into my mouth and sucked him hard.

He groaned. I reached around with one hand and dug my nails into his buttocks as hard as I could. He could be rough? Well, so could I. I tongued and sucked and almost gagged when he drove in deeper than I was used to. He was so damn big.

I got control of my breathing and sped up, wondering if I could make him come. I wanted to. But I also wanted to tease him. I jerked my lips off him and leaned back. I might be on my knees, but I felt powerful. "Not so fast, big guy. Let's see how long you can stretch this out."

Unlike some guys he didn't look irritated—instead he laughed and hugged me to his thighs for a second. "You got it, babe." He lifted me right up off the floor and laid me backwards on the bed, with my legs hanging off the edge. Then he dropped to his knees between my thighs and returned the favor.

In keeping with his "slow and smooth," he started at my ankle and kissed and licked his way up my leg, my knee, my inner thigh. Just as I was arching my pelvis toward his maddening mouth, he chuckled and ducked down to the ankle of my other leg. He pursued a similar path, with the added variation of giving me light—oh so devilishly light—caresses between my legs with his fingers.

"Oh my God," I muttered, along with similar exclamations. But no way was I shouting out his name. I wasn't going to give him the satisfaction of meeting that cocky prediction. I didn't have much trouble keeping my noises inarticulate.

When he finally tongued my clit, I was so close to the edge that I could barely keep from spinning out of control. And I'm usually so much *in* control. Shane was unleashing feelings in me that were typically contained and private.

I was on the edge when he pulled back and flipped me over onto my stomach, so my knees were on the floor and my upper body sprawled crosswise on the rumpled bed. I heard the sound of a condom wrapper ripping, then his fingers again thrusting inside me. "Such a sexy ass," he crooned, rubbing me while I flexed the muscles there. "I'm gonna remember this fine ass for a long time to come."

Then he lifted me slightly and drove his cock into me from behind. I felt my pussy clench as he filled me…so full, so sweet. He got one of his hands under me and strummed my clit as he pumped into me. I saw stars. He pounded against me and I pressed just as hard back at him, flying high. "Come for me, princess." He did something amazing with his fingers on my swollen clit. Then he added wickedly, "Say my name."

I nearly did. But I was face down on the mattress and thankful for the folds of the sheet that gagged me enough to prevent it. I keened instead as my entire body soared into climax.

He was right behind me, and, in a way, I won. Because it was he who groaned, "Fuck, Cassie, fuck!" as he went rigid with his own orgasm.

I didn't tease him about the name thing, though. I was too dizzy with delight. My body kept vibrating and the pulses in my core went on and on. I couldn't remember any time when I'd been so thoroughly pleasured. I felt as if I was glowing from the top of my head to the tips of my toes. Wow, this guy might be every kind of arrogant jerk, but he sure knew what he was doing in bed.

CHAPTER 6

Shane

I GLANCED DOWN AT CASSIE'S naked ass, plump, juicy, wide hips. Perfection. Since this was officially my last night of freedom, I planned to throw down a few more rounds with her before I kissed her goodbye. The night was still young.

"Put your clothes on, babe."

"You told me to stay naked? Are you kicking me out already?"

"You're not going anywhere until I say so. Let's get some food."

"You're taking me to dinner?"

"No, princess, I'm not taking you to dinner. I'm grabbing a bite to eat and you're coming with me because I'm not through with you yet. I've worked up an appetite from that dive, and from fucking your sweet pussy." This wasn't a date—it was a hookup. I wasn't cheap, but she wasn't my girl, she would never be. Before this weekend was over, I'd be on the other side of the world. But at least for tonight, she'd be mine.

She dressed quickly, and we left my apartment. She started

walking ahead to my bike, but I put my arm around her and led her into the greasy bar next to my place.

The waiter knew me and waved. I sat in the closest booth. When the waitress came by, I ordered a burger and a craft beer, Cassie ordered a quesadilla and a glass of Malbec.

Her eyes studied the bar the same way she had studied my apartment, no doubt doing some type of character profile of me. This place was a dump—classic dive, pool tables and an old school jukebox. A far cry from the bass-heavy dance clubs just a few blocks away, close to the beach.

We sat in awkward silence. Luckily the classic rock jams were loud enough to provide a perfect excuse for our lack of conversation.

When we finished eating, I threw down money for the bill.

She stood up. "Thanks. I guess I'm gonna go."

"You're not going anywhere but back to my place."

I grabbed her, and kissed her on the lips. A long, deep kiss. My arms squeezing her ass.

Once outside, I pinned her on the side of the building, my cock pressing against her warmth. "Can you handle another round?"

"Yes. Yes, please."

God, I loved that she said please. Within a few minutes we were back at my place. This time, she was less nervous. She stroked me above my jeans. Her fingernails were short, not painted. The kind that spent their days in salt water, not in nail salons. She was beautiful, naturally pretty. Most of the chicks I fucked in San Diego were bleached blond with fake tits, fake nails, fake lives. Though they were technically enrolled in school they barely attended class, never worked and instead chose to spend their days at the beach and their nights at the clubs. It was refreshing to meet a girl who was passionate about something other than having a good time.

Even so, Cassie sure knew how to have a good time. She

was incredible in bed. She seemed to love sex, to enjoy pleasing me, and to be confident enough to tell me what she wanted. I loved it. With one arm I lifted her to me, wrapped her legs around my waist and placed her on the top of my sofa.

I peeled her jean shorts off, ripping her black panties off with my teeth. Her hair was neat and trimmed into a perfect triangle. Her lips were soft, pink, and swollen. I knelt on the cushion, and drove my face into her pussy.

"Yes, please!"

She gasped as I began to lick her, focusing first on her lips, then her beautiful clit. I showered her with kisses, probing her with my fingers. I took off the top and she started rubbing her nipples. "Ohmygod. Please don't stop."

My tongue lashed at her, my fingers circling her clit. She reached down and grabbed my hair, pulling me into her pussy. I let her use my tongue however she wanted. She pressed herself deep into me, moaning, biting her lip.

"Baby, you taste so fucking sweet. Come in my fucking mouth." I reached my free hand to her round ass, squeezing it. Her breath hitched, her back arched, and her belly quivered.

I couldn't get enough of her. Her tanned thighs wrapped around my face as her moans quickened, until her hips jerked. Her hair thrashed around, her nipples hardened.

"Oh, yes! I'm gonna come."

I buried my tongue in her pussy, lapping at her. She tasted incredible. The more I licked, the more she moaned, until she let out a final scream. She collapsed on the sofa, and I held her in my arms, her pussy still pulsating.

She was now grinning. I took a moment to appreciate how beautiful she was. How lucky I was to have her as my last girl before I deployed.

After a few minutes, she rolled over on my lap, pulled my pants down, and released my cock.

"It's your turn. Let me return the favor."

I relaxed back and she stroked my cock. Her mouth widened over the head and she took in my full length. Her tongue flicked around my tip as she sucked harder, deeper.

"That's it, baby. Suck me hard."

She obeyed my order. Sucking, stroking. Her eyes looked up at me and she gave me a wicked smile that almost put me over the edge.

My hand reached around the back of her head, and I touched the nape of her neck. Pulling her into me, forcing her to take me deeper. She didn't let up, her tongue flicked around my head, her throat took me deep, her lips created a tight seal around my width.

I could go on like this forever. But I pulled out of her mouth. "I want to watch you ride me."

I dashed to get a condom, and when I returned, she was sitting on the edge the couch, legs spread.

I kissed her neck, her small but soft breasts. Everything about her was perfect.

"Please don't make me wait."

Yes, ma'am. I flipped her on her back and climbed on top of her. One slow thrust into her tight pussy. I wanted to savor this moment, remember every second of being inside of her. She gasped, her pussy clenching around me. I held her hips up with my hand, making sure to take her deep. Harder, faster, I was almost there, but I wasn't done with her yet.

I turned her around, and I sat upright on the couch, positioning her body on top of mine. I pulled her down on my cock.

"Ohmygod. Yes, like this."

I let her control the rhythm, one hand on her ass, my mouth sucking on her nipples. Her hips swiveled around my cock, clenching, pulsating. I pressed her deep and held her still for a moment.

I stared deep into her eyes, dying to connect with her. By this time tomorrow, I'd be heading to the danger zone, maybe on a one-way ticket. I hated to think about it, but this could be the last time I ever had sex. For once, for a fleeting moment, I wondered what it would be like if someone missed me while I was gone.

She tossed back her hair, thrashing down on me. She was so close, she bit her bottom lip, her eyes were hooded.

"Ohhh, yes don't stop, yes!"

She was right on the edge so I sucked on her nipples hard.

"Fuck, Cassie." We came together, but she wasn't done. I cradled her through another orgasm, mesmerized by her beautiful body.

She collapsed on me and whipped back her head. I kissed her and pulled the hair out of her eyes.

We both remained silent for a few minutes. I pulled on my clothes, headed to the bathroom to throw out the condom, then came back, careful not to sit next to her. Though I could fuck her all night, I had to pack and report to the base by six.

She must've sensed that I wanted her to leave. She gathered her clothes and headed to the bathroom, emerging a few minutes later.

After a few more awkward moments of silence, she shrugged her shoulders and scribbled something on a notepad I had on the counter in the kitchen.

"I left my number, just in case you want to tour the aquarium."

I gave her a reassuring head nod. "Thanks." I had no intention of calling her, ever.

She swallowed hard, her shoulders slumped. "Okay, I'm gonna go. There's a cab outside that bar next door. It was nice meeting you."

"Bye, Cassie." I gave her a kiss on the cheek and an extra long hug—it was the least I could do so she didn't go home feeling like a slut.

One final glance at her sweet ass as she walked out my door

and I knew I'd never see her again.

I collapsed on to my bed, the sheets smelled sweet and salty, like she had. She hadn't held back, a perfect memory, a perfect night. Special Forces still didn't have women in our units so I wouldn't taste another pussy until I returned stateside.

Cassie was different than anyone I'd been with—she dropped hints that she was a daddy's girl, rich and educated, and completely out of my league. It was cool that she was a marine biologist, even if she was stupid enough to try to save that sea lion. Older guys on the Teams always told us to only date women who had an interest in something other than SEALs, that way the girlfriends would keep busy and wouldn't cheat while we were gone. Well, in all fairness she was interested in seals, but the kind that had flippers instead of tridents.

It didn't matter. She was gone, I was about to be gone. By the time I returned, she would forget all about the guy who blackmailed her into having sex with him.

This blissful moment we shared. For all I knew, tomorrow another guy could fuck her. Hell, she could even have a boyfriend.

Unfortunately for me, the image of her ass as I took her from behind, the sensation of her tight pussy pulsating around my cock, and the scent of her hair brushing against my chest as she rode me would have to last me a long time.

CHAPTER
7

Cassie

HE DIDN'T CALL. OR TEXT. Or make any attempt to arrange another hookup. I hated, absolutely hated, that this bothered me.

I don't know what I'd expected.

The guy was a jerk. So what if he'd been good in bed. Good, if you like crude. If you like rough. If you like filthy descriptions of everything you're doing, like a play-by-play commentary. That's probably exactly how he saw it—sports sex. He'd have liked it even better if it had happened in that sleazy dive he'd dragged me to because fucking made him hungry. Maybe on the pool table with the Big Game on the wide screen TV.

And he'd been so arrogant. "I know, princess, you just can't help yourself, can you? No way to argue with the best sex of your life."

Prick.

And yeah, it had been good sex. Okay, great sex. Okay, I had come more than once. More than twice. I wasn't going to count these things, dammit.

But at least I had never screamed out his name.

I did kinda know where it had gone wrong. But not because I'd gone over every single word that had been said between us a few hundred times! I was pretty sure he'd iced over when I'd told him about my father being a professor. I never should have mentioned the sailboat, either. That had probably come across as bragging or something. Not that I'd meant to brag. It wasn't my boat. I didn't even like to be out on it anymore. It reminded me too much of my mother.

When Mom died four years ago, Dad had pulled the sailboat out of the water and stuck it in storage. I'd been the one who had urged him to get the boat fixed up and ship it out to San Diego when he'd decided to move here from Boston. I'd also encouraged him to begin sailing again. I'd thought it would be good for him, especially when I wasn't around because of school and work and stuff.

Dad had moved out a year before I had, when I'd still been in my senior year at Penshurst College in Massachusetts. I'd already planned to do my graduate study at UCSD because of the Oceanography Institute, and he'd been lured with a really great offer of a chair at the private school, University of San Diego, so it had seemed the right decision.

I knew he went deep sea fishing sometimes, to relax. I'd even gone out with him here a couple times. I never caught anything and I was always too worried about accidentally hooking some species that was already fished out and should be left alone. I didn't like messing with the local ecology.

Lately Dad had been going trout fishing, too. Fly-fishing, catch and release. He loved it, but I'd rather be snorkeling or diving, admiring the marine life, than trapping and killing it.

Anyway, Shane hadn't liked hearing about my father. I got the impression that he wasn't too impressed with my graduate studies, either. During the rare moments when he'd engaged in any conversation that wasn't sexually oriented, he'd seemed intelligent, even though he hadn't gone to college. "Self taught," he'd claimed. That was cool. But maybe he had a chip on his shoulder about the whole thing. Or maybe he imagined that I thought I was better than he was because my dad had a university job and I had a good education.

Had I given him the impression that I was slumming by having sex with him? *Did* I think that?

Well, he hadn't exactly behaved like a gentleman. What did he expect me to think?

Bottom line, I didn't know much about the guy. He hadn't revealed whatever he was really thinking. He'd been too busy exercising his thick dick. Give the old pelvic muscles a workout.

Maybe he was one of those man-whores who only did it once with each woman before moving on to the next. Hungry cock types who only got off on the chase and the conquest. Incapable of ever having a real relationship.

A real relationship? Listen to me. It was a hot hookup. Get over it, girl.

It took a while, but after a few weeks of nothing, I stopped checking for texts that never came. Weeks turned into months without a word.

Clearly I hadn't been as memorable an experience for him as he had been for me. My bad for being fool enough to hookup with an obvious pussy-chaser who didn't give a shit whose body he sank into as long as she was female and willing.

Jerk.

CHAPTER 8

Shane

Nine Months Later

I WOKE UP, SPRAWLED IN my bed. First good night's sleep I'd had in nine months. After a hellish deployment with my smelly brothers, not a pussy in site, I was so happy to be back in San Diego.

I walked into my bathroom and my eyes focused on something on the sink. A hair tie, black, with a few red hairs in it. It was hers.

Cassie. Sweet Cassie.

Fuck. I couldn't get her perky ass out of my head. Her soft skin, her full lips, the shade of green her eyes turned as she looked up at me while blowing me. Being alone in a dirt hole in Afghanistan for days at a time, nothing to do but jerk off had given me plenty of time to fantasize. I remembered the way that black mesh thong of hers split her ass into two perfect ovals, like a goddam heart. She had a fucking heart-shaped ass.

I'm sure she'd already found someone else. Some other douche bag was fucking her from behind, staring at her heart-shaped ass.

I threw on some civilian clothes. Wearing shorts and sandals seemed so liberating after sleeping in my crusty cammies
and boots for weeks on end.

I grabbed my keys and saw the note pad on my counter, her
name and number written in cursive.

Cassie Bennings.

No heart dotting the "i", no overly flowery letters, just sleek
and to the point. Like her. Fuck, why was I still thinking about
her? I grabbed her note and threw it into a drawer. Time to go.

A few minutes later, I was already at my go-to dive bar. It
was all decked out for Christmas—a decorated tree in the corner,
some colored lights hung on the walls, an "Elf on the Shelf"
creepily staring at me from behind the bar. Before I could sit
down, the bartender embraced me, thanked me for my service.
He handed me a beer, which was on the house and I sat at the
bar. Kid Rock played on the jukebox. I stood up to start a game
of pool, when I saw it.

Like a flame.

A wisp of red hair. The back of a girl's head, sitting in the
farthest booth, with a couple of girl friends.

No, it couldn't be. She didn't even seem to like this place,
although I didn't blame her. She was probably used to fancy
five-star dinners overlooking the bay.

I had to know. I walked over to the table. The girl's head
whipped toward me, but it wasn't Cassie.

I eye-fucked the group. A blond, a brunette, a redhead. But
Red looked nothing like Cassie. This chick had way too much
make up on, her lips were painted a frosty pink, and she had
huge fake breasts. Before I could say anything the redhead started speaking.

"Hey, what's your name?"

"Shane." I really wanted to get some pussy so I figured I'd
play along.

"Hi Shane, I'm Veronica. I saw you staring at me from the bar. You're hot. I'll let you buy me a drink."

"Let me? Sorry, princess. You're not that hot. And I'm not drunk." Fuck that. I could get laid by any girl in here. I called the shots. In everything, in my life, in my career, in the bedroom.

This chick was vain, nothing like Cassie, who didn't even seem to have a clue how fucking beautiful she was. Fuck, there I was again thinking about her.

Maybe, I should call her. I could see if she was up for a re-match. But I'd never told her I was a SEAL about to deploy. She had moved on, I'm sure, that fine ass was bound to have plenty of men after it. Educated men, rich men, not men who killed other people for a living.

After I downed my beer, I thanked the bartender and left, headed back to my place.

Once inside, I rummaged through my seabag until I found my notebook. After my dad left us, I'd been consumed with anger. My teacher taught me how to express myself by drawing, and I'd been sketching ever since. In Basic Underwater Demolition /SEAL training, I'd been elected class cartoonist, and doodled funny events from our days. I thumbed through my sketchpad, staring at the drawings. Cassie with the sea lion, Cassie on the back of my bike, Cassie sitting on my sofa. I'd tried to convince myself that my obsession with her was based on the fact she'd been the last girl I'd been with, but I wondered if there was something more.

I shed my clothes, and stepped into the shower. The warm water cascading down on me. I reached for my cock and stroked myself. I'd gotten off so many times during the deployment, re-living our epic night. The way her pussy clenched around my cock every time she took me deep inside her, fuck, I barely had to stroke myself. The image alone of her wicked smile as she rode me was about enough to get me there.

The heat rose to my dick, my hand a poor substitute for her

tight wet pussy. I clamped my hand at the base of my cock, and closed my eyes. I loved the shape of her body, her firm thighs, her juicy ass. Her breast—real breasts, small, soft. I didn't need more than a mouthful. I could almost feel her riding me, smell her intoxicating scent. Salty and sweet. An image of me taking her harder deeper filled my mind. In my head, I could see her swiveling her hips around me, biting her lip down, her face flushed in ecstasy, coming again and again.

Cassie!

I cleaned myself up, this letdown worse than the others.

I got out of the shower, redressed, and left my place again. I climbed on my bike and headed to the cove.

Tonight, I'd go on a nice dive, and maybe Cassie would be there fucking around with the sea lions again.

CHAPTER 9

Cassie

"MOLLY'S COMING DOWN TO STAY for a few nights," my father announced.

I felt a twist of panic. He'd been seeing Molly for several months now, but I'd been so busy with school that I'd been able to pretend it wasn't going on. But with Christmas coming up soon, I'd have to deal with Molly directly. And that was a bit of a problem for me.

It wasn't that I didn't like Molly. I'd only met her once, but she was down to earth, friendly, and she struck me as much more confident and independent than any of the other women Dad had dated since Mom had died.

She was a vast improvement over the San Diego hussies, as I called them—the women who had first started chasing after Dad when he'd moved out here from Boston. It had been as if word had gone out over the Country Club hotline that a lonely, well-to-do widower had come to town. Every single chick from age 30 to 60 wanted to get her brightly-painted nails on my dad. When they'd seen that he was a good-looking guy for a man in his fifties—fit and active and still with a full head of hair—they'd been even more eager.

At first, to my disgust, Dad had done some dating with those local barracudas. When I'd expressed alarm, he'd laughed and told me not to worry—he wasn't serious about any of them. I'd remembered that Mom had once told me that Dad had been a player before they'd married; she had an old picture of him dressed in a leather jacket and kissing my mother up against a motorcycle. It was such a different image than I usually associated with my professorial father that I'd forgotten all about it until he started taking what the women here were offering him.

I didn't blame him for having some fun, and at least he'd waited a decent interval after Mom's death. I knew how much he'd adored her, but she'd made him promise on her deathbed that he wouldn't stop living just because she was gone. She'd wanted him to be happy. To find another partner to brighten up his twilight years.

Fine. But I didn't have to like it. If he'd taken up seriously with any of the botoxed bitches who hung out at the golf course, I think it would have broken my heart.

Molly was different. She wasn't from Southern California. He'd met her when he'd gone on a trout fishing trip to Montana last May. She had been his fishing guide on the Big Horn River. A woman. I'd thought that was pretty cool when I heard about it. I guess they'd spent several days in the wilderness together, and he'd come back all charged up.

He'd gone back a few weeks later, with Molly guiding again. I didn't want to think about what else she might be doing. Pretty soon Dad was finding all sorts of excuses to go fishing, and it had to be Montana because that's where the best trout were. Until it got cold up there and he started inviting her down to California.

At the rate they were going, Dad and Molly were both racking up a lot of frequent flyer miles between San Diego and

Billings, Montana.

Molly was almost as old as Dad, and similarly fit and active. She didn't bother with all the fripperies of Southern California women, though—her hair was dark and mixed with grays that she didn't bother to dye. Good honest laugh lines around her eyes and mouth. And she didn't take any shit from anyone, not even Dad.

The one time we'd met at a local restaurant, Molly had insisted on paying her own way. "She's very independent," Dad told me later. "She's run her own hunting and fishing guide service for years, and she employs a staff of eight. She's quite the entrepreneur."

I knew that was a compliment coming from Dad, who was an economics professor and did some independent consulting for various business ventures.

I shied away from the idea that he might be getting serious with Molly. I knew it was silly. I didn't want Dad to be lonely. But it was really hard to think of any other woman taking Mom's place in his life.

"How long is this Molly coming for?"

My dad pursed his lips, looking the way he did when he had something serious to say. Uh oh.

"She's not 'this Molly.' Just Molly, okay? She'll be staying through the weekend. Maybe a little longer. I'm going to take her sailing and we'll probably do some deep sea fishing as well."

Sailing? Shit. That was something we'd all done together, the three of us, when Mom had been alive. Sailing reminded him of Mom. It reminded me of Mom, too. And of happier times.

I felt that deep ache inside that never seemed to go away. I beat it back down. My mother had died and bad shit like that happened. Life sucked sometimes. But other people had their problems, too. "No self-pity" was my mantra.

I wasn't going to let my father know it bothered me that he was taking her sailing. It was his life, right?

"Are you saying you'd like me to make myself scarce for the weekend?"

He actually seemed embarrassed when I put it that way. "No. No, of course not. In fact, we would like to invite you out to dinner this Saturday at the Del Coronado."

We would? "Um, sure. What's the occasion?"

I could have sworn my father flushed a little. What the hell? "Nothing special. I just thought it would be nice if we all went out to dinner."

I wished I could say no, but no good excuse came to mind. When I agreed to go out for a nice dinner with him and Molly, my father beamed.

Looking back on it, I feel as if I ought to have known what was coming.

Maybe, in a way, I did know. The mind is strange. Things get put together deep down underneath the surface, where they don't quite rise into our awareness. Little things that don't make any sense to us rationally, like the quirks of a smile or the shape of an eye.

The night before the dinner, I had an erotic dream about last spring's one-night sex fest with the barnacle-diving dude, Shane. He was fucking me, slowly and deliciously, and I could see his cock between us, sliding in and out of me while I jerked my pelvis against him.

I woke up in a sweat, my core fluttering. Damn, damn, damn. I needed sex. A boyfriend. A partner. Just a wild and crazy fuck. It had been so long! Had I ever gone this long without having an actual man between my thighs? I'd been making do with my vibrator for so many months now that the thing must be worn smooth. It worked for making me come, but, damn, I wanted to be cuddled and kissed and held.

What I really wanted was Shane. I didn't even know why I wanted him. I didn't even like the guy!

But, damn, that boy could fuck.

CHAPTER 10

Shane

"MOM, I TOLD YOU, I can't. I'm working all night."

And no, I didn't want to meet her fucking boyfriend, even if I hadn't been roped into a twenty-four hour shift on the base. It was Hell Week after all and I had to train these jackasses how to survive on five hours of sleep during five and a half days. If these guys thought BUD/S was hard, they didn't have a clue what was in store for them. Training was nothing compared to being stuck out in the middle of the ocean, no clue how long you'd be trapped in the water before you could break your cover. I'd rather be busting their balls to ensure they were able to watch my brothers' backs than making nice with the guy who was fucking my mom.

I cocked my head, half listening to my mom rambling on about how I had to meet Henry. I'd heard it all before, another one of my mom's boyfriends who would come into her life and fill her head with false promises. Ever since my dad left when I was a kid, I'd been dealing with these pricks.

Though I had to admit—it had been years since she'd been

serious about someone.

"Shane—we could make it dinner right near your work at the Hotel del Coronado? That way you could just run up from the beach and say hello." Her voice cracked, this was important to her.

Fuck. "Fine mom, I'll stop in and say hi, but I can't stay longer than a few minutes."

Henry. She hadn't stopped talking about that dude since she'd met him. Rich, pretentious asshole from San Diego. Even owned a mansion on the beach in Coronado, which was minimum a cool three million. Had a daughter, probably one of those liberal Ivy League bitches who hated the military and saw us SEALs as psychos. Though not all rich girls were like that—Cassie didn't seem to be stuck up, though I barely knew her. Nine months later, I still couldn't stop thinking about her sweet pussy.

I needed to get laid soon, and erase her memory from my mind. The other night had been a waste. No sign of Cassie on the beach during my dive, so I'd called it a night.

My recruits stood in front of me in the sand, their bodies shaking from being wet, their muscles trembling from physical pain. Time to kick some ass.

These men had a long week in front of them—basically being wet, sandy and miserable.

For the next six hours, we schooled the recruits. Smoke grenades blasted, sirens wailed. Pushups, flutter kicks, surf torture, mind games. My fellow SEALs and I tormented these men. It was a blur, a rush, a chaotic mindfuck. And I loved every second watching them squirm. But it wasn't because I was a sadist—our training exercises were necessary to give the tadpoles the skills they needed to keep their fellow SEALs safe. This wasn't some fucked up reality show trying to play the "my dick is bigger than yours" game—this was real life, this was training for war.

I'd almost forgotten about my promise to my mom. I

glanced at my watch, fuck. It was six-thirty and I told her I'd be there at six. When I reached into the pockets of my cammies and grabbed my phone, yup, it was lit up like a glow stick with texts from my mom. "Shane, are you coming? We're sitting on the patio. Please, this is important to me."

I turned to my buddy Pat. "Hey, I have to run up to the Del and say hi to my mom. Be back in ten."

"No worries, man. I got your six." I smiled; my brothers always had my back. We were more than Teammates—we were bonded for life. These men would do anything for me, and I'd give my life for them.

My camel-colored boots treaded through the sand. It was so fucking hot today my body couldn't tell if I was in San Diego or Afghanistan. My long-sleeved blue tee shirt clung to my chest. The tourists were wearing sundresses and khakis even though it was the beginning of December. Yup, I'd fit right in.

I walked past the Del's wintertime ocean view beachfront ice skating rink. I scanned the patio, searching for my mom. The outdoor seating area was huge, all tables facing the glorious Coronado sunset. The grand resort loomed in the distance, the place that L. Frank Baum based Oz on: Victorian architecture, red roofs, white wooden cabanas. Everything looked even grander at Christmas time, decorated with 100,000 glittering lights, a humungous Christmas tree. I'd spent so much of my life staring at this building during BUD/S; rich playboys relaxing on the same beach where SEAL recruits were being tortured never sat right with me.

My mom waved and walked over to me. I almost didn't recognize her—instead of wearing her usual uniform of cargo shorts and tank tops, she was dressed in white linen pants and a flowy pink blouse. I don't think I'd ever seen her in pink. Fuck, this guy was already changing her from a Montana salt of the earth woman to a So Cal socialite.

"Shane. You made it! Thank you. They can't wait to meet

you."

They? He brought his daughter? We walked toward the table and a silver-haired man stood up to greet me. Turned away from the table, was a girl—with hair as bright as a flame.

Cassie?

No fucking way. It couldn't be. I studied Henry's face—same fair skin, same emerald eyes, same shape of mouth.

For a cruel second, I thought this was some kind of joke set up by my buddies, roping my mom into it. But I quickly dismissed that thought—none of them had ever met Cassie, and though my mom definitely had a mischievous streak, this was no prank. This was just straight fucked up.

Her head whipped around when her father put his hand on her shoulder.

My Cassie.

One glance at me, and her face went pale.

"Shane, this is Henry. And his daughter, Cassie."

"Nice to meet you, Henry." I shook Henry's hand.

"Nice to meet you, son."

I walked around the table to Cassie and kissed her on the cheek. "Pleasure to meet you," I said out loud. Then I whispered under my breath, "I can't wait to fuck you again." She bit her lip and her chin quivered.

Fucking hot. She looked even sexier than I remembered. Her skin was tanner, her hair longer, her lips fuller. The image of her riding my cock, her face flushed with pleasure, flashed through my mind.

What were the odds? There were hundreds of thousands of chicks in San Diego and I happen to find and fuck the daughter of my mom's boyfriend. Guess both Cassie and her dad liked to go slumming.

One of the Victorian carolers the Del hired was singing "Deck the Halls" with her hands in a fur muff—the only muff I wanted to put my hands in was Cassie's.

Fuck—I had wanted to see her again, but not like this. Though I had to admit, I found this whole situation funny as shit.

I pulled the chair out next to Cassie and grabbed the menu. Cassie's ears were turning red. The tablecloth covered our legs, and my hand clamped down on her thigh. I was making her uncomfortable. As for me, I was just happy to be sitting next to the girl who had starred in my fantasies for the last nine months.

A waiting waitress ran over. "Can I get you something?"

My mom interjected. "Oh, I don't think he can stay very long."

I had no intention of exiting this scene early. I texted my instructor buddy Pat to tell him I was taking a dinner break. "No mom, actually I'm starving. I'll have the New York Strip, medium rare and a martini. Make it dirty."

CHAPTER 11

Cassie

IT WAS AS IF I was seeing everything through wavy glass. Or through a face mask at 50 feet below the surface where the depth of the water makes everything too dark. Shane, the man I had stranger-fucked or maybe hate-fucked. Whom I'd stupidly given my number to. Who'd never called, never texted.

Shane the asshole, Shane the dick. Shane the bad boy stud who still made guest appearances in my most erotic dreams.

Through my fog, I was a little slow to get it. Shane wasn't just strolling through the restaurant, maybe checking out the chicks for his next mark. He was here, with us, being introduced as if Molly knew him. Which, of course, she did. As his blue eyes burned into mine, I saw how similar those eyes were to Molly's blues. And his mouth—god damn, it was her mouth. Shane was Molly's son.

My stomach lurched in horror. I'd had sex with Molly's son. Molly was with my Dad now. So that was—Jesus, I didn't know exactly what that was, but it was enough to make my head swim and my eyes glass over.

What if they found out? I had to keep it together. If I passed out here at the table, everybody would know something was wrong.

Oh god, oh god, oh god. How had this happened? I'd fucked exactly one man in the past year and he'd been Molly's son?

I'd learned during the meal that the jerk was a Navy SEAL. Which must be one of the reasons why Molly had been so happy to meet my dad. Her son was located in San Diego with his Team. San Diego was where he lived and worked and preyed on foolish women like me.

"Would you like another drink?" the server asked me.

My glass wasn't entirely empty, but I gulped it down now. "Please." My voice didn't sound like me. My heart was pounding so hard I could hardly speak.

He had kissed my cheek! I was still burning from the brief contact. Pretending he didn't know me, huh?

God, I was so tempted to blurt something out to prove that he did know me. He knew my whole damn body. I had an image of him looming over me, his pecs bulging as he held his weight on his raised arms and thrust his hips against mine while I writhed beneath him, driven into a frenzy by the quick, hard pressure of his cock.

But I controlled myself before I could make some wiseass remark that might reveal the whole messed-up situation. How bad was it? Shane and I had fucked once. Well, maybe it had been more like four times, plus a couple of blowjobs and some other stuff. It had been a busy night.

But my dad and his mom had been seeing each other for months. *They* were fucking. Did that make what Shane and I had done that night incestuous?

I think all the blood had drained from my head when he'd first appeared, but it must be back now because my cheeks were hot and I was blushing. That happened too often. My red hair, I guess.

Not incest, I told myself. Shane and I weren't related. We were adults. We hadn't grown up together or anything weird like that. There was nothing wrong in what we'd done. Stupid, yeah, but not wrong.

How were we supposed to know that Molly and my Dad were about to start a relationship?

Through the fog I started being able to make out what everybody was saying. Only a few seconds had passed, but the way my brain had processed it all, it seemed as if time had gotten sticky. Everything slowed to a crawl. I guess I'd smiled and nodded and made the appropriate noises while the introductions were going on, but now I was going to have to participate in the conversation. And I saw at once that Shane wasn't going to make this easy for me.

"So, Cassie—that's your name, right—what do you do for a living? Or do you stay at home and play golf with your father?"

"I'm a grad student at UCSD. I study marine biology." He was stroking my thigh under the tablecloth, his fingers slowly drifting up toward my crotch. I wanted to jerk away, but I was self-conscious about making any sudden movements. Everyone was looking at me.

"Marine biology? So you must know all about the laws concerning marine animals around here, right? I hear there's a real problem with the tourists and even some of the researchers from SeaWorld and Scripps messing with the sea lions over in the Children's Cove. Thinking they can save the sick or injured ones, instead of letting nature take its course."

If looks could kill, asshole, SEAL or not, you'd be dead meat. "And you, wow, you're a Navy SEAL? Are you even allowed to talk about that? One of my friends was going out with a SEAL, and he told her he scraped barnacles off boats for a living."

I noticed that Dad and Molly were giving us funny looks, so I dialed it down a bit. I couldn't let them find out. That would be horrible in so many ways.

I tried to smile at him, as if I were impressed with his SEALiness. I wasn't. Big deal. So that's why he was buff and hard-assed and full of himself. I knew the SEALs did dangerous missions in hot spots all over the world and I respected them for their service. They were amazingly versatile and talented—only the best of the best passed the rigorous requirements of SEAL training. But I'd also heard from a couple of friends I knew who'd dated Special Forces types that a lot of them were arrogant, aggressive and prone to screwing around. They had tough jobs, no doubt, but all the pressure they were under probably didn't make them good boyfriend material.

Boyfriend material? Who was I kidding? Shane had been a quick and dirty fuck, not a boyfriend.

And now? Now I didn't know what the hell he was.

It got worse. When all our drinks had been refreshed, Dad and Molly exchanged a meaningful glance. He reached over and took her hand in his. It was then that I noticed she was wearing a huge rock on her left hand. I was pretty sure that wasn't the sort of ring a Montana fishing guide could afford.

Oh my God. I realized what was coming. My glance cut to Shane's as I briefly panicked. He looked oblivious. Typical male. He might have superior night vision and be able to leap tall buildings in a single bound, but wouldn't even notice a diamond ring.

"We had a special reason for inviting you both here today," my father said. "We have an announcement to make."

He and Molly beamed at each other. A frown line deepened Shane's forehead. Yeah. He was getting suspicious at last.

"I've asked your mother to become my wife," Dad said, looking first at Shane and then at me, "She has said yes, and—" I caught a flicker in Dad's eyes that revealed that he was nervous about my reaction. "—and I hope you'll be able to share my happiness." He looked back at Molly and grinned at her, "*Our* happiness."

I swallowed. My stomach was rebelling against it, but I knew what I had to do. No matter how I felt inside—and I was a complete and utter mess—I couldn't hurt my dad. I had to be supportive, no matter what it cost me.

I reached across and patted his free hand. "Wow. Congratulations to both of you."

Shane stood up from the table. His lips were tight and his eyes were angry.

Shane, the Navy SEAL.

Shane, my prospective stepbrother.

CHAPTER 12

Shane

MARRIED? CASSIE WAS GONNA BE my fucking stepsister? Fuck my life. No way, this was like one of those bad romantic comedies my mom used to force me to watch.

"Why would you want to get married? You're going to move out here? What about your business in Montana? Our house?"

My mom rubbed her white pants and gave Henry a sharp glance. "Well we haven't worked out all the details yet. But no, I won't be giving up my business. We'll be having a thoroughly modern marriage, with some long distance commuting built in. The important thing is that we love each other."

I gazed at Cassie, her lips parted. She took a nervous sip of her drink. I had another use for her lips. Fuck, there I went again. I had to get the fuck out of here.

But I needed to talk to her now, alone. She was almost hiding behind her hair, which hung over her face like a curtain, as if she was desperate for a way out of this mess.

I waited until our parents were distracted and leaned down

and whispered in her ear, "Meet me on the beach in five minutes."

"I got to get back to work." I glanced down at my mom's blinding diamond, which clearly cost more than I made in a year risking my life to fight terrorists. Was this what she wanted now? Designer clothes, flashy jewelry, mansions on the beach? What was wrong with her life, our life? Simple, hard working, filled with purpose and in harmony with nature. Mom was a fishing guide in Billings. Now she was going to fill her days spending this jackass's money?

I threw forty dollars on the table. He wasn't going to pay for my dinner.

"Shane—" my mom grabbed my hand.

I held my hand up to stop her. "Congrats, Ma. I'll call you later." Her eyes pleaded at me, as if to beg me to be nice to Henry, not to ruin her chance of happiness.

I gave him a curt nod. "Henry."

"Cassie, it was nice to meet you. Welcome to the family." My words dripped with sarcasm.

"You too." She looked up at me through her eyelashes, like she had the night we met at the cove. But this time she wasn't looking at me with lust, her eyes were confused, hurt even.

I walked toward the beach and waited on a nearby bench, out of sight of the patio. Cassie showed up a few minutes later.

I could almost see the outline of her thong through her dress, her nipple buds hard in the ocean breeze. I needed to feel her wet pussy clench around my cock.

I stood up and clutched her shoulders, pressing her body into mine. Her thin dress clung to her, and despite my anger, my only thought was ripping off her panties and taking her right there in the sand. She attempted to jerk away, her nostrils flared.

"From your reaction at dinner, you didn't know about our parents' bullshit, either, right?"

"I didn't have a clue. But even if I had known, I had no way of contacting you. I gave you my number, but you didn't call."

"I was deployed. We can't text during firefights, despite what you see in the movies." But even if I hadn't been deployed, I would never have called her. We were too different—way too different.

"For the record, Shane the SEAL, the only reason I agreed to leave the restaurant with you was to set down some rules."

"Rules?" I laughed openly at her. "You're giving me rules?"

"Yes. We will probably see each other at family events. You and me, whatever the hell that was, can never happen again. And Dad and Molly can never find out. Promise me you won't say anything."

I laughed. "Listen, sweetheart. If I want to fuck you, and you want me, which you do, nothing is gonna stop me."

"Go to hell."

But I wasn't done talking to her yet. I grabbed her hand and pulled her along with me we continued down the beach.

"Dammit, Shane, the only reason I'm not running away from you is because I'm not leaving until you swear to me that you won't tell your mom about that night. Or anyone else."

I released her hand and playfully pinched her. "What makes you think I haven't bragged about you yet? Our night was epic."

"So the rumors I've heard about SEALs are true—you guys are a bunch of misogynist pricks who can't keep your mouths shut."

My Teammate Kyle noticed my return first. "Is this the red-head you won't shut up about?"

I raised my eyebrows at him. "Sure is. Cassie, meet my buddy Kyle. Just found out that Cassie is going to be my stepsister."

A look of horror flashed on her face.

Kyle let out a deep laugh. "Stepsister? That's a good one, Instructor Tyler. Laughing my fucking ass off. Let me know how that works out for you."

One of the recruit's eyes lifted toward Cassie, a full body eye fuck.

"Hey Pinhead, are you checking out my stepsister?"

"No, Instructor Tyler."

"You calling me a goddamn liar? Get in plank."

The guy dropped into the sand. I grabbed a hose and blasted him with water. Fuck him, no one was gonna look at Cassie while I was around.

"If your body isn't straight, put your ass in the air." I yelled at the motherfucker. But I wished Cassie were the one writhing in the sand, her ass in the air as I took her from behind.

Cassie stood back, her shoulders dropped. I was probably scaring her but this was my job.

I dropped the hose. I had to get back to work. I turned around to her.

"I doubt they'll get married. I know my mom—she's too independent. Been single so long she won't go through with it. It will implode and then we'll never have to see each other again."

Her eyes scanned the beach. "I don't know, Shane. I mean my dad has never been serious about anyone except my mom. She passed away years ago. They seem pretty happy."

My gaze followed hers out to the shore. Fuck, one of my recruits was in trouble. "Hey, don't go. Wait here for a second."

I ran down the beach; one of my men looked like a ghost. Lips chapped, biting his lip, clutching his body.

I pulled him out of the water, took my flashlight out and shone it in his eyes. His pupils weren't focusing. Signs of hypothermia were setting in.

"How many fingers am I holding up?"

He didn't respond.

I lugged him over my back and ran up the beach to a tub we kept to warm our recruits in. I immersed him. After a few minutes in the tub, his eyes started to focus.

I repeated my question. "Fingers?"

"Two, Instructor Tyler."

"Get the fuck back down there."

The guy scampered down the beach like Cassie's hurt sea lion. I picked up the microphone. "You're wet and cold—you're going to be wet and cold for a week. You better all start laughing."

The kid hooked his arms with his swim buddy and started cackling like the Joker. The laughter would warm up their bodies. I wasn't a sadist—if these men thought ocean in the winter in San Diego was cold, they'd never survive the sub-zero temperatures when we did missions in Alaska.

I returned to Cassie. She was standing there next to the instructor truck, a surprised look on her face.

"I need to get back to work. I won't tell my mom, but I'm not going to lie and tell you that I'm never gonna touch you again. When you're ready for a second round, let me know. Bye, Sis."

She stalked away from me, sand flying under her angry feet, and stormed back up the beach. My eyes lingered a little too long on her curvy ass. She'd looked so fucking incredible in her cotton dress, and I knew that every man on that beach wanted to fuck her, but they had thought she was mine. Which she had been, for a minute.

I wanted to carry her away and take her back to my place and fuck her brains out. The sooner, the better. I hadn't been able to stop thinking about her since our night together. Was it really only because she'd been the last girl I'd fucked? I'd been stateside for almost two weeks now and still hadn't gotten laid. I didn't have relationships; I rarely slept with a woman more than once. A Navy SEAL never makes the same mistake twice—why was I breaking my rules for Cassie? I didn't know—the only thing I was certain of was that I had to taste Cassie again. And nothing was going to stop me.

I didn't have time to deal with this mess. Not now. Not

when my men needed me.

The sun began to set. I spoke into the microphone. "Say goodbye to the sun, gents. It's gonna be a long night."

CHAPTER 13

Cassie

AS I WALKED AWAY FROM the sand-caked would-be SEALs on the beach and their asshole instructor, I didn't know what to feel. The truth was that seeing Shane, walking beside him, listening to his low, sexy voice had brought that sexual yearning boiling to the surface again. There was an ache in my belly and that damn traitorous dampness between my legs.

What was wrong with me? I couldn't allow myself to have such feelings. Not now. Not ever. Was I some kind of deviant or something? Shane was my stepbrother. Or he soon would be.

I couldn't ever be with him again.

I couldn't even permit myself to think about it. Dream about it. Fantasize about it.

I had to put the guy completely out of my mind.

Anyway, how could I be attracted to such a full-of-himself jackass? He'd been barely civil at the dinner, and the moment he'd gotten me out of sight of our parents, he had grabbed me and pulled my body against his. If he'd jammed his mouth down on mine right at that moment, I'd have kissed him back. Seeing him was like watching shards of lightning, up close, despite the danger.

A SEAL. He could probably kill me with his bare hands. He'd survived the training those recruits back there were enduring. And I'd heard—everyone around here knew it—that most members of every new SEAL class washed out. Quit. The instructors did their damnedest to make you quit. You had to be really tough and stubborn to graduate from that self-imposed torture class.

A lot of girls around here were hot for SEALs. Would drop their panties if one of them so much as grinned at her. I'd thought that was really asinine behavior. Like I'd never do such a thing. Oh no, not me!

God. No wonder I'd never heard from Shane after our night together. That must have been an easy hookup for him. Order a woman to fuck him and she'd be, "Yes, Sir, How Hard, Sir?"

Shit, shit, shit! Even before this latest mess, what must he have thought of me? Just another ho. Only this particular ho was about to become his stepsister. He probably figured my dad was just as empty headed and sex obsessed as I'd appeared to be. Why would he expect my father to treat his Mom right, when he clearly had such a shallow daughter?

And yet...and yet. Sex had felt so right between us. It had been different, special. It had felt as if we were meant to find each other and be together.

Yeah, right. Stop it, brain! Someone turn a hose of cold water on me.

By the time I'd gotten back to the hotel, my father and my new stepmother—I nearly gagged at the thought—were nowhere to be seen. Fine. I got in my car and drove back to my apartment. Somehow I had to learn to live with having a stepmother.

And a stepbrother I had fucked and, deep in the darkest part of my heart, wanted to fuck again.

CHAPTER 14

Cassie

DECEMBER SEEMED TO CRAWL ALONG. Molly was staying for Christmas. And New Year's. Damn. She was practically living here.

She kept trying to be friendly and I kept trying to tread the thin line between being tolerant and polite to her and fleeing the situation at top speed.

I didn't want to hurt Dad's feelings, but watching him planning his wedding to another woman really got my panties scrunched. Even if she hadn't been Shane's mother, it would have been hard for me. The only Mom I was ever going to have died when I was a freshman in college. My dad had been so broken up about it that I'd had to do most of the funeral arrangements myself. He couldn't stop crying. I'd never seen my dad cry before. All I'd wanted to do back then was collapse and howl myself, but someone had to keep it together, and I'm not quite sure how that someone had turned out to be me.

Maybe I hadn't forgiven him for that yet.

I don't know.

Or maybe I couldn't forgive the idea that he could be in love when my own grief for Mom had been made raw all over again. I couldn't deal with the thought of him standing up in church with Molly and pledging to love her for the rest of his life. If he was so desperate for companionship and sex and stuff, why couldn't he just bone her? That would be private and none of my business.

This past year, when I knew he was seeing her, I'd ignored it. Denied it. Who the hell wants to think about their father having sex? But now I couldn't seem to *stop* thinking about it.

Especially since it was obvious that Dad was getting a whole lot more sex than I was. The only man I wanted was now forbidden to me.

Despite all my good resolutions, my stupid brain remained fixated on Shane. Every time I got myself off with my trusty BOB, all I could envision was him.

Not that Mr. Fuck Me, Babe even cared.

As it turned out, it wasn't going to be a big wedding. They decided to do some intimate thing down in Baja… just the family. Dad and Molly were going to sail Dad's boat from San Diego to Cabo in Mexico, have the ceremony at a little church where an old friend of Molly's was now the priest, and then cruise back for their honeymoon.

The wedding would be right after New Years, before Dad and I headed back to school after winter break. Shane and I were expected to show up and Dad had offered to pay for our plane tickets. But I didn't think Shane even knew about the plans. I'd overheard Molly, practically in tears on the phone with him, trying to get him to make a little time in his busy schedule to talk to her.

Asshole. Yeah, I didn't like it either, but at least I was trying to be nice about it. If people fell in love, they fell in love. There was nothing Mr. Super SEAL could do about that.

Suck it up, Sand-Boy.

CHAPTER 15

Shane

I RAN ON THE BEACH to Mr. Bennings' mansion. On Ocean Boulevard. He had a fucking house on Ocean Boulevard. What the fuck did he want with my mom?

I'd been too busy for this full mind fuck since dinner at the Del. My officer *volun-told* me for a training exercise in Arizona. Away from my mom. And her fiancé.

And Cassie.

Cassie. I couldn't wait to see her again. The anticipation of fucking Cassie was killing me.

I hadn't had a girlfriend since high school and I was in no market to find one. My only focus had been getting through BUD/S and becoming the best Navy SEAL I could be without any distractions. No woman to try to make happy, no months in the desert worrying whether or not she was being fucked by someone back home.

My buddies had warned me to stay the fuck away from Cassie—that it would only end badly. They encouraged me to go find someone else, anyone else, but Cassie was the only one I wanted.

But now I was starting to think my friends were right. The thought of another man touching Cassie made me insane. And she wasn't even mine. What if my mom went through with this wedding and Cassie became my stepsister? Flashes appeared of future holiday dinners with my mom, Mr. Bennings, Cassie and her preppy husband, probably some jackass trust fund baby who never worked a day in his life. I didn't need that kind of distraction, I didn't need a constant reminder of our one epic mind-blowing night shoved in front of me for the rest of my life. But the damage was already done, we couldn't go back in time. We already fucked, so what was the harm in going for a second round?

Tonight was gonna be my first glimpse into a future with Cassie, my stepsister. It was Christmas Eve. My mom insisted that I "join the family" for Christmas Eve dinner and to exchange gifts on Christmas morning. I had an idea for a present for Cassie—my dick in a box.

I knocked on the massive wooden door, painted bright red. This place looked like something out of a Norman Rockwell painting. Would a butler answer?

Fuck. Even worse. Cassie opened it. She was wearing a fitted green sweater with a white reindeer over her chest and tight jeans. If she was trying to turn me off by wearing an ugly Christmas sweater, it wasn't working. She was so fucking hot. Her hair was damp, as if she'd recently showered. I could still picture the beads of saltwater on her ass when I'd first seen her.

"Nice of you to show up. Your mom has been trying to get you to come over for ages."

"I'm busy, Cassie, training the most elite warriors in the world. I'm sure you're enjoying your winter break—maybe you spend your days at the Del: relaxing at the Spa La La getting a Peppermint Mistletoe pedicure, sipping English breakfast tea while snacking on finger sandwiches, or having Santa serenade you on the gondola. But some of us work for a living."

I waited for her smart-ass response, but she just bit her bottom lip. I wanted to bite that lip, taste her blood, make her scream as she came over and over again. I glanced up at the door and saw we were standing under mistletoe. I pointed to the doorframe and grabbed Cassie, pressing my lips on hers. My hands cupped her face, my tongue explored her mouth. She tasted sweet and spicy, like cinnamon and chocolate, and I wanted to drink her up.

She twisted her face to the side. "What are you doing?" she said, under her breath.

"What's going on here?" I looked up and saw Mr. Bennings, a scowl on his face.

Cassie pulled away from me. Her face went blank. I'd handle this. "Nothing, old man. Mistletoe?"

My mom appeared around the corner, glancing around, trying to assess the situation. "Oh that, sorry Henry, that mistletoe is my fault. It adds some holiday spirit." She hugged me. "Merry Christmas Shane, I'm so glad you could make it."

"Merry Christmas, Ma."

Mr. Bennings must've calmed down, but he still looked at me funny. "Ahh. I didn't notice that there. Welcome Shane. Merry Christmas. Please come join us in the living room." He placed his arm on my shoulder, some type of paternal pat. But I stepped away—I'd never known my own dad, and I was not about to let this guy attempt to take on a fatherly role.

In the living room, one of the frosted white Christmas trees was tucked in the corner, behind the grand piano. I placed the gifts under the tree. It was decorated with blue and white ornaments, very beachy. I missed our holidays in Montana, just my mom and me, a pine cut from the woods, homemade decorations with strung popcorn and cranberries, hot chocolate in our mugs.

My mom handed me a beer, and Henry made small talk with me about a recent SEAL autobiography he'd read. I just rolled my eyes—another one of the fame-hungry former SEALs violating our honor code—we were supposed to be silent warriors. These days, I wondered if our trident came with a book deal.

Dinner was finally ready. Molly and Henry dominated the conversation, alternating between thrilling topics like the economic impact of the recent legalization of marijuana and the looming prediction that California would run out of water due to the drought. Cassie and I mostly stayed quiet. At least my mom had prepared my favorites—stuffed mushrooms, grilled salmon, pumpkin ravioli, apple bread pudding with moonshine crème sauce. I gobbled down every bite, though I noticed that Cassie didn't touch her salmon. She was weird, and I was sure I made her nervous.

"So Shane," she said after swirling her glass of wine, "why did you want to be a SEAL?"

Nope, not gonna happen. I was not going to open up to her. "To shoot guns, blow up stuff, and jump out of planes."

My mom shot a glare at me. "Shane always wanted to help people. He's a corpsman actually. It's like a medic for the Teams. He had to go through extensive advanced field medical training. Maybe one day he'll get out and be a doctor."

Cassie's mouth softened and she tilted her head and smiled at me. "Wow, that's fascinating. What kind of training?"

I didn't want to answer her questions, but I figured enlightening her that I really wasn't a dumbass would help me get into her pants later tonight. "It's pretty intense, almost a year long after you become a SEAL. Rotations for surgery, dermatology, pediatrics, orthopedics, radiology. Even large animal veterinary care—so we can treat sea lions."

Cassie ignored my last comment and pressed her palms against her cheeks. "I had no idea you guys did all that. I'm impressed."

"It's not a big deal. It was a pain in the ass but anything to save my men's lives." I fidgeted in my chair. I was done talking about myself. "I'm beat."

I excused myself from the table and my mom showed me to my room on the main floor. It looked like a hotel suite, huge king bed, view of the ocean, and a marble bathtub. I noticed Cassie slipping by us and heading upstairs.

Tonight, she would be sleeping in the same house as me.

Well, after I fucked her.

CHAPTER 16

Cassie

I HEARD A SOUND AT my door—a very slight sound, but it was enough. I sat up with a jerk as the door swung inward and Shane slipped into the room, with a wicked grin on his face and a knowing look in his eyes. Damn him! Somehow he sensed that I wasn't as immune to him as I was pretending to be.

"What are you doing in here? Get out," I whispered, afraid to scream it at him. Terrified that anything we did together, our parents would hear. Not that we were going to do anything together. Did he really think I was going to let him touch me again?

He waltzed right over to my bed, all six feet two of his gorgeous rock-hard body, and sat down beside me. "I've seen how you look at me," the arrogant prick said, grinning that soul-softening grin. "I know you want me."

"I do not want you." I was trying to forget how good that quick mistletoe kiss had felt. "Are you crazy? Our parents will hear you. My dad is already suspicious."

With one arm, he flipped me under him, and pressed me down flat on the bed. God help me, but the feel of his body, his muscles, and flesh and his bone brought back sharp memories of how it had felt that amazing night last spring, when he'd catapulted me up into an erotic wonderland. I had never felt such insatiable desire, nor had I ever come as hard or as long as I had with his thick cock inside me.

Stop thinking nonsense, I yelled at my unruly mind. What was wrong with me?

"I don't care who hears us," he said. His mouth came down on mine and he kissed me hard and deep. When I fought to turn my face away, his hand slid into my hair. He lifted his lips just above mine and murmured, "God, I love your taste." He ran his tongue over my lips—sending sparks shooting all through me, and then he kissed me again, more sweetly.

Oh god, oh god. Why did he feel so good? Why was my belly already burning and my core softening and turning wet?

"You're not my stepsister yet."

He slid one hand down over my breasts, my waist, my hip and in between my thighs. I tried to squirm away from him, but I didn't try too hard. He arrowed right in, parting my pussy lips. He made an approving sound as he discovered I was already hot and wet.

"Stop it! I mean it, Shane. I told you—we can't do this. We can't ever do it."

I slid out from under him and turned on my side. I brought my knees up. I think I was shaking a little. I could feel my hair in my eyes and my heart pounding. He continued stroking me and my traitorous pussy clenched. I was on the verge of tears. What happens when you want something so much, but you know you can't have it? My heart felt as if it were cracking in two.

"Cassie," he breathed in my ear. He kissed the back of my neck. "I can't stop thinking about you. About us. That incredible night we had. It was amazing. It can be like that again. You know it can." His hand closed over my breast, rubbed, teased, caressed. "It's so hot between us. You can't deny it, babe."

"Oh please. You never even called. You've been back from deployment for over a month now. You've probably fucked half the sorority sisters in San Diego."

He chuckled and said, "Truth is, I haven't been with anyone since you. You're the only one I want."

I punched him lightly in the arm. "You're such a jerk. I don't believe you."

"It's true. There's been no one. Not while I was deployed and not since I've been back."

He sounded sincere, if only because he also sounded puzzled by his own behavior. As if he didn't believe it himself. What the hell did that mean? It wasn't as if he cared about me. And, anyway, he couldn't care about me. Not in that way. Not now.

I tried to pull away and sit up. "It doesn't matter. We aren't doing this. It's wrong. It's impossible. So please, Shane, just get the fuck out."

I said it as fiercely as I could, because I was fighting myself just as much as I was fighting him.

"Listen, babe," he said, the voice of reasonableness. "Enough of the good girl act. I'm not going to beg. Either admit that you want me, or I'll walk out of here and never ask again."

There was something in his tone that told me he was serious. That was good, right? He would leave and this agony of yearning would be over. It wasn't as if he was going to force me.

I rolled over to face him again. He was right there, lying on his side on my bed, his long body relaxed, his head propped up on one hand, his blue eyes gazing seriously into mine. *Admit that you want me.* I couldn't do that. I wouldn't. He was my stepbrother. My father was fucking his mother.

I gathered breath to say the words, "I don't want you," but it would be such a lie. And he knew it. How could I lie to that beautiful face that was so close to mine? My body sure as hell wasn't going to lie to his body.

"I hate you," I said, because that was, in a way, true. I hated him for making me feel things I didn't want to feel. That I shouldn't feel.

His thumb brushed the surface of my bottom lip, and my words turned to an abject moan.

That was all it took. He moved his mouth closer and then he was kissing me. And I gave in. I surrendered. I couldn't give this up...not now...not yet. I kissed him back with every bit of the yearning that had been dammed up for so long. I'd wanted him so much and now he was here, in my bed.

At last.

Everything happened quickly after that. Clothes were mutually shed and tossed aside. Our mouths engaged, our tongues teased, our fingers explored and our limbs flailed. The first time he rocked his hips against me, the bed squeaked loudly and I panicked.

"Oh no, they'll hear us!"

He had the nerve to laugh softly. "I doubt it. They're down the hall, not underneath us."

"What if they wander by?"

"I locked the door."

"Stop laughing. You're talking too loudly."

"I don't wanna talk at all."

"I think you're getting off on the idea that this is forbidden and we might get caught."

He laughed at that, too. He kissed me into silence. The only sounds were the gasps of our breathing and the tearing of the condom wrapper before he lifted my hips and impaled me on his cock.

It might have been wrong, but it felt so good, so hot, so right. My legs wrapped around his waist and we slammed together in rough, wild rhythm. I rubbed my clit against him, desperate for more pleasure and feeling it arc through me. When I felt like screaming, I pressed my mouth against his throat to gag the sound. My fingernails dug into his ass. I was probably hurting him, leaving marks. Good. I wanted to leave my prints on his hide.

"Say my name," he whispered, "and I'll let you come."

I moaned something, but not his name. He had already won one victory tonight and I was damned if he'd win that one.

He laughed softly. "Okay, babe. I'll let you off easy this time. But only because I want to hear you scream my name, not just whisper it."

I think I laughed a little, too. Even when we were both nearly out of our minds with pleasure, he was still a cocky badass.

He lapped and sucked at my nipples, not missing a beat of our rhythm. I was close, so close. As his cock drove hard into my clenching pussy, he said, "Come for me, baby."

And I did. I would have cried out if his mouth hadn't pressed down on mine. I shot over the top and lost myself in bliss.

Shane let himself go right after. I felt his balls tighten and his cock turn harder still. My pussy was still bearing down on him when he erupted, our bodies thrashing together and then quietly melting into stillness as we both tried to catch our breath.

As soon as I came down, I started feeling bad about it.

I tried to push the feelings aside. Couldn't I just experience the sheer erotic skill of the man I was nestled against, my face on his chest and my legs entwined with his? Couldn't I just have this moment? This night? The gift of his body in my bed on Christmas?

My arms tightened around him. I didn't want to let him go.

There was a light tap on my bedroom door. I stiffened. Shane must have heard it, too, because his body switched instantly from lazy, relaxed mode to tense and alert. Neither of us moved.

After a pause, the tap came again, a little louder this time. "Cassie?" said my father's voice.

CHAPTER 17

Cassie

I WAS HORRIFIED, EMBARRASSED AND ashamed all at once. We were going to get caught and everything would be ruined!

I pushed Shane off me. At least he moved quietly. But he also clapped one hand over my mouth and leaned up on his elbow beside me. He put one finger to his lips, which was hardly necessary. What did he think I was going to do—scream?

I mouthed the words, "Did you lock the door?"

He nodded, looking impatient. He had told me that when he'd first come into the room.

I pushed up on one elbow, too, and signaled for him to remove his damn hand. He did. I whispered against his ear, "You should hide. In the closet...under the bed...somewhere." I was looking around the dark room, panicking.

Shane rolled his eyes and whispered back, "Fuck that. I am not hiding. What the hell is he doing out there?"

"Cassie?" my father said, again, his voice still very quiet. "You sleeping, sweetheart? I didn't want to miss our Christmas

Eve carols."

Oh God. Tears pricked my eyes as I realized. I wanted to throw open the door and hug him for remembering. But I couldn't do that.

Every Christmas Eve when I was a child, Dad and Mom used to come into my room as I waited for Santa, all excited and restless, and sing me Christmas carols. Daddy had a really nice tenor voice.

The Christmas carol lullabies had stopped when I'd declared them "cheesy" as a teenager. But after Mom died, Dad started coming to tuck me in when I was home from college for the holidays. Mostly we would just hug each other and cry for Mom, but sometimes he would sit down on the end of my bed and sing. It was good for both of us—taking us back to happier days when she had still been alive.

On Christmas Eve, my father would always sing O Little Town of Bethlehem and Silent Night, two of my favorite carols.

He had done it last year.

Now he was here to do it again, and part of me yearned for it. I guess I'd figured that now that he was with Molly, he would forget.

Shane seemed far more relaxed about this disaster than I was. He had lain back down again, looking smug. I don't think he'd really give a shit if we did get caught.

He pulled me down, too. "Just pretend to be asleep. What's he gonna do—break down the door?" he breathed in my ear. Then he started fondling my breast again. When I squirmed, he murmured, "Don't make a sound." He stroked my nipple with his fingertip, sending pleasure shooting through me again. "Better control yourself, babe," he taunted, adding a little pinch to my pebbled breast. "Don't want Daddy to hear you."

Dammit! What was wrong with him? If we were caught it would be terrible. Embarrassing. Worse than embarrassing—it would horrify both my father and his mother. It might even ruin their plans to get married. Tear up Dad's relationship with the only woman he'd loved since my mother had died.

Was that what I secretly wanted?

No! I missed my mom—I ached every time I let myself think about her—but I'd already come to like Molly a lot, and I wanted my dad to be happy.

All this went through my head at lightning speed, making me even more ashamed for not kicking Shane out the moment he'd entered my room. He probably thrived on risk, stealth, living on the edge. He didn't care about our parents' happiness. He just wanted to get his rocks off. Sexual fulfillment. Gratification. That had been all he wanted from the start.

And I'd surrendered. Just because he had those merry blue eyes, that roguish smile and the best male body I'd ever seen naked. Not to mention a certain natural talent for fucking my brains right out of my head.

There were no further knocks on my door. I heard Dad's footsteps moving away down the hall. He hadn't wanted to wake me up.

When I heard his door click shut, I sat up and glared at my partner in crime. My pussy was still clenching from the nipple play and his nearness, but I couldn't let him win this round. He was so smug. He didn't give a damn. This couldn't go on.

"This can never happen again. I mean it, Shane. It's over."

He rolled his eyes. He pulled away, but not before giving me another long, sweet kiss on the lips.

I watched in silence as he gathered up his clothes, dressed. He even took the used condom with him, wrapping it in a tissue and stuffing it into the pocket of his jeans. He wasn't leaving it in my bedroom to incriminate me.

God, I felt like a guilty teenager.

"And don't let my father see you or hear you. If he knew what we were doing, it would break his heart."

"I don't give a shit about your father or his heart. But I do care about my Mom, so don't worry." He did not say this in a comforting manner, but rather in a snarky one. He laid one finger over his lips. "This'll be our little holiday secret. Merry Christmas, Sis."

He exited my room as stealthily as he had entered it.

I rolled over, punched my pillow furiously, and tried to go to sleep.

CHAPTER 18

Shane

THE NEXT MORNING, I WOKE and showered. I headed across the hall to the living room. Cassie was sitting on a white leather sofa. I remembered her legs spread on my sofa, my face buried in her pussy, her fingernails running through my hair, pulling me closer to her core as I edged her to pleasure.

My mom and Henry emerged from the kitchen and placed a platter on the coffee table. I was starving so I helped myself to some bagels and orange juice.

I handed Cassie a bagel. "So, do you live here?"

"No. Just during winter break. Campus is closed so I thought I'd come spend the holidays with dad."

Well that was convenient. I could come fuck her on my lunch breaks. Or she could run over to base and blow me in the compound. The possibilities were endless.

"So Shane, how did you sleep?" my mom asked.

I smirked. "Great, best night I had in ten months."

Cassie fidgeted and avoided eye contact with me.

"Well, you're welcome to crash here whenever you like."

My mom placed her hand on my back. "I hate that you drive across the bridge after working all-night shifts."

"Maybe I should just move in? We can be one happy family."

Cassie choked on her orange juice.

My mom leveled me with her eyes. "Shane, stop. I just worry about you. It would be nice to spend some time together."

Cassie quickly changed the subject. "Time to open gifts."

She played Santa, dispersing the gifts. My mom gave me a leather bound sketch pad and a new set of pencils. I noticed Cassie focusing on that present and I wondered if she remembered the framed sketches I'd had at my place. I offered my mom a simple thanks and looked away from Cassie.

After opening all the others, she paused and glared at me before unwrapping mine.

She smiled when she viewed the title. "Oh Shane, how thoughtful. *The Proper Care and Feeding of Sea Lions.*"

"Glad you like it." I ripped open the small box she handed me. A fucking barnacle scrapper. "Thanks Cassie."

She smirked. "You're welcome, thought you could use it for your SEAL boats."

Smartass. I loved the way she teased me. I wanted to teach her a lesson, put her in her place—under me.

Our parents seemed a tad baffled, looking back and forth between us.

"Why did you buy him a barnacle scraper, sweetheart?" Henry's tone was tense. "I'm sure these men have professionals cleaning their boats for them."

"Barnacles can cause damage to their zodiac boats. I thought this could help him."

Old man was catching on about the vibe between Cassie and me.

My mom pursed her lips. "Shane, I know this is short notice, but we've set the date for the first weekend in January. I'm hoping you'll be able to get the time off to come to our wedding."

"What's the rush, Ma? Are you pregnant?"

My mom blushed. "That's enough, Shane. We just don't see the need to wait. It's January and we all have a little time off, so we thought we'd seize the opportunity. I'm not getting any younger."

Whatever. I didn't care. I didn't want to know the details. "Sorry. I can't make it. We just started a new training phase."

My mom put her hands on my shoulders. "You haven't taken any leave since your last deployment. It's on the weekend. In Cabo. You can fly in Friday night and be back to work by Sunday. I'd really like you to be there."

Cassie couldn't resist getting a word in. "Shane, it's our parents' wedding. All you have to do is show up."

I could tell this was important to my mom, and I didn't want to disappoint her, but I was damned if I'd be treated as a family obligation by Cassie. I'd never had a sister and I didn't want one—her, least of all. "The only person I take orders from is my commanding officer. I won't be there. Enjoy your picture-perfect family Christmas—without me."

I walked right out of that mansion, and slammed the huge door. I didn't fit in their world, and I didn't want to. Before I could run back to the compound, I heard the door open behind me.

CHAPTER 19

Cassie

WHEN SHANE STORMED OUT OF our Christmas celebration, I went running after him. I couldn't believe he was being such a jackass. "Look," I said when I caught up to him. "This is not about you. Why are you being so cruel to your own mother?"

"Poor little rich girl. It's about you, then? Your feelings, your wishes, your demands? Forget it, babe. I'm no sucker for female crocodile tears."

I V-fingered my own two eyes. "You see any tears, there, asshole? It's not about either of us. Not you and certainly not me. It's about them. Our parents love each other."

"Look. I told you. This marriage will never happen."

"You're in some kind of denial. It's happening. And yeah, it's freaking me out because of everything I've been stupid enough to do with you, but that is over. I mean it. Stop smirking at me. It's done, it's history. We have to forget it and let them live their lives." I paused for breath. "I'm not standing by while you singlehandedly sabotage their wedding. And on Christmas, too!"

"Yeah, well I'm not letting your rich-ass father ruin my Mom's life. He's using her. I want nothing to do with that fucking circus."

I couldn't believe the guy could be this stubborn. "Are you blind? Haven't you been watching when they are together? They've been seeing each other ever since last spring."

"Bullshit."

"It's true. While you were off stalking terrorists or whatever you do, our parents were screwing their brains out, both here and in Montana."

"Jesus! Don't say that."

"What, it's okay for you to fuck everything that moves, but the ground's going to surge up and swallow the city if your Mom gets some too?"

I knew I was pushing. I mean, this wasn't something I wanted to think about, either. But double standards much?

There was fury in his eyes, but it was banked, as if he was counting to ten or something. I guess it was a good thing I wasn't one of those SEAL trainees, because he'd have me down on the floor giving him twenty.

Oh no, don't think stuff like that, brain! If he ordered me down on the floor, it wouldn't be to do pushups. He'd tell me to kneel, and I'd do it. He'd proved that last night. Even though I knew it was wrong, I couldn't seem to stop myself. I probably wouldn't even hesitate before sliding down his zipper and pulling out his big, juicy, delicious cock.

Shit! I was truly pathetic. I hated this jerk, but it didn't stop me from yearning to lick him all over.

"Look, Mr. Badass Navy SEAL, like it or not, you are going to that wedding. We are both going to show up and be supportive and grit our teeth and smile. We will wish them well and be polite and do everything that is expected of a stepbrother and a stepsister at their parents' wedding."

"Right," he snarled. He looked incredulous. "Are you giving me orders? I don't know what kind of fantasy world you're living in, doll, but I am not gritting my fucking teeth and I am not going to any goddamn wedding."

"I won't let you ruin my father's happiness."

"Yeah? How are you gonna stop me?"

Clearly this approach wasn't working. Dammit. I had to be smart about this. I thought about the various sea mammals I'd worked with....how they learned...how they taught their own pups. Lead by example was one way, but that depended on a strong mother/pup bond and the expectation that the animal wanted to learn. Positive reinforcement? Rewards? Challenges worked sometimes, too.

"You tell me," I said. What would constitute a reward for Shane? Was there anything I could offer him as a positive reinforcement that might alter his behavior?

He stopped looking quite so aggressive. I'd finally gotten his attention, at least. "What do you mean? I tell you what?"

"You tell me what you want. What it would take to make you stop being such an ass and go with me to the wedding?"

"Oh, now you want to go *together* to the damn wedding?"

"No, no, I didn't mean that." I didn't like the way he was smirking. "I just meant, what can I offer you to make you change your mind?"

As soon as I spoke the words, I knew I'd made a huge freaking mistake. And as the smirk grew wider on his face and the mischief lit up his blue eyes, I also knew he was going to make me pay. Just the way he had on the night we'd met. Saved you from the angry sea lion mama, girl. Now you have to show your gratitude in my bed.

And on his floor. And ass up across his coffee table. And up against his wall.

He sauntered closer to me and fisted a hunk of my hair. He pulled me right up against his hard, murderously hot body. "Tell you what, babe. I'll behave myself all you want, show up at the damn wedding, and play my part in the farce if you road trip with me down to Mexico. And not on a plane, because I'm not spending my money on that shit and I'll never take anything from your father. You come with me, on my Harley, your tight little belly jammed up against my ass and your arms around my chest."

"That's crazy! I'm not doing that. I can't do it. We are about to be stepsiblings, Shane! Don't you *get* that?"

He ignored me and continued, "and the whole way there, however long it takes, you do everything I order you to do. Just like one of my BUD/s trainees. Your ass is mine for the whole trip." He reached around and dug his fingers into my ass. And God help me, my pussy gave one long agonizingly pleasant clench.

"If you mean—"

"That's exactly what I mean. As I told you last night, we ain't stepsiblings yet."

"That's impossible. We can't travel together. Our parents will know. They'll think we're doing..." my voice trailed off.

"...exactly what we will be doing," he finished.

"Well, they can't know what. They can't *ever* know that!"

"Yeah, yeah, stop worrying. They'll be too wrapped up in each other on their little sailing cruise to think about us. All we have to do is show up at the damn wedding. They aren't going to know or care how we got there."

He was probably right. Ever since Molly had come into his life, Dad had been preoccupied with her.

"One last joy ride, you and me, Sis. After that, they are married and we are quits."

Oh God. I hated myself. I was going to say yes. If we road-tripped down to Cabo, we'd be alone. Complete privacy...no way we could get caught by his mom and my dad. We'd be safe. No one would know about it but us.

Maybe it was wrong, but I needed his body between my

thighs. One final time. I could do that. Right?

He wasn't my stepbrother yet.

"Couldn't we take my car?"

"Nope. We take the bike. You can be my old lady for a few days. Yeah. I love that idea."

"And you'll respect the wedding? You'll be polite? You'll treat my father well and be nice to your Mom? You'll be good?"

"All of the above, sure. 'Cept the last. I won't be good, doll. With them, but not with you. With you, I'm gonna be real fucking bad."

I was gonna be bad, too. For once in my life, I was gonna be *so* bad.

PART TWO

CHAPTER 20

Cassie

WHEN SHANE SHOWED UP IN the semi-circular drive of Dad's place on the morning we were starting our road trip, my heart groaned at the sight of him. Tall, tan, and built like some kind of classical god. Even the way he dismounted was hot. The bike itself was sexy. Oh, God, I was a goner already. How was I ever going to get through the next few days?

He sauntered on up to the house, the helmet hanging from his fingers. He was wearing the boots, the tight jacket and pants, the sun shades. Shit, my knees were going weak and he hadn't even touched me yet.

His ass was amazing. I was going to sit pressed tight to that ass all day? How was I gonna stand it? I was tempted to invite him in to start this whole thing off with a bang, just to take the edge off.

But then he grinned slyly at me and said, "Good job, princess. I see you got yourself outfitted properly." He tossed me his extra helmet. I caught it. Just. "You'd better follow the rest of my instructions, too, babe. That's part of the deal, so don't forget it."

"There's nothing wrong with my memory."

"Good. Where's your stuff?"

He had emailed me a long list of things to bring on the road trip. It was accompanied by a note to "pack efficiently. Don't bring extra clothes. You won't need them anyway."

Screw that. I was going to a wedding. But after thinking it over and reading up on the web about motorcycle trips in Baja, I decided to give my dress, shoes, most of my cosmetics and jewelry to my Dad to pack in one of his suitcases. He and Molly were going on the boat, so they ought to have lots of room.

Even in January, it would be hot in Baja. But I was still supposed to have long riding pants, boots, a jacket and a sunhat. Shane would provide the helmet. When I asked why I couldn't ride in shorts and a T shirt, he laughed at me. While we were on the road, he assured me, I'd be cool enough because of the wind factor.

So I went to a shop and bought the motorcycle traveling clothes, much to the amusement of several hardass dudes in there who were buying leather duds for themselves. I packed a couple of light changes of clothes, simple stuff. Shorts and T-shirts for when we weren't riding. A sundress and sandals in case he ever took me anywhere nice. Some toilet paper. Antibiotics in case Montezuma's Revenge hit. My Kindle. My phone. Condoms, in case he ran out. My birth control pills and some lightweight toiletries. Sunglasses. Bathing suit. Towel. Sunscreen. Passport.

He'd also ordered me to bring a sleeping bag and a small tent. He'd provide other camping gear. Camping? Jeez. Couldn't we stay in hotels? It was a thousand-mile trip from San Diego to Cabo. To me it already sounded like a thousand miles of torture.

Still. I was excited. It sounded kick-ass to go biking in Baja. I'd been working super-hard at school this year and I was due for an adventure.

The other thing I was due for was the smoky hot sex that

Shane was sure to provide. No one had ever fucked me the way he had, and for another chance at that, I was willing to put up with his annoying personality.

The good thing about riding tandem on a motorbike was that I wouldn't be expected to make conversation with the jackass along the way. I was pretty sure talking would be impossible. The only time I'd have to speak to him would be when we were stopped, and when we were stopped, we'd probably be all over each other.

Our parents left the day before we did, which was fine with me.

I had lied to my father. He'd offered to buy me an airline ticket for the trip to Cabo, but I'd told him I'd decided to drive. I wanted to see Baja, I explained, and I had time off because of winter break, so it was the perfect opportunity.

Dad had been dubious about me going alone. When he warned me about bandits and drug cartels and all the horrible things that could happen to a single woman in Mexico, I'd weighed the odds and taken a risk. "No worries, Dad. I could ask Shane the SEAL to watch out for me. He's probably leaving around the same time."

At first I thought I'd made a huge mistake because Dad had said, "Please don't tell me you're thinking of traveling with him."

"Nah, not officially. We'll just be on the same road and maybe he could keep an eye on me, that's all. I don't even like the guy."

"I don't trust those SEALs, not with my daughter. I've seen them on the beach, harassing their trainees, and I've seen the way the women hang around them. I know Shane is Molly's son, but he's got a real bad attitude. I think you should stay away from him, Cassie."

I'd laughed. "We can't stand each other, Dad. But you gotta admit, a SEAL is a good guy to have around if there's any risk of bandits or drug cartels."

I could tell Dad was torn. Shane had behaved badly from the start and that kiss under the mistletoe hadn't helped. "I don't like it. And I don't like him."

"Well, don't let Molly know you feel that way about her son. That could really hurt her feelings. She obviously adores him."

He'd grunted and said nothing more.

When I handed Shane my kit, he proceeded to grill me on the whole list. I smirked when he'd run through everything and there was nothing I'd missed. So far he had no reason to criticize me.

The back of the bike was packed with stuff. There were two side carrying metal cases and another one at the back. As he took my sleeping bag and my backpack, I strolled around to the back and watched him rearrange things.

He stuffed my things into a carrying case in the rear of the bike. He already had a lot of gear in there, so he mashed it all together.

"What is all this stuff?" I had stressed over every item I'd brought, finding it hard to stick to his requirements. I'd left out things I'd really wanted and now my scrunched up clothes would be wrinkled to shit. "You told me to pack light so you could bring the entire contents of your apartment?"

"It's gear. Necessary gear."

"We're not going into combat."

"You never know. We'll be in the desert. We need water. We need shelter. We need protection from the sun."

"Well, if we'd taken my car, we could have put all that gear in the trunk and I could have brought my favorite dress, shoes, and jewelry."

"Are you going to bitch all the way to Cabo?"

No, I wasn't. In fact, I decided right then and there not to complain about anything. I was betting he intended to harass me the way he'd harassed those recruits on the beach. Just because he could.

Well. We would see who cried for mercy first.

I could be just as stubborn and determined as any SEAL.

CHAPTER 21

Shane

WE WERE READY TO ROLL. Cassie wrapped her arms around my waist, her chest pressed against my back. I'd never taken a road trip with a woman, but I was looking forward to the break, the time away from my job, the time alone with her.

In a way, this was the best of both worlds. Instead of my usual one-night stands, I would have one week of endless sex with Cassie, and nothing could come of it. Our parents were getting married, so we wouldn't have to have the talk about our future. We could just say this long goodbye.

I'd mapped out every minute of this trip—1000 miles to Cabo, broken into five 200 mile legs. Tonight we would stay in San Quintín, then we would spend nights in Guerrero Negro, Loreto, and La Paz before continuing to Cabo San Lucas. I'd always wanted to ride the Baja Coast, but I'd never gone further than Ensenada, and that had just been a drinking trip with my buddies.

I needed this vacation, I needed her. Our Christmas Eve rendezvous had only whetted my appetite for her. I planned to fuck her every way I'd fantasized about over the last ten months. Whatever she wanted, I was game. Rough, dirty, sweet, sensual.

I exited the freeway at Camino de la Plaza, clearly labeled in yellow as LAST USA EXIT. I had to purchase Mexican Insurance and fill up the tank with the last clean tank of fuel we would be able to purchase for this trip. We pulled into gas station. Cassie removed her helmet, her hair wild in the wind.

"Shane, I'm going to stretch my legs."

Shane . . . I loved the way she said my name. Slow, breathy. Before the end of this trip, she would scream my name, as she already had so many times in my dreams.

Cassie

WHILE SHANE WAS FILLING UP on gas, I walked around, studied the landscape and felt ever more excited about our adventure. It wasn't just being with Shane, which I was appreciating more than usual after clinging to his fine ass for the past half-hour. I was excited to be in Mexico. Since he lived in Southern California, it was probably no big deal for him, but I'd only been to Mexico once, for a brief visit over the border. I'd been reading blogs and studying maps of the Baja peninsula ever since he'd suggested the road trip.

I pulled out a road map, since I had nothing better to do while I waited. Shane was tinkering with the engine and he certainly wasn't going to consult me about that.

When he finally looked up, I pointed to a spot on the coast and said, "If we can fit it in, I'd like to explore around here. I was reading this blog about two guys cycling in Baja and they had some really cool pictures of an old Mexican guy—I think he's descended from Mayans or Aztecs—who has a little camp on the coast. He grows beans and vegetables, catches fish, and lives off the land. He prays to the ancient gods of the sun and the moon. He's a shaman and a seer."

I glanced up at Shane. I couldn't even guess what he was thinking behind his heavy sunshades. "A shaman and a seer? Old gods? I thought you were some kind of scientist."

"I am. But that doesn't mean I can't have a spiritual side."

He snorted. "You want the guy to tell your fortune or something?"

"I just thought it would be cool to talk to someone who believes in ancient traditions that are lost to most of the residents of the land. He's probably a wise man, even if he isn't really a seer."

"Yeah, well, it's out of our way. The trip's already a thousand miles, and I'm not going to make it even longer so you can go bow down to the Aztec gods."

"Fine," I said, snapping the map closed. What a jerk. I left him and walked over to a battered old soda machine that I hoped was working. The sun was hot and my throat was parched.

"Hey, baby," a low voice said from the other side of the soda machine. "Need some help with that, little girl?"

I instinctively backed away from the voice even before I saw the guy. He stepped around, a huge man with greasy dark hair and massive tattooed biceps. He looked like a serious biker, and not the kind you wanted to run into if he was with his motorcycle club buddies. Or even if he was by himself. Thuggish, with a nasty gleam in his black eyes.

"No thanks," I said, grabbing my soda and turning back in Shane's direction. He was paying for the gas.

Another dude came up behind Biceps. He was younger—maybe late teens and didn't look quite as vicious. Behind him I could see two huge shiny motorcycles, all snazzed up with lots of chrome and various emblems and skull and crossbones type stuff.

Biceps sidled after me. Yuck, he had wicked BO. "Who you ridin' with, girly? The Cub and me could use a fine old lady like yourself."

The emphasis he put on the word "use" gave me the shudders. I didn't look back, but hightailed it over to Shane. He looked up, saw me and the two guys, and his expression turned ice cold. It was a subtle change, but I felt it. He didn't move; he didn't speak, but there was something in his body language that made the two bikers hesitate.

For the first time ever, I was aware of what it meant to be with a Navy SEAL. If I should ever need protection on this trip, I had it.

CHAPTER 22

Shane

I PLACED MY ARM AROUND Cassie's shoulder, clutched her to my side, and led her back to my ride.

Bikers. I didn't recognize their club patch, but in SoCal we had plenty of motorcycle gangs, mostly offshoots of the Hells Angels, or the Mongols. Either way, I didn't want to fuck with them—I never went looking for trouble, but I was more than capable of handling any chaos they sent my way.

But I didn't like the way they looked at Cassie. She was my woman, and I'd be the only one to look at her like that.

We entered Mexico and the *Federales* didn't stop us. I wanted to stick to the toll roads despite Cassie suggesting that we take the coastal road. I didn't even have to argue with her because the coastal road was closed. My bike barreled along the highway, the view of the coast on our right side. I'd never taken a road trip with a fine ass woman on the back of my bike, her arms clutching around my waist, attached to me like human velcro, her heat contrasting with the ocean breeze. Her body just fit with mine, her sexy hips opened for me, her luscious thighs clinging clenched around me, her tits bouncing against my back. Every sensation was heightened, and Cassie's body filled me with lust.

An hour later, I turned into Puerto Nuevo. I loved this place, this quaint fishing village, still unmarred by tourists. It reminded me in a way of my home in Billings, Montana. Great food, nice people. I could see myself getting a place down here, catching my own supper, drinking Coronas while watching the sunset.

I parked the bike and she took off her helmet. Her hair cascaded like a curtain down in her face. Sweaty, fiery, wind swept, she looked like I'd just fucked her all night. Which I was about to do. But not yet.

"Wow, Shane. I didn't figure you for the romantic beach hotel but I like it. I've always wanted to come here, explore the marine life."

"We're not staying here—just getting lunch. I'm sure you're used to five star resorts with pool boys spritzing your face with cucumber water and feeding you fresh pineapple skewers, but that's not how I roll."

"I read Ortega's has the best hand-made tortillas. Let's go, I'm hungry."

I tried to fight a smile but my lips involuntarily widened. She was always fun, bright, cheery. A big contrast to all the heavy stuff in my day-to-day life. I could get used to someone always trying to lighten up my day.

"I'm hungry too but we're not going to Ortega's." I took her hand and led her down to the beach. I knew a few of the lobster divers from my last trip. I left her on the shore and went over to one of the boats and negotiated a deal, using my best Spanish.

As I walked back toward Cassie, I noticed that the hem of her tight pants was now tinged with sand. I could see the outline of her thong and couldn't wait to rip it off with my teeth. I wondered if she was freshly waxed or she was still sporting the neatly trimmed triangle look. Either way, I couldn't wait to taste her again.

"Let's go, babe."

"Go where?"

"Get lunch. We're diving for lobsters. Get in the boat."

Her eyes focused on the boat. "What? It's illegal. Only Mexican citizens can take crustaceans from their waters."

I raised my eyebrow at her. "Juan is a Mexican national so it's fine. It's not like you would want to violate any marine laws now, would you?"

She swallowed hard. That skill would be useful later tonight. Now it was time to hunt for lunch.

CHAPTER 23

Cassie

THE WHITE BOAT SPED DOWN the waters, and I focused on the blaring sun in the distance.

Juan had provided all the equipment. Despite his repeated assurance that the gear was properly maintained and the tanks had plenty of oxygen and no leaky valves, Shane was doing a detailed inspection.

I didn't really want to do this. Why had I told him that first night that I was an experienced diver? Was I trying to impress him? I do talk too much when I get nervous. I wasn't scared, but I had no desire to rip these beautiful crustaceans from their homes. Lobsters have feelings, they scream when they are boiled, they mate for life. It just seemed cruel.

The boat slowed. Juan said something to Shane, who replied in perfect Spanish. Where had he learned that? I was impressed.

"Okay, Cassie listen up. There's a group of rocks near this cove that the lobsters hide in. Now usually, they hide under sea urchins, but if you're lucky and go deep enough where it's dark, they could be out looking for a date."

I scowled. Poor lobster looking for love and we're going to snatch him. Fuck this.

Shane continued. "If you see one, swat it—like this." He held his hand out over my wrist. "Grab the body, and slam it against a rock. The lobster is gonna fight you, gripping for life to the rock. Keep shaking it until its antennae loosen."

Great—now I was going to play tug of war with a lobster. He handed me some gloves so I wouldn't get sea urchin spines lodged into my hands. We put our equipment on; Shane attached a glow stick into my mask.

We climbed down the boat steps and descended. Shane kept me close to him and took out his dive light, which was fluorescent green and resembled a gun. Around 30 feet down, we saw a patch of rocks, a lone antenna peeking out of the rock. Shane motioned me to go first. I didn't hesitate. I reached into the hole and grabbed that poor lobster by its body and slammed it into the rock. He didn't put up much of a fight, and once I loosened his antennae I threw him into the bag.

Shane gave me a high five. He dug into that hole as if he was the lobster boss, grabbing two of the lobster's buddies. He saved the last one for me. He put up a bigger fight, probably because he'd just watched all his friends being kidnapped.

We made a slow, careful ascent to the top of the water and climbed back into the boat. "Not bad, for your first time."

I didn't respond. Instead, I stared at our bag of four scrambling lobsters, fighting for their lives, spending their last few moments on this earth trapped in a plastic bag with their friends and loved ones.

I knew I shouldn't be so sentimental, but hell, sea life was my passion. I wasn't even going to eat the things, so this just seemed wasteful to me.

CHAPTER 24

Cassie

WHEN THE LOBSTERS WE HAD personally trapped showed up piping hot at our little table in the nearby restaurant that cooked them for us, I took a big swallow of beer and stared at mine. Again, I thought of it swimming around, doing lobsters things just a little while ago. It hadn't known its existence was about to come to an end in a boiling pot.

"What?" said Shane, who was already digging into his.

I grabbed a tortilla and shoveled some black beans into it, then dumped some guacamole on top. I rolled it up. "I probably should have told you."

"Told me what, doll?" He was giving me that once-over again. Now that I was in my bathing suit and cover-up instead of the motorcycle duds, he'd been eye-fucking me constantly.

"I don't eat shellfish. I'm a vegetarian."

He looked dumbfounded. Ha! "Are you fucking with me?"

I shook my head and took a bite of my beans and rice.

"Damn. You helped me dive for these things!"

"You ordered me to. Just keeping my end of the bargain. I

figured you had a craving for lobster. Isn't it supposed to be good for the libido? Or…no. Maybe that's oysters."

The corners of his mouth took on a dangerous slant. "I don't need any kind of help."

I smiled cheerily. "Cool. I would be disappointed if you did."

He shook his head slowly. "You're digging yourself deeper and deeper, you know that?"

"I'm reckless like that. That's me, Motorcycle Mama—I'm all about living on the edge."

I wasn't, of course. I've never lived on the edge. I was usually cautious, thoughtful, analytical. Despite my yearning for a bad boy lover, I'd always been pretty much of a good girl. Good grades, healthy lifestyle, no smokes, drugs, or excessive partying. When my mom had taken sick in high school, her illness had changed my life. Her death could have destroyed me, so crazy with grief had I been at the time.

But I'd held it together because I had to. Dad had no one else except me, and I knew he wanted me to prove to him that I could still do well in school and make a good life for myself. So I'd tried.

Now, against all expectation, Dad had fallen in love.

So what did that mean for me? I wasn't sure. I had no clue. But in a weird way, I felt as if I could do anything now. Anything I wanted. For this one week before the wedding, I was free. I could be crazy and contrary and wild, because why the hell not? Our parents would never know.

Ever since the first time I'd seen Shane, my body had gone into a hormone-drenched state of high alert. I knew a little about the biology and chemistry of sexual attraction. Clearly his body and mine had a lot of compatible molecules. We'd formed a strong physical bond that transcended anything our minds were capable of feeling. I wanted him and he wanted me.

So here we were, a graduate student and a Navy SEAL,

with nothing in common and no possible future except as reluctant stepsiblings, sitting across the table in Mexico engaging what amounted to pre-coital banter.

I expected he would fuck me just as hard and just as dirty as he had the first two times.

I hoped he would.

I didn't like the guy, but I craved the release he could give me.

"If you're really not going to eat that, push it over here."

"Fine. I'll take your beans and rice."

We made the exchange, with him frowning the entire time. I think he took it personally that I didn't want his precious lobster. "Your father is into fishing. Are you telling me you won't eat the fish he catches?"

"He mostly does catch and release. Like your Mom. Isn't she a catch and release fishing guide?"

"Yeah, but she's not some kind of weird-ass vegan. She eats everything."

"I'm not vegan. I eat some dairy. I even eat sushi sometimes. I just don't eat shellfish, meat, or fowl."

"Why? Are you one of those animal rights crazies? That's probably why you were trying to help that baby sea lion. I'm surprised you didn't pull him out of the water and trundle him off to SeaWorld to be taught to do cute tricks for the tourists."

"I'm a scientist. Not an animal rights nut. And I would have let nature take its course that day if it hadn't meant he'd die a long, slow death of strangulation. That wouldn't have been nature at work, but man, dumping his trash into the oceans and polluting the ecosystem."

I was getting hot under the collar now. I took a pull of my cerveza and ramped my emotions back down. "Anyway, I'm not here to listen to your critique of my eating habits. It's none of your business what I eat. So back off."

He reached across the small table and gripped my wrist. His

thumb somehow found its way to a spot where it could scrape gently across my palm. Uh-oh. That touch. It put me in mind of all the other intimate things he had done to me. And of everything I hoped he'd do tonight.

"You're a firecracker," he said, low. "Must be that red hair. I love the idea of tangling my fingers in that hair while you wrap those luscious lips around my cock." His eyes caressed me. "And that long, slender throat of yours. How deep can you take me, babe? We're gonna find that out tonight, aren't we?"

Shit. I couldn't look away from his burning blue eyes. Fine. I wouldn't. Let him do whatever he wanted. I was on board with it. So *very* on board.

Shane

I RELAXED BACK INTO MY chair for a final few minutes before we hit the road again. Cassie surprised me, again. Hadn't bitched once, captured lobsters like a champ even though she was a vegetarian.

Five days and five longer nights. Cassie had no idea what was in store for her tonight. I couldn't wait to have my way with her, fuck her brains out, make her scream my name. On her knees, on all fours, from behind, riding me cowgirl. Every fantasy I'd had about her during deployment was about to come true.

A beautiful woman to fuck was one thing, but I planned to camp in my tent under the moonlight alone, count the stars, a cold beer in my hand. Some of my Teammates had wives who adored them, were faithful and loving, but that type of love was not in the cards for me. Not only had I never had a serious girlfriend, but also my dad left when I was young so I'd never really seen a healthy partnership.

This was just sex, that's it. That's all it could ever be. She was going to be my sister for fuck's sake. That was more certain now than ever. And my mom deserved to be happy without me fucking up her relationship.

But if after this trip my dick couldn't stop craving Cassie's pussy, I would do what I had to do—move on. I could always apply for one of the East Coast Teams. Otherwise being her stepbrother would be the one type of torture this Frogman would be unable to endure.

CHAPTER 25

Cassie

AFTER PUERTO NUEVO, WE CLIMBED back on the bike for what Shane warned, with a touch of sadism, would seem like a long ride. He was right, the road was a lot narrower after Ensenada—we were really in Baja now. It was an agricultural area with farms and some vineyards. Wine and vegetable country. Apparently they grew a lot of tomatoes here.

We could see mountains on our left and the road got hilly—some of the sharp curves scared me a bit. But Shane seemed in absolute control of the bike and I didn't think we were speeding.

The sun was beating down, and even though it was January, it felt hot. I couldn't imagine what it would be like to do this trip in the summer.

Shane had warned me it would get a lot chillier in the evening, and I could feel the land cooling down when we got to San Quintín, where he planned to spend the night. I began looking for a good hotel as soon as we hit the town, but Shane was more interested in another gas station. When we finally did pull into a small restaurant, I was dismayed. It looked like a real dive.

I said nothing, though. Besides, we'd already had one good-sized meal today. Him especially, considering he'd eaten all the lobsters.

After we'd finished our supper, which was surprisingly tasty, he motored to a barebones motel. I was dubious about it, but Shane insisted the place was "nothing fancy, but good enough for me."

Okay, fine. That meant it had to be good enough for me, too, or I'd look like the rich girl snob that he already thought I was. At least it was on the water and tucked away from the usual touristic traffic.

When we got inside, though, I checked the mattress for bedbugs. There are certain places where I am not going to sleep! No sign of insect colonies, to my relief.

"What are you doing?"

"Nothing. Just tucking in the sheet. Military tight corners."

He gave me a suspicious look as he schlepped in the carrying cases with our belongings. Mostly his belongings. Between the cases and the water carriers, he had a shitload of stuff. I think he would have brought the bike, in too, if the room had been big enough, but he settled for locking its wheels together with a thick chain.

"I thought we were camping out," I said, just to annoy him.

He surveyed the small room he'd rented for the night. Its entire furnishings consisted of one double bed with a saggy mattress and a single wooden chair. An old air conditioner rattled in one window. Instead of a closet, there was a recessed area with a bar for three wooden hangers and a ragged curtain. The other amenity was a small bathroom with toilet, sink and tiny shower stall.

"I need a shower," he said. "You could probably use one too."

"Gee thanks. Are you telling me I stink? It's lovely having a future stepbrother who is so deft with a compliment."

He sidled up to me and thrust his nose and lips along the line of my neck. "I like your smell. And shut up with the step-brother talk."

One of his hands found and gripped my breast. He squeezed. Not gently. I swayed toward him. Who needs gentle? I'd been clinging to his back all day. Feeling his ass and thighs bounce against mine. Enough of this tease—I wanted him. I'd done my time riding his bike. Now I wanted to ride his pelvis.

I dropped to my knees and tore at his trousers. Screw the shower; we'd already been in the sea today, so we were reasonably clean.

I got him out of his pants and underwear in record time and sucked his amazing dick, already thick and hard, into my mouth. He tasted fine to me—warm and a little salty. The head of his cock was velvety and the ridges and veins were fully engorged. I played at the rim and then greedily swallowed as much as I could of him. He filled me completely and I had to focus on breathing through my nose, but it was hot as hell.

Shane groaned and slid his fingers into my hair. He held my head still and drove even deeper into me several times, claiming me, using me. He was rough, but I didn't care. I thought about the way he'd fucked me on the night we'd met—the way he'd taken control. It had been new to me, and strangely exciting. Would he do that again? Why did I want him to?

I needed the mental blankness that came with fast and furious sex with Mr. Hot-Ass SEAL. Everything in my life was so planned and controlled, so neat and tidy. That was the way I liked it. It made me feel safe. Planning kept the demons at bay.

But this week, I didn't have to plan anything because Shane was giving me orders. I didn't necessarily plan on obeying all his orders, but when it came to sex, I liked it. This was way hotter than any other sexcapade I'd ever had.

I worked him with my mouth and tongue, sucking hard while I twirled my tongue around the head and the sensitive underside. I also slid my hand over his balls and caressed him there while bobbing my head on his dick. It excited me, kneeling before him. Even though I wouldn't necessarily put giving head at the top of my list of sexy things to do with other guys, I loved it with him. I wanted to get him off. I was putting some real effort into it when he groaned and jerked himself out of my mouth. "Shower first, babe."

"No." I tried to take him back, but he pulled away. "Why? I want to please you."

"Because I said so, that's why. You wanna please me, you obey." He pulled me up from the floor and pushed me in the direction of the bathroom. "Get in there."

"Are you coming too?"

"You bet I am."

Shower together? Okay, I could live with that. The stall looked pretty tiny for anything too adventuresome, but we could probably make do. "Wait, I need my shampoo."

"Fuck your shampoo." He turned on the water and undressed me with the skill of a man who has undressed a whole lot of women. Then he pushed me into the stall, shook off the remainder of his things, and joined me in the small tile-lined space.

"Are you some kind of clean freak?" I asked, remembering his spotless apartment back in California.

"Nope." He was sudsing up his hands. "I just like the slippery feel of soap over skin." He proceeded to demonstrate. He pushed me back against one wall and devoted considerable attention to my breasts. He had magic hands and it didn't take long before I was panting and squirming against the shower tiles. I don't think my nipples have ever been so clean, or so hard.

I tried to wash my hair while he was caressing me, but I ended up with soap in my eyes. He laughed at me, the big jerk. "Settle down and let me do it. You just won't quit, will you?" he added when I reached down with soapy hands to massage his dick. I wanted to torment him as much as he was tormenting me. "Stand still before I punish that wayward ass of yours."

I laughed at him. "Yeah and that's supposed to make me follow your orders? You've got a lot to learn about me."

"I reckon I do." He ground himself into me, all his hard wet muscles and his irresistible cock smashed between my belly and his. "But right now I wanna learn how the sweet inside of your pussy feels."

For a moment I was afraid he might thrust without a condom and I panicked a bit, but all he did was rub and tease me until we were both gasping for breath and pressing our mouths and bodies together frantically.

When we finally got out of there, the hot water had gone cold and our bodies were both rigid. Drying off was something of a joke. He brought a towel with us to the bed and tossed it down beneath us, then he grabbed a condom pack, tore it open with his teeth and rolled it on. I was touching myself between my legs in the meantime. I couldn't help it—I was so wet and ready and the sensations in my clit were driving me out of my mind.

When he crawled between my thighs and saw where my hand was, he laughed low and said, "I like watching that. But stop touching your clit. Slide your finger down inside and fuck yourself with it. Show me how you get off when you don't have a man in your bed."

"I usually use a vibrator." I said this to taunt him, too, since most of the guys I'd known seemed to hate the thought of a woman using a vibrator, as if it were some kind of battery-powered challenge to their manhood. But Shane just grinned even wider. "I'd like to see that, too. In fact, I'd like to fuck you in the ass while you rub your clit with that vibrator. Did you bring it with you?"

Whoa. My future stepbrother wanted some anal action, too? This was going to be one wicked road trip. "Nope. I didn't see vibrator on the packing list." I stopped the self-pleasuring to take a good hold of his dick. "I'm expecting this will serve the purpose. You wouldn't want to disappoint me, now, would you?"

"Babe," he said, pushing aside my hand and drilling the tip of his cock into my opening, "When I get through with you, you're not gonna have any energy left to complain."

He kept his promise. The first bout was fast and furious. We both had explosive orgasms, but I hoped we weren't done. Turned out that Shane didn't need much in the way of recovery time. He was young and so was I, but even so, it was amazing how fast the need came rushing back again. We built it more slowly the second time.

That sense I'd gotten before of him liking to control the bedroom action got stronger. I didn't think of myself as submissive, not at all, but something about his penchant for dominating me in the bedroom really got my wheels spinning.

"Get on your hands and knees, babe."

The mattress seemed a little bouncy for that, but I started to do it when he gave me a slap on the ass. "On the floor."

I grinned at him. "If you are going to tell me to crawl around, forget it."

He laughed and slid to the edge of the bed. "Just kneel. Remember your ass is mine all the way to Cabo."

"Fine, Master," I said, kneeling between his legs and going for his cock. I was pretty sure "suck my dick" was going to be the next command. "But my ass is sore from sitting on a goddamn motorcycle all day, so be gentle with me."

"Ha! Not a chance," he said, fisting my hair and driving his cock into my open mouth. I wasn't gentle either. I sucked him as well as I could and did a few fancy things with my tongue as he pumped in and out of me. Then I gave him just the tiniest hint of teeth, which made him hesitate. My turn to laugh.

Looking up I could see the merriment in his eyes. It showed up there every now and then, confirming that the boy had a sense of humor buried somewhere. "You give great head, Cass, but seems you've got this tiny streak of aggression, doncha?"

"You'll get used to it."

"I like it fine," he retorted, hauling me back up on the bed and pushing me down. A moment later he dived between my legs for some impressive tongue action. "You're hotter than hell, girl," he said, next time he took a breath.

But I was already flying so high I had no words to answer him. He made my core ripple and burn. By the time he started fucking me again I was already tumbling headlong into erotic nirvana. He kept me right on the edge, though. I'm not even sure how he did it. He varied the rhythm just enough that I couldn't come. "Not until I say you can," he said, with an evil smile. My body should have ignored him, but for some reason it seemed to hang on his every word.

"Dammit, I'm almost there," I moaned.

"Say my name."

Oh god, oh god. I wouldn't. My body went stiff and I was in that almost-there area where the slightest thing can push you over the edge. But he slowed to a stop, leaving me hanging.

"Say my name and I'll let you come."

"Jackass!"

I felt him chuckle. Just the movement of his laughter was enough—my entire body convulsed into something that could have won the Orgasm of the Year award.

He didn't seem to mind, and it didn't take him long to follow me over that knife edge of pleasure.

Afterward, we cuddled. It felt fine. I liked the way he could laugh during sex. Make me laugh, too. Maybe he wasn't so awful, after all.

CHAPTER 26

Shane

CASSIE'S HEAD RESTED ON MY chest. I stared at her naked ass, still bruised from my hand clutching it. Her fingernails were tapping on my chest.

"Shane, why'd you really become a SEAL?"

Hell no, not again. I flipped her body off from me. "To kill people."

She didn't flinch. "No seriously. The adventure? To prove something to yourself?"

"Special Forces are still the only branch in the military where we don't have to deal with women asking us stupid questions, like you're doing now."

She snuggled up to me. "I get you, I do. It's the ultimate challenge. So few make it. I respect your determination."

"I'm gonna take a walk. Rest your mouth because when I return it's gonna be sucking on my cock." I pulled on my shorts and walked out of the hotel room, desperate for some fresh air.

I hated being psychoanalyzed. It was like when I came home from a fucking deployment and I had to be interrogated by the navy psychiatrists to make sure I wouldn't run off and kill a bunch of schoolchildren. I fed the quacks what they wanted to hear—killing the enemy didn't bother me, I slept well at night, I was able to relate and have functional relationships with partners, friends and families.

Which was all bullshit. I was beyond fucked up. I had nightmares, brutal vicious nightmares starring the faces of the men I'd killed. The only people I could trust were my mom and my Teammates. I'd never trusted another woman, and I doubted I ever could. And despite how great Cassie made me feel, I doubted that she could ever love a killer.

I dealt with stress my way. Casual sex being my favorite therapy. I'd rather put a bullet in my brain then discuss my feelings.

Once outside, I sat on the sand in front of the hotel. I planned to stare at the ocean for a while, then pitch my tent and crash—alone. I felt a twang of guilt for expecting her to sleep solo. It was what it was.

I heard footsteps behind me. Cassie emerged from the hotel. She didn't even acknowledge me, and slowly stripped off her clothes. The moonlight illuminated her incredible body. I thought she was going to try to talk to me, but she just ran toward the water, her breasts bouncing, her heart-shaped ass leaving me behind.

I took off my shorts and joined her, pulling her to the surf, wrapping her legs around me. This was more like it, no words, just raw sex, the rhythm of the waves guiding the cadence of our bodies.

CHAPTER 27

Cassie

AFTER WE'D FOOLED AROUND IN the surf and on the beach, I'd stumbled back into the little hotel room, taken another quick shower to get rid of the sand, and crawled into bed. I heard him come in a few minutes later and I heard the shower running as he, too, cleaned up. But I must have fallen asleep before he got into bed.

Shane awakened me the next morning, pounding on the hotel room door. Why was he outside? I could tell it was around dawn, far before my usual rising time, but he'd said we had to get an early start because of the heat. The plan was to travel in the morning before the sun reached its zenith, then stop and rest in the shade for lunch before continuing on later in the afternoon, when it was a bit cooler.

As I rose from the bed, I noticed his side hadn't been slept in. At least, it didn't look as if it had.

"Why're you outside?" I asked when I unlocked the door.

He strolled in and headed for the bathroom. "Get packed up. We need to leave soon."

I saw his small tent set up in the sand a few feet outside our door. "Wait. Did you sleep in the tent?"

"Yeah, I did. So?"

I looked at the bed, puzzled. It wasn't huge but it was big enough for two. "Was I snoring or something?"

"I wouldn't know." His voice was cool and clipped. "I sleep alone."

I blinked. Was that why he had ordered me to bring my own tent? Holy shit. I thought he wanted an extra one to store all our gear when we were camping out.

He was already in the bathroom, but I wasn't about to let this go. I pounded on the bathroom door. "We have a perfectly good hotel room and you slept in a tent? What the fuck, Shane? Are you mad at me for some reason?" I remembered how pissy he'd gotten when I'd tried to probe a little, find out more about him, like why he'd decided to become a SEAL. He'd made it clear that he didn't want to talk about anything too intimate.

"It's got nothing to do with you. Personal habit. I don't share a bed."

"Not even with a lover?" I remembered how he'd kicked me out on our first night together. I hadn't really wanted to stay with him that night. I'd been a little embarrassed about my reckless behavior, so I'd been glad to get out of there. And on Christmas Eve I'd been so afraid of getting caught that I'd wanted him to leave. But now...we were traveling together now.

"I don't have lovers. I fuck. That's all this is, Cassie. Get packed."

Before I could say another word, the water in the shower came on.

Well fuck you, too!

But I had to brush a stupid tear out of my eye. We'd had fun yesterday. We were still bickering, yes, but it had such a sexy edge to it. And our lovemaking—er, our *fucking*—had been so amazing. I'd thought we were connecting, even if it was mostly physical.

When he held me and stroked my hair, his touch had seemed tender and caring. He listened to me when I chattered away, and he never sounded bored. But as soon as we stopped sexing for a little while, he pulled back and put up his walls.

I'd hoped we could be friends, at least. I'd even started liking the jerk a bit. We were going to be stepbrother and stepsister. Didn't we have to have some sort of relationship?

I got dressed in my motorcycle duds, tied back my hair, and started rubbing sunscreen all over my face. By the time he got out of the bathroom, I had myself back under control. He wouldn't see that I thought there was anything weird about his obsessive need for space and privacy. What did I care if we slept in the same bed? I could casual-fuck him all the way to Cabo and then wave goodbye without a qualm. I didn't need a big, bulky SEAL in my nice little tent.

But deep down inside, something felt almost scarily empty. I was not going to let myself feel anything for him, dammit. Attachments led to pain and the terror that I might lose someone. I'd never thought my Mom could get sick and die. She'd been completely healthy until, one day, she wasn't. The cancer had taken her quickly, too. I'd never had the chance to get accustomed the idea, and, bam, she was gone.

I wasn't going to let myself get accustomed to Shane. That would only lead to heartbreak. Even if we ended up liking each other, we could never be together—our parents had made certain of that.

I was outside with my stuff before Shane even got out of the bathroom. If he could be ready to leave at dawn, so could I.

CHAPTER 28

Cassie

SHANE HAD WARNED ME THAT the second day's ride would be tough, and he wasn't kidding. First of all, I was stiff. I'd known my ass would be sore from sitting on the bike, but I was surprised to find my legs and knees hurting, too. So many hours in one position, I guess. I felt as if I'd spent the previous day horseback riding.

Shane wanted to get to the Guerrero Negro area by nightfall, which was more than 200 miles. At first the road ran along the coast, passing through some small towns. In one of these villages, I saw a couple of guys on motorcycles blow by, leaving dust in their wake. They didn't slow for the pedestrians; they weaved around them or just went full tilt, scattering people. One of them almost ran over a woman who was pushing a stroller, which caused several of the townsfolk to cry out and shake their fists at the bikers.

Assholes, I thought. I was pretty sure they were the same two creepy bikers who had tried to chat me up just before the Mexican border. Those guys were bad news.

After about an hour, just past El Rosario, the road turned inland. The mountainous landscape was barer, more like scrub desert, and not as developed as the former vineyard region had been.

We had to stop for gas, but there were no gas stations. Instead we found a dude selling gasoline out of drums in the back of his truck. I felt far from home, yet charmed at the same time. We were really in Baja now.

We didn't quite make it to Guerrero. I'm sure Shane could tell I was tired and hurting, although I was determined not to grouse about it. He decided to stop at a sorry-looking campsite on the outskirts of town. Since there was a cantina that actually looked as if it had a bathroom, I was happy to climb stiffly off the bike. Damn, I thought as I hobbled in search of bladder relief, why hadn't I insisted we take my car?

"So this is where we're camping, huh?" When I got back from the john, I surveyed the sandy campgrounds with some dismay. It did boast a few scrubby trees, but it wasn't exactly scenic.

"Yup. It has everything we need." As he said that, he looked at me as if he dared me to deny it. I wasn't going to give him the satisfaction.

"Fine with me," I said, trying to sound as cheerful as possible. "What do you want me to do?"

"You can help me set up the tents."

Tents. Plural. So we were camping in a desolate campground and that's how he wanted to play it? Okay. But I was going to have some input into this idiocy, too.

I did everything he told me to do. When we got the tents erected, side by side, he unpacked the gear we needed, and ordered me to gather fuel for our campfire. It was getting cool, so I guess having a fire made sense. I gathered a bunch of sagebrush, twigs, and broken branches while he walked over to the cantina to fill our empty water bottles and get us some supper.

I hadn't made a campfire for a while, but I wanted to show him that I wasn't a slouch when it came to camping out. I think I did okay. Other than suggesting that I dig the fire pit a little deeper next time because there was so much dry scrub around, he didn't have much to criticize.

I enjoyed my bean and cheese taco.

"You can eat this, I hope? It isn't meat or shellfish," Shane said, and I nodded, happy he'd remembered.

We had some great local fruits and veggies with our tacos and a couple of cold beers. Later he made coffee over the fire and we enjoyed that. It was simple, but everything tasted delicious.

When darkness fell, the stars were amazing. So bright. You never see stars like this in Southern California, or back in Boston, either. No city lights out here to mar the view. "This is fun," I said, lying back on the ground to trace the familiar constellations with my forefinger. "It's been a while since I took a vacation, and an even longer while since I've been in the wilderness."

"The sky is beautiful, isn't it?" He pointed out some of his favorite constellations. He was knowledgeable about the stars and we started chatting randomly about space and the possibilities of parallel universes and the unlikelihood of faster-than-light travel. He was well-informed and more scientifically literate than I had expected. I remembered him telling me he was self-taught. We talked about some books we had both read, and it began to get through to me that Shane was actually quite bright.

I asked him about his mom, and he talked a bit about her. It sounded like they had a close relationship. He was proud of the guide business she had built up in Montana, and I told him I thought it was pretty cool, too.

At some point, silence fell between us, but it felt comfortable. Then Shane rolled over and kissed me, nearly sabotaging the plan I'd come up with on the long and winding road.

Oh God, this was going to be difficult, but I forced myself

to pull away. No, no, my body screamed at me, but I ignored it.

I don't have lovers. I fuck.

Okay, buddy. Let's run a little test.

I yawned and stretched, then I pushed myself up to my feet. I jerked my top back down, covering my breasts and adjusted my pants, trying to pretend my sex wasn't already soaking wet and aching for him.

"Hey. Where're you going?"

"To my sleeping bag, of course. Much more comfy. Plus I think a mosquito just bit me." I opened the flap of my tent and crawled in. Shane apparently thought my words were an invitation, because he started to follow. Before he could fill my tent with his big body, I pulled the flap down right in his face. "Sorry, dude. I sleep alone."

There was a moment of explosive silence, then Shane pushed the flap aside. "You're not sleeping yet."

"Oh, yes I am. I'm tired."

"Bullshit. Don't play games with me." He took my chin in his hand and pulled my face to his. He planted one on my lips. I sighed and kissed him back. Then I pushed him away.

"I've decided separate beds make total sense, dude. After all, we're about to be brother and sister, aren't we? So be a good boy and go lie in your own tent."

"Cassie—"

"Don't worry. You're right next door, so I'm sure you'll be able to protect me from any dangers of the desert. Coyotes or jackals or snakes or whatever. I have complete faith in you."

"Quit foolin' around, princess. I know you want exactly what I want. You're wet for me, aren't you? And I am hot and hard for you."

Damn. His voice was enough to make me melt. What I really wanted was to melt all over his fingers, all over his tongue, and most of all, all over his cock. "I don't have lovers," I said, quoting him. "But I don't just go out and fuck a lot of guys, either. What I do do, you can still appreciate from your own tent. I'll probably make quite a clamor."

"What the fuck, Cassie?"

"I'm going to play with myself. Self-pleasure. Masturbate. Whatever you want to call it. You're welcome to listen. You can even shout encouragement. Why don't you jerk off in your own tent, too? Maybe we can time it so we come together."

He growled and burst through the flap of my tent, fell on top of me, and then rolled me over so I was straddling him. I started to laugh. He swatted my ass a couple of times and I laughed even harder. Then he was laughing, too.

Then we fucked. Or maybe even made love, at least a little bit. When I fell asleep, he was still there, holding me tightly. I could feel his heartbeat, slow and steady against my chest.

But next time I woke, he was gone.

Sure enough, the jerk had left me and gone to sleep in his own tent.

Wow. He was such a stubborn hardass. I wondered what had turned him into such a solitary man.

CHAPTER 29

Shane

I TOSSED AND TURNED IN my tent but I couldn't fall asleep, even though I was tired as fuck. Long ride, marathon sex session, yet the sandman eluded me.

I barreled out of my tent and patrolled the campsite. A few other tents, some smelly surfer looking dudes smoking weed by their filthy RV. This place blew—I hadn't wanted to stop here, but I could tell Cassie was getting tired. I'd been heading toward this nice site in Guerrero Negro. Had a restaurant, wifi, and even whale-watching tours. I was even thinking of surprising her with an early dawn excursion. Maybe we could even still make it if we left at dawn.

I wasn't trying to be romantic, but I did want her to have a good time. She'd gone along with all my plans so far, so I'd wanted to do something nice for her.

I knelt outside of Cassie's tent—maybe if I snuck back in there and wrapped my arms around her tight little body I could drift off to sleep. Or better yet, she'd feel my rock hard cock pressing against her ass and we could go for another round. But she looked so peaceful, her chest slowly contracting, her body curled into a small ball, her hands tucked under her chin in some sort of prayer position. I wondered what she was dreaming about—could it be me?

Fuck it. Back to my tent. I couldn't figure out why this woman was getting to me. I didn't trust her, or her dad for that matter. She was one of those academic types, like my father had been. He'd been a geology professor. Met my mom when he was a professor at Montana State University in Billings. My mom loved him, or so she said, though they never married. I don't fucking remember him at all. The second he was offered a better position at some university in bumfuck Idaho, he bailed. Though his child support payments arrived on time, I never saw him again. He didn't know a fucking thing about me—he didn't even know I was a SEAL.

The starlight shone into my tent and I decided to use the illumination. I rummaged through my pack and grabbed my sketchpad and pencils. The fast, dark lines filled the page. I drew the moonlit sky, the stars, and of course, Cassie sitting under the constellations.

Some softer strokes added the luscious curves to her body, and I accentuated her features with short, dark marks—almost like exclamation points.

I never understood exactly why drawing calmed me down, and it didn't matter. Creating a picture was more powerful to me than explaining my thoughts in words.

Finished. A final examination showed the Baja mountain landscape in the distance—a looming contrast to Cassie's lithe figure. This trip would be nothing more than a memory by the end of the week, but I'd preserved this moment in time.

CHAPTER 30

Cassie

ON THE THIRD MORNING, AS we folded the tent and stowed our gear, I noticed that Shane was once again withdrawing into inscrutable silence. He'd been the same yesterday morning, too. Cold. Controlled. Distant. It reminded me of how he had behaved on the night we'd met. At least he'd been polite then, even if it had been clear he wanted to be rid of me. Now he couldn't get rid of me, so he didn't even bother to be nice.

Why had I ever agreed to this crazy idea? A road trip, sex, and camping with a man who didn't like me any more than I liked him? What a brilliant plan! Yet another example of how stupid humans could be when they let their genitals do their thinking.

"Not like that," he said sharply as I tried to stuff my sleeping bag into the Harley carry-all. "That's not how you do it."

"Fine." I tossed the bundle to him. "Sorry for screwing up. You want me to roll around in the sand until every inch of my skin is covered with it?" That's what they did when their SEAL trainees messed up. Actually, that was one of the milder punishments.

"I want you to sit down and shut up while I finish packing. We are carrying a lot more gear than usual, thanks to you, and it has to be balanced. We're not driving a fucking limo, or whatever you're used to."

"I only brought what you told me to bring."

I hated the way he assumed that we were some sort of rich, spoiled assholes. It wasn't true. Dad was a university professor who made extra money doing consulting. He had always worked hard and saved. Our home back in Massachusetts had been nice, but not a mansion. I'm sure my background was more privileged than Shane's but it wasn't as if we were part of the one percent.

In Rolling Meadows, my hometown in Massachusetts, I'd gone to the public school and my friends had come from a broad swathe of different incomes. I'd worked part-time in high school and college like everyone else. I had student loans to pay off. I lived in a modest apartment near campus in La Jolla during the academic year and I earned a little extra cash working at the Birch aquarium.

As for Dad's house overlooking the beach in Coronado, we didn't own that place. Dad had done a house trade with some wealthy dude who was doing a visiting professorship in Boston for the academic year. We got that guy's gorgeous mansion overlooking the beach, and he'd taken our more modest home back in Massachusetts. Dad was planning to sell our old house and buy a new one out here, but it wouldn't be anything as expensive as the Coronado place, because California real estate on that level was out of his price range.

I'd considered making this all clear to Shane, but what was the point? I didn't care what he thought of me. If he'd seen my dad's sailboat—the thing Shane kept calling his yacht—he'd have to adjust his fantasies. It was small, kinda old, and could probably have used a good, thorough barnacle cleaning.

Now I was in a bad mood, too. I plopped myself down on a

nearby boulder and sulked while Shane did the final packing. "Let's get started," he snarled, even though I'd done exactly what he'd told me to do. He climbed on the bike. "Hurry up. Put on sunscreen, and don't forget your sunglasses. Get your helmet on."

"Save the commands for the bedroom." I jerked on my helmet and climbed on behind him. If we could have ridden without my touching him, that would have been fine with me. Dick.

But of course I had to fold my arms around his strong chest. I had to press up against that firm back, that rock-hard ass, those amazing thighs. Damn him. I wished he'd take his stupid pheromones and get the hell out of my life.

Long-term, even the thrill of pressing my belly and chest against Shane's firm back got monotonous. We were in a hot desert climate with the sun beating down, but the breeze from the draft of riding was enough to keep us relatively cool. But in this part of Baja, there wasn't much to see but scrub and cactus, road and more road.

The ride today was long, too. We grabbed lunch in San Ignacio, which was an oasis compared with the desert we had just ridden through—there were even date palm trees. We restocked on gas and water and I got into a short debate with His Lordship over my desire to take a side trip down to the lagoon where the gray whales come to breed at this time of year. When I showed him the map and how to get there, he rejected the idea.

"That's almost fifty miles in the wrong direction. We'd have to stay here for a day, maybe two. You want to miss this wedding you've insisted on dragging me to?"

Obviously I didn't. "I just want to see some whales."

"We'll soon be riding down the east coast. Maybe you'll see some there."

Shoving the map back under his nose, I pointed to a spot off the main highway on the east coast between Mulegé and Loreto. "Okay, well, let's take this smaller road off the highway and camp by the sea tonight instead of going all the way into Loreto. Maybe we'll see some whales or dolphins in the Sea of Cortez. And even if we don't, it's supposed to be beautiful there."

He looked at me suspiciously. "Isn't that the spot where you claimed some old fortune-teller guy hangs out?"

"Somewhere near there," I admitted. I had read about the old Mayan shaman on one of the blogs I'd consulted before the trip. "He's a whale-whisperer."

Shane rolled his eyes. "I'm not even gonna ask."

But, to my utter amazement, when we finally got down to the area I'd indicated on the map, late in the day, he swung the bike off the main road and onto a dirt road heading east.

Whoa. He was doing something I'd asked for? I could hardly believe it.

I hugged him harder than usual. I was clinging to him happily with my cheek pressed to his back for quite a while on the rough road, wondering when we were going to see the sea. We hit a bump. It felt like a big bump. I hung on tightly, seeing the road race by alongside us, not particularly rutted. It wasn't a good road, by any means, but now it felt as if it was coming apart under our wheels.

Shane stiffened and slowed down. The shaking continued. Got worse. What the fuck? Maybe we had a flat tire or something?

The bike started to skid. Or turn. Or something. I wasn't sure what was happening. I just hung on as we leaned over to the right and slowed and bucked and then there was a sickening sensation of something very, very wrong.

The bike shuddered and jerked. I was slammed against Shane and he was sent forward. Fuck, fuck, fuck. We pitched up and then down. Everything was confusion.

Next thing I knew the bike seemed to slip out from under me and I was rolling on the ground, pain of all types shuddering into me. I let out a moan of fear because I thought I had stopped but I kept bucking up and down—me, the ground, the sky and where was Shane? I wasn't clutching his body anymore. I was curled on my side on a patch of ground that wouldn't stop shaking. It was making an unearthly noise, too.

Maybe if I'd grown up on the West coast instead of in Massachusetts, I'd have realized what was happening. It wasn't until I managed to push myself up on my hands and knees and feel the earth still shuddering beneath me that I got it.

Earthquake. Oh my God, it was an earthquake. A big one. A very big earthquake that had sent us careening off the road.

CHAPTER 31

Cassie

SHANE. WHERE WAS SHANE? I was about to scream his name when I heard my own being yelled:

"Cassie? Cassie!"

He was there, behind me. In my blind spot. I grabbed my helmet and yanked it off. My arm hurt. My shoulder hurt. My legs and ass and back all hurt. But I didn't see any blood or any bones sticking out.

Shane was also on his ass, pushing himself up on his arms. I could see a tear in his sleeve. Some blood. A lot of blood. He looked even more dazed than me, but it didn't stop him. He pushed himself to a squat and then rose shakily. He rocked as he stood. I couldn't tell if it was the ground still rocking or if he was injured.

He limped the few steps to me and went back into a squat. "Are you hurt? Cassie? Are you okay?" He actually sounded as if he cared.

"You have blood on your arm." He had blood on his leg, too, I realized. Same side. Another place where his bike riding clothes were ripped. He must have landed on a rock or something. "Shane, you're hurt."

"I'm fine. Don't move. Let me check you out. I'm a corpsman."

I obeyed because I was still confused and I honestly didn't know if I was hurt. I thought I was just shaken up. He told me to move this and lift that and he looked into my eyes and took my pulse both in my throat and wrist. He then had me move my limbs and point my freaking fingers and toes, all of which I could do.

Meanwhile, red blood was seeping from wounds on his right arm and leg. It wasn't gushing, though. Or pulsing. That was good. Not arterial wounds then.

"Sit," I commanded when he had finished examining me. "I'm okay. You're bleeding. Let me examine you now. Tell me what to look for."

"I'm fine," he repeated, but he started putting pressure on the wound on his leg. As he bent over to do this, though, the blood coming from his arm increased. I squatted down beside him and looked more closely at the arm. His jacket was torn and so was his skin—there was a gash on his forearm that must have been close to four inches long.

"I'm putting pressure on this," I told him, doing so as calmly as I could. He had pushed aside the fabric over the leg wound. It wasn't as bad as the arm wound, but both were still bleeding. "Shane. I think you need stitches."

He looked again at the arm wound. "Fuck. We usually don't suture wounds in the field. We stop the bleeding with pressure bandages."

"And then what?"

He looked a little sheepish. "Then we evacuate the wounded to a medical facility. But that's for the big shit. These are just scratches. I mean, sure, they could use a suture or two, but it's not necessary. They'll heal without stitches. I'll just have a couple more scars to decorate my body with. Calm down."

"I'm calm," Actually, I was panicking. There was nothing around us that I could see. We were alone in the desert and Shane was hurt.

He obviously realized how scared I was because he looked at me steadily and said, "It'll be okay. I have a great med kit. I'll take care of everything."

Yeah right. How? His right arm was the one with the wound. Not even an experienced corpsman could patch himself up left-handed, could he?

"Get my med pac and I'll show you how you can help. I'm fine with the leg, but I could use a bit of assistance with the arm." He gave me another assessing look. "But not if you're squeamish. I don't need you fainting on me."

"I'm not squeamish," I said through gritted teeth.

"Good. Biggest problem with wounds is the possibility of infection. That's more important than a damn suture. So we're gonna wash, disinfect and seal me up with a pressure bandage. I'll heal just fine."

"That was an earthquake, right?"

"That was a fucking Big One. I had to steer off the road. Look. It was breaking up."

I was a little better oriented now. We were off in the dirt on the side of the road. About 20 yards ahead of us, the packed dirt track had buckled up in a slope that wasn't supposed to be there. Beyond it was a jagged fissure with a smoke or dust cloud billowing around it. If we had hit that we'd have had a much worse spill.

I didn't even want to think what might be inside that crack in the earth.

The bike was on its side a couple of yards away from us. It didn't look too messed up. He must have slowed it way down before it had skidded out from under us. I guess we were lucky that it hadn't landed on any part of our bodies.

"I've never been in an earthquake before."

He gave me an incredulous look.

"I'm from Massachusetts." I managed to stand and limp toward the bike. "Where is the first aid kit packed?"

"Rear container, left side. It should pull right out."

The fact that he hadn't insisted on getting it himself worried me. Was he doing the I'm-so-tough-I-don't-feel-pain thing? Of course he was. He was a SEAL.

The carrier was battered from the crash and didn't open as easily as usual. My hands felt slippery with sweat as I struggled with it. Sweat wasn't good. We were in a desert climate. The sun was low in the sky now, but it had been hot during the middle of the day. Night was coming on and it would get chilly.

What if we were stuck here? Shane had made a big deal about carrying plenty of water, but water would go fast if the motorcycle was too damaged to drive.

A big fucking earthquake. Where was its epicenter? Here in Baja or someplace else? Maybe we hadn't even felt the worst of it. Maybe it was a big disaster? Had it been felt off the coast? What if it had caused a tsunami and my Dad and his small sailboat had been caught in it?

I felt dizzy and really scared as various horrible possibilities swept through me.

Calm down, I told myself. What did my mother always say? It's no good worrying about things that will probably never happen. Yeah. Like cancer killing you when you were only forty-one.

"Did you find it? Do you need help?"

I pulled myself together. Had to think and act smartly. "Got it." I grabbed one of the canteens and the Mylar blanket from the pack, too, then returned to Shane, who was sitting on the ground, still applying pressure. The leg wound appeared to have stopped bleeding, but he was still losing blood from his arm.

He showed me a rock. It was rounded on one end and pointed on the other. It had reddish stuff on it. "Blood," said Shane. "That's what cut me. I must have landed on it. See? It's pretty clean. Once I irrigate the wounds to get the dirt out, they should be good. They aren't deep, so stop worrying. This is totally minor shit."

"You still lost blood," I said stubbornly. If I wanted to worry about him, I would.

"Listen to me, Cassie. It's no big deal. I haven't popped any arteries, so that's good." He tore open a sterile pack and pressed it to his leg, then put another on his arm. "Put your hand on that and hold on hard."

I did so. Shane's blood was on me now, lending a coppery scent to the air. There were other unfamiliar smells too from dust and plants being stirred up in the desert by the force of the tremor.

"Where's your cell phone?"

With my left hand, I pulled out of my pocket.

"Check for connectivity. Don't panic if we don't have any. Cell service often goes down in an earthquake."

"There's no signal."

"I figured." He was fishing through the medical kit. "Get me some water." He looked up at me. "You brought a sun hat, right? Find it and put it on. Find mine, too."

"The sun's going down."

"Then we'll need our hats to keep our bodies warm. We are no longer on the main highway, as you may have noticed. We are, in fact, out in the middle of no-fucking-where."

I said nothing to this. We were here, I knew, because of me. If we were lost in the damn desert, it was my fault.

When I gave him the water, he told me to take a few good swallows. "It's been ages since we stopped to drink. Need to stay hydrated." He drank a large swig too.

"But what if we run out?"

"We'll get more."

He didn't say how.

Shane was all business: "First we'll patch me up. Then I'll need to see what kind of shape the bike is in. If we can travel to a more sheltered area, we will. If we can't, we'll figure out a way to shelter here."

I looked around nervously. I saw nothing in any direction except scrub and cactus. This wasn't good.

CHAPTER 32

Shane

BAD. THIS WAS REALLY FUCKING bad.

Didn't matter that I had extensive training, I mean fuck the
Navy had spent over half a million dollars to train every one of
us, even more to train me since I was a medic. But an earthquake, middle of the desert, in a developing country with an un-
stable government meant we were royally fucked.

"Start the small camp stove and boil up some water. Don't
waste any. Just enough to fill this plastic bag."

She did as she was told without speaking. In the meantime,
I'd grabbed a pair of gloves from the med kit and used sterile
gauze to clean out as much gunk from my wounds as I could—
dirt and dust and gravel from the road. When Cassie poured the
water in the bag, she turned off the stove and returned to me.
"Now what?"

I handed her another pair of sterile gloves. "Cut the corner
and flush both wounds. You can control the flow by pinching the
bottom."

The hot watered burned my gashes but I didn't flinch.

"Good job, babe. Now scrub it with this liquid soap. Not too rough."

The soap stung like fuck but again I kept still and breathed deep.

When she finished, she applied some anti-bacterial ointment and I explained how to close the wounds with my pressure bandages. They oughta stop any residual bleeding. I'd trade them off for regular bandages before too much time went by. Fortunately, I had a good kit and adequate supplies.

"Come here." I kissed her. "You did a good job, Miss Nightingale."

Our kiss lasted longer than it should've and I noted that it was our first kiss that didn't lead into sex. I pulled away from her, and relaxed on the ground. I needed to rest.

I must have dozed for a while. After I woke, I checked my wounds. I felt okay so I checked again on Cassie, to make sure she didn't have anything wrong with her that I'd missed. But she seemed fine so I didn't bother to wake her.

Next I inspected my bike. There was a hole in the tire, but I had a puncture kit so I wasn't worried about that. I turned the bike upright. That's when I noticed the damage.

"Fuck my life!" I cursed.

Cassie roused from her sleep and bolted up. "Shane, you okay?"

I didn't answer. The right side carrier had been bent by the weight of the fallen bike. "Fuck," I said again as I dug through the carrier, my hand grasping on the remnants of our lifeline. "Sat phone got damaged."

"You brought a satellite phone? Do SEALs carry stuff like that everywhere you go?"

I ignored her and started tinkering with it.

"So it's not working?"

"No," I snarled. "Fuck."

"So…" her brow furrowed, "That means you can't call in air cover or something?"

I shot her a look. I was not in the mood for her smartass comments.

Her tone softened. "No quick rescue, I guess, then?"

"No. We're on our own."

The engine started up, but when I applied the front brake, the lever barely resisted my pull. It must've blown the seal on the brake when it hit the road split. We were fucked without a front brake. I could probably make it to the next town if it was only a leak. Either way, I would need to get parts to fix it.

We were nowhere near any towns, with limited water, in the desert heat, during a natural disaster.

I walked back over to Cassie. Before she said a word, I could tell by the look in her eyes she was anxious.

"Cassie, we're going to be fine. I got this. I'm not going to let anything happen to you. We need to conserve our energy." I held her in my arms and kissed her head.

Over the past couple days I'd been withdrawing from her, trying to deny the feelings I was developing. Like the fact that I was dreading my mom's wedding, not only because I thought she was making a mistake, but also that I didn't want to end whatever was happening between Cassie and me. But I didn't even know what I was feeling. The sex was incredible, but it was more than that. The way she listened to me, the way she saw through all the smartass remarks I dished out, the way she seemed to really want to know the real me.

The other girls I'd slept with since I'd been a SEAL were just interested in being fucked by a SEAL. But Cassie didn't seem to care about my job; she respected it and admired my strength, but she kept trying to connect with the man under the tough exterior. Asking about my family, delving into my interests in medicine and nature.

We applied sunscreen and sat down together. "No reason to worry—we're going to be fine."

Her lips and chin trembled a little. My stomach felt rock hard and a spike of adrenaline bolted through me. I'd been on many missions, saved my brothers' lives, and fought the enemy. But the most dangerous enemy, the one that wouldn't surrender to guns and fear, was Mother Nature.

CHAPTER 33

Cassie

SOME SORT OF ICY CALM had come over me. It felt as though I were drawing strength from Shane. It had been his steady voice that had gotten me through the patching up his wounds thing. He'd been in pain—he couldn't hide the way his muscles had tensed every time I touched the injured areas. But if he could control his pain, I could control my nerves.

Fortunately, I wasn't squeamish about the sight of blood. At school, I'd put in some time as a lab assistant for a vertebrate anatomy course. I'd dissected plenty of mammals and I knew some physiology.

Still, I'd been worried that I'd do something wrong. Make his situation worse instead of better. But it had all gone well.

I had set up camp. Right there on the side of the road. It would be getting dark soon and we needed shelter and a camp-fire.

He wouldn't allow us to get too far from the road or from the motorcycle. "You should always stay with your vehicle," he explained. "And even though this isn't the highway, there might be other travelers. I'm not going to start out doing something stupid." He grimaced and added, "Stupider. This whole fucking trip was stupid."

"Yeah, too bad we didn't fly," I shot back.

"Too bad we didn't stay home."

It was also too bad about the broken satellite phone. I hadn't known he had one. What other shit had he brought? SEALs prepared for anything, right? If I had to be stuck with a guy in the desert because of a natural disaster, who better to be stuck with than him?

"We don't know how bad this earthquake is yet or how wide an area is affected," he said. "If we had stayed on the highway, there would probably be other travelers and a bigger chance of rescue. Here, that's not as likely."

Right, I thought. Don't rub it in, dammit. "At least we have water." No longer would I question him for taking up valuable space in the carrier with his multiple water containers.

"Not enough."

I knew we had two full gallon canteens because I'd filled them myself. I had another 16 ounce one and so did he. That sounded like a lot to me. But then I remembered that a human needs 64 ounces of water a day to survive. More if it's hot, which it was, or if they need to expend energy doing things like, uh, surviving. That meant we only had enough water for about one and a half days. Maybe less.

"We're not that far from the Pacific, so we should get some breeze coming off the water. And there is high ground," he pointed to a hilly ridge that didn't look too far away. "Water runs downhill. There is quite a lot of vegetation, so there is probably a fresh water source."

"If we can't find water, can we drink from a barrel cactus or something?"

He rolled his eyes. "No. That's a myth. Most barrel cactuses are toxic."

I thought about the plants I knew of that were safe to eat. There definitely were some. I knew a fair amount about ocean vegetation. I didn't know a lot about cactuses, though, having come from the Northeast.

I had once taken a course with Dad on survival in the wilderness. If I probed my brain I could probably remember some of the things I'd learned. Water was vital no matter where you were. As were fire and shelter.

"What about solar stills?" I asked, remembering being taught about digging holes in the ground, filling them with vegetation and covering the hole with plastic. The sunlight would shine through the plastic and photosynthesis from the plants would produce a water vapor that could be captured in a container placed in the hole.

"Stills cost energy to build and don't collect enough water to bother," he said. But he looked faintly surprised that I had even heard of solar stills, just as he'd been when he found out I knew how to SCUBA dive. Hadn't this guy ever met up with a woman who could take care of herself? It seemed odd, considering that his mother was an outdoorswoman.

"We can look for water in the morning. You need some help with those tents?"

"Nope. I'm used to doing it now. Keep resting for a bit longer." I pressed one of the canteens on him. "Drink some more. You lost blood."

He didn't argue. He drank.

I kept checking my cell, but the service remained down. This worried me because cell service in Baja had been amazingly good so far. Shane kept cursing over the broken satellite phone. I guess SEALs didn't go anywhere without prime communications in the field.

But this wasn't warfare. It was looking increasingly like a disaster zone, though. The jagged fissure that had split the land extended on both sides of the road. It got wider to our left and narrower to our right until it petered out.

I wasn't getting anywhere close to the thing. Although I knew I was being silly, and it wasn't a crater that descended down into the center of the earth, it still freaked me out. If we'd been going just a little bit faster, or if Shane hadn't reacted as quickly as he had, the earth could have swallowed us up.

I had just finished securing our tents when that ground jerked and shook again, sending me sprawling to my knees. "Just an aftershock," he assured me, but it rattled me. What if that crevice widened? It could still swallow us, maybe? Or a new one could open?

Shit. I wanted to go home to Massachusetts. I didn't like this earthquake crap.

I clamped my mouth shut, though. I was not going to complain. Not going to give Shane an excuse to get all patronizing with me again. If he could get through this without panicking, dammit, so could I.

We sat together in front of the fire. Shane gave me some dried fruit and nuts. I ate without comment. It wasn't a large meal, but I knew the reason for that. Digestion required energy and hydration. You can survive without food a whole lot longer than you can survive without water. If water was scarce, we should not eat too much.

After supper, Shane got up to tinker with the motorcycle. He insisted he was feeling better, and it did look as if the color was back in his cheeks. He really was a tough guy—a couple of lacerations weren't going to keep him down.

"I've got the engine running well enough to take us a short distance," he said a little later. "We'll get up early, before the sun. I'd head back to the main highway, but I doubt the bike will hold up that far. I just hope there's some settlement near the water. Your fucking whale-whisperer dude if nothing else."

I hoped so, too! "So we should try to get some sleep, huh?"

"Yeah. Sleep is good."

We huddled together in one of the tents, and despite everything I was worried about, like whether I'd be alive tomorrow night or not, touching Shane made me yearn for him again. "We probably shouldn't," I said when he started touching me back. "You're hurt."

"I'm not that hurt," Mr. Badass insisted.

"But it takes energy. Burns calories. Causes sweating and the loss of other body fluids."

He snorted. "We'll be fine. I've been in much worse situations than this." A more violent than usual aftershock shuddered through the tent, and I clung to him. "At least there aren't guys shooting at us. Or dropping explosives on our location."

I thought of the damage that an earthquake of this size could do. The people crushed or trapped in fallen buildings. I hoped not too many had died. Shane and I were lucky. We weren't that bad off and tomorrow we'd find water. Nothing to fret about.

I hoped our parents were okay. Oh God…it was too terrible to even consider any other possibilities.

"Shane." I slid my hips against him and found him hard and ready. "I need you. Please. I need you now."

His mouth came down on mine and his hand found its way between my thighs. "We'll take it slow. Calm and cool. No sweat."

"No sweat," I agreed, kissing him back.

Yeah, we burned some calories, but it made me feel a whole lot better. Shane left me alone in my tent again, but at least he waited until I was sleeping.

CHAPTER 34

Cassie

HE WOKE ME UP BEFORE sunrise. He gave me water and an MRE.

I looked around. Even though the sun hadn't risen yet, there was already a lot of light. But it was such a desolate location. I didn't see anything but desert and hills in all directions.

There had been no traffic on the dirt road since we'd crashed. No low-flying planes overhead. It was as if we were alone in the world, and it was a spooky feeling, as if we were the only two survivors of a global disaster.

He allowed me to check his wounds. I rubbed on more antibiotic cream after he confirmed that they were healing. We were both bruised and sore, but nothing, he insisted, that would stop us from moving on.

We took down the tents and he packed everything back on the bike. He was basically ignoring his wounds today, now that the bandages had been changed. I hoped that would be okay. It still scared me to think he might be hurting.

He got the engine going and I climbed on behind him. The

bike was making clattering sounds that it hadn't made before. This increased as he sped up and took us into the desert, along the border of the fissure the earthquake had left in the earth. When we rocked and bucked, I wasn't sure if it was the terrain or another aftershock. I just hung on as hard as I could and hoped for the best.

When the fissure jagged to a close, we were able to cross to the far side and arc back in the direction of the road. I'd thought the dirt road was rough, but it was nothing to jolting over the scrubby earth. Several times he had to swerve to avoid rocks and cacti, and once we almost got stuck in the sand. I was hot, sweating and wired with adrenaline by the time we reached the road again.

We rode for a while, our progress slow. The engine was making loud sputtering noises, and I could hear Shane muttering curses. From the sound of things, this vehicle was not going to get us all the way to Cabo without some major repairs. Or even to the next town.

The road was climbing the hills between us and the coast now. Eventually we had ascended enough that I caught a glimpse of the ocean in the distance.

Thank goodness. The sea would at least cool us, right? Even though we couldn't drink its salty water. The sun was high now and the temperature felt as if it was going to be even hotter than yesterday.

When the road crossed a dry and narrow wash, Shane turned off into the scrub again and gunned it toward some small trees. They looked bushier than the other vegetation, and the terrain along the wash was rocky. I didn't see any water in the wash, but I did see a lot more greenery. Where there was abundant vegetation, surely there would also be fresh water?

The engine whined and coughed. We rolled to a slow stop.

"Good place to look for water," Shane said cheerfully as he stood and steadied the bike. "These broad-leafed trees might be trapping water in their root systems. If we're really lucky, there might be a creek or a stream. See the birds? They hang out at water sources, same as humans."

We set up shelter, doing everything together. At one point, he nodded and complimented me. "You learn fast."

I smiled at him, grateful for his praise. "Thanks."

When we were finished with that, he insisted we sit down in the shade, rest and drink some water. We were going through our supply fast. I wasn't super thirsty, yet, but I would be soon.

Thirst would be bad. If we were thirsty, we were already dehydrated.

CHAPTER 35

Cassie

"NOW THAT WE'VE RESTED A bit," Shane said, "I'm going to look for water."

"I'll come with you."

"No. There's no point in both of us wasting energy. You stay here in the shade and conserve your strength."

"Let me go while you conserve energy. We might need your strength later, since you have more survival skills."

I thought this was a reasonable suggestion, but Shane didn't agree. "Don't argue with everything I say."

I bit back a retort. I hadn't been arguing with him much at all since the earthquake had hit. But if I argued now, he'd claim it proved his point. "Well, please be careful."

"Aw. You worried about me?"

This was sarcastic, so I rolled my eyes.

"You'll be okay," he said, as if he realized I was apprehensive about being alone. "I won't be gone long." He handed me a couple of items from his survival kit. One was a whistle. There were a couple of chemical light sticks. The third item was a knife. "If there is any trouble, blow the whistle three times. Break the light tubes to start them glowing and wave them in the air. I'll be able to see that."

"And the knife?"

"That's just to make you feel kick-ass," he said with a grin.

I laughed. "You'd better keep it then, I wouldn't know what to do with it."

"I have another. You'll be fine and I'll be back soon. I am not going far, I promise. Just to the top of that rise. You okay?"

"Yup."

"Be careful where you step and keep your pants legs rolled down. There might be spiders or even snakes. We have a snake-bite kit with the first aid stuff. You know what to do if you see a snake?"

"Run screaming in the other direction?"

"Cassie. This isn't funny. Stop clowning around."

Dammit. "If I don't find something to clown about, I'm afraid I'll break down."

Wow, that was honest. I wasn't sure what had induced me to admit that.

He laid one hand on my shoulder. "Repeat after me: we are going to be okay."

"How can I repeat that when we don't know what's going to happen? We don't even know how bad this is. How many cities and towns have been destroyed. We don't know where our parents are, or if they're safe." I squeezed my eyes together. I was not going to cry.

"Repeat it."

I blew out a shaky breath. "We are going to be okay."

He leaned down and kissed my lips lightly. Despite everything, lust spiked through me. I coiled my arms around his neck and kissed him back, hard. When his tongue slid into my mouth, my body started yearning for him.

"Stop that," I said softly.

He raised his eyebrows.

"I'm talking to my vagina, not to you."

A grin slip his face. "What are you saying to your vagina? Or is that too personal a question?"

"I'm telling it not to get all gushy. Because I don't want to waste body fluids!"

"We'll find water," he promised, "And then we can let your vagina have some fun."

CHAPTER 36

Shane

I TRAMPED UP THE WASH, which sloped at a gentle uphill angle toward a rocky outcropping and some higher hills. The land here was greener than the flatter area where we had camped last night, but so far I hadn't found any moist ground.

I grasped my small folded shovel, a tool I'd nearly left at home. But I knew from long experience that it was unwise to take a road trip without a few basic tools. It wasn't just my SEAL training that had taught me this. My mom and I had camped in the Montana wilderness frequently when I'd been a boy.

She was a skilled outdoorswoman, and she had taught me to love and respect nature. We'd always spent considerable time planning our hikes, and she'd always insisted on having a well-stocked emergency kit. SEAL training had taught me to survive in all climates and all terrains. But when you were running low on water, the need to find it trumped everything else. Not even a highly trained Navy corpsman could keep people alive without adequate hydration.

I was pretty impressed, actually, with the way Cassie had behaved so far in this mess. She hadn't bitched or complained, at least not out loud. If clowning was her way of coping, that was a helluva lot better than tears.

I tried to imagine one of the girls I occasionally fucked marooned in the desert. Those women would be useless. Nothing but a burden. But Cassie had drunk what water I'd ordered her to drink and she hadn't complained when I'd offered her little in the way of food. She understood what we were doing and why. She obviously knew the dangers, too, but she was keeping it together.

In a way, she reminded me of my mom.

At the base of a broad-leafed tree, I unfolded the shovel and dug a hole, trying not to expend too much energy. The earth was moist a few inches down, so I dug a little deeper. Water didn't start rising in the hole, but it might if I waited a bit. Promising, but not great. I left the hole open and moved on.

I examined rocks and crevasses, looking for hollows where rainwater might have collected. But it must not have rained for a while. Frequently, I looked back in Cassie's direction and listened in case she was calling or whistling for me. I could no longer see the camp because of the twists and turns of the wash and the outcroppings of rock.

A rock cliff rose around the next bed, falling from a large outcropping of granite. I stood still, listening. Overhead I saw a dove, and I thought I could hear the buzzing of bees.

I scanned the rock surface. Pigeons and doves required a water source. Bees built their hives within reach of one. The cliff wall was sheer, but I could scale it with some effort. I hadn't brought climbing rope, and doing it without Cassie nearby would be foolish, because if I fell and hurt myself, she'd be left alone out here without water. That wasn't an option.

I prowled around the side of the outcropping, noting the greenery and listening for the sound of flowing water. An aftershock shook the earth, and stones crumbled from overhead. I ducked out of the way as a rock the size of a baseball just missed hitting me.

Fuck. I hoped Cassie was okay. That had been a big damn aftershock. I listened for her when the earth gods quieted again.

I was listening so hard for any trickle of water that I was startled when I heard a different sound. It sounded like an engine. It was coming from the other side of the ridge, off to the north. I recalled from the map that there was a large peninsula up that way that was pretty undeveloped.

I wasn't sure if there were any roads there. Well, more dirt roads, probably. Those weren't all on the map. Could we be near someone who could help us? If I didn't find some water soon, we were truly fucked.

I climbed a little higher, but except for the cries of the birds and the buzz of insects, all seemed quiet. Then I heard it again, far in the distance. The revving of an engine—a car, or maybe a motorcycle. Sounded like it was headed in the opposite direction from us, though.

I remembered those two hulking motorcycle club dudes we'd seen a couple times. Those guys had been bad news. I wouldn't want to run into them again while Cassie and I were strung out like this.

There could be other bad guys around, too, especially on these less touristy shores. Baja was a popular place for bikers, both the good and the bad kind. I wished I'd stayed on the highway. In a disaster, there would be military vehicles on the roads and planes overflying the area, assessing the damage.

That's what comes of trying to do Cassie a favor and taking her to visit her damn whale-watcher dude. I couldn't believe I'd been such a sap.

And we would've been better off driving down in my truck, but there was no way I could have anticipated this disaster.

There were no more engine sounds. But when I walked a little farther, what I heard was a trickle. It took me a few moments to locate it—it was around yet another granite outcropping: a small flow of water was sliding down over the rock face from ledge a few yards above. It wasn't much, but it was water. I propped one of the canteens under the flow and waited for it to fill. Then I bathed my hands and face in the moisture.

I leaned against the cliff in the shade while the canteen filled. It took about twenty minutes to fill my 40-ounce container. I also had a gallon container that I decided to leave here to catch the flow. There was a risk that animals would knock it over, but I propped it up as well as I could.

I needed to get back to Cassie. The water was cool, so it was probably coming from a spring, especially since I didn't see any other sources of rain run-off. If it were a spring, it would probably keep producing.

I'd hoped for a creek or a stream, but this was good. We could survive with this, as long as the spring kept flowing. But we were in the middle of nowhere, and we couldn't count on being rescued out here. Unless cellular came back or I could repair that satellite phone.

Feeling tired and hot but reassured, I headed back to Cassie. Like I promised her, we were going to be okay. Nothing was going to happen to Cassie, not on my watch.

CHAPTER 37

Cassie

SHANE CAME BACK BEFORE I got too antsy, thank goodness. It was nerve-wracking, but apart from a couple more aftershocks, nothing horrible happened while he was gone. I hated that I felt so dependent upon him.

He smiled as he handed over a full canteen. "Oh my God! You found some!" I jumped up and hugged him hard. He hugged back, and then pulled away.

"A small spring. It's not great, but it's better than nothing. I left the gallon container there to fill. In the meantime, we have to purify this."

Right. We couldn't just drink it.

Shane removed a small plastic bottle from his emergency pack. "Bleach. A few drops will do the trick. I'm going to strain it first, though. Give me that other empty container."

He used his bandana to strain the water. He then added the chlorine and let it sit. We'd be drinking water that tasted like a swimming pool, but at least it would be free of pathogens.

"You rock."

We both drank, and I felt a whole lot cheerier. Dying of dehydration a couple days before my father's wedding had really seemed an unpleasant fate.

"We should probably move closer to the sea. If we cross that ridge, it'll be downhill to the ocean."

"Cool. We can catch fish and suck fresh water from their eyes and spines."

He looked at me. "Have you ever done that?"

"No, but my dad and I took a survival course once."

"I'm trying to imagine you sucking on a fish eye."

I gave him a big grin. Finding water had made me feel a whole lot better. "I can think of things I'd rather suck on."

He laughed. He hadn't laughed that often since the earthquake and it lit up his face. "So you're game for setting out for the sea?"

"If you think it's our best bet, yeah, I'm game."

"Okay. We have water and can get more, so let's stay here for a siesta and then head out. I think we can get to the shore before nightfall. Where there's water, there will be wildlife. I don't want to run into something in the dark that I might not be quick enough to protect you from."

I was beginning to realize that he was all about protecting me. I liked it. But I knew it was the SEAL thing. It wasn't as if he actually cared about me. It was his duty to protect someone he figured was weaker than he was.

He went back to the spring to fetch the container he'd left there. When he returned, he was excited. "I went a little higher, to get a better look. We're even closer to the sea than I thought. There's a creek—almost dry but with a trickle of fresh water. But better still, I saw smoke."

"What sort of smoke?"

"I couldn't see. It's behind a ridge near the shore. I think it's a camp of some sort. Maybe it's your whale-whisperer."

"Oh, I hope so!"

"Whoever they are, they might have supplies or communications. We'll have to be careful, though, in case they're unfriendly."

"Will people really be unfriendly in a disaster zone?"

He looked at me with eyes that had seen a lot of nasty stuff. "You'd never know," was all he said.

CHAPTER 38

Shane

IN MY LINE OF WORK, there was no room for luck. We trained extensively; we were intricate machines, human terminators. Part of the reason that BUD/S training was so intensive and brutal was that we were taught to survive anything. SEAL: Sea, Air, Land. But today, I prayed for some good fortune.

We were dehydrated and hungry. Cassie's lips looked ashen, her eyes tired. I was dizzy and had a headache, not sure if it was from the extreme heat, the rationing of water, or limited food, more likely from a combination of all the elements.

I motioned for her to get back on my bike. She seemed a bit shaky and I wanted nothing more but to hold her in my arms, promise her I would keep her safe. I had a fleeting thought what it would be like to protect her not just through this trip, but forever. But I didn't make promises I couldn't keep.

A mile turned into ten, my eyes focused on the road. Hoping for some sign of life or the smoke I'd seen in the distance.

But what I found was something better. A sign. An actual sign.

A sign with no letters—just a pictograph of a crescent shaped moon with a whale underneath.

I kicked down the stand.

Cassie's lips brush over my ear. "Shane! This is the place I was telling you about. A moon! Meztli means moon in Nahuatl."

Nahuatl? At this point I didn't care what the fuck language this guy spoke, as long as he had water. But as we exited the road, the first thing I noticed was bricks—huge adobe bricks, collapsed over what seemed to be some type of dwelling.

Cassie and I drove up and took off our helmets. I pulled out my knife, I didn't know who I was going to encounter here, even the so-called whale-whisperer. Besides, I hadn't forgotten those motorcycle engines I'd thought I'd heard.

I motioned Cassie to stay silent. There was a decaying truck with what looked like herbs growing out of its back, a broken down motorcycle, and a stacked rock fence. I heard the distant sound of a coyote baying; the howl almost soothing. The ground had no fresh tracks, so I assumed that no one else had been here since the quake, which alleviated my fear of looters.

I decided it was safe enough to call out. "*Hola. ¿Hay alguien ahi?*"

Silence. I held Cassie to my side, and pushed in the door to the hut. "*Hola.*"

A Chihuahua seemed to fly out of dwelling, running frenzied in a circle, nipping at my ankles, as if she were pulling me inside.

I scanned the house, clay pots strewn everywhere, broken stone dishes. I waded through the mess to the back where I spotted a man, early fifties, long black hair streaked with silver, an ice chest pressing on his chest.

I lifted it off him, noticing the gash on his leg. "Cass, get my kit and our water."

She ran to the bike as I laid the guy out and elevated his legs with a chair I found. I reached down to his wrist and detected a pulse. Airways, Breathing, Circulation. I pressed my ear to his mouth, and could hear a shallow breath.

I tilted his head back, and he coughed. I checked him all over for broken bones. He was lucky—I found none.

I noticed the man's tattoo, some Aztec god. "You're gonna be fine, old man. I'm a medic."

He didn't say a word but squeezed my hand. After he had a sip of water, and I cleaned and bandaged the wound on his leg, he finally spoke.

"*Tlasohkamati*. Thank you. You have a polished eye. Your woman looks like an angel."

"Well we've had it pretty rough last few days. You may be able to repay us. Do you have food and water here?"

"*Mi casa es su casa*. But you're going to have to help your-self."

I kissed Cassie. I helped the old guy up and then I transferred him over to his mattress so he could rest. He said his name was Meztli. He told me the layout of the place; where he kept the food, the supplies, the well out back, the outhouse. I told him we'd take care of him.

My first stop was the well.

The cold water tasted so fresh and sweet. After I was hydrated, I got down to business. Still no reception on our phones. I needed to get in touch with my command and also see if my mom was okay. But for now, I just wanted to stare at this glorious sunset and drink some more water, with my angel by my side.

Meztli had recovered well enough to move around. But the best news was he had an extensive tool kit. After an hour of work, I was able to fix my satellite phone and check in with my command.

My command was fine. I had taken official leave after all and had asked for permission to come to Mexico, so I was in the clear. My buddy gave me the 411 on the quake: the epicenter had been in the desert very close to our location, and the quake registered at 7.2 on the Richter scale. There was extensive damage and casualties throughout the Baja region, but due to the ruralness of the area, the full impact of the quake was not known yet.

Of course, my buddies offered to sweep in on a helo and save us, but Meztli had an extensive supply of water and food and believed he could find the parts to fix my bike. So Cassie and I decided to take a day to rest and head to Cabo tomorrow.

We hadn't been able to get hold of our parents. I tried to assure Cassie that they probably were also lacking reception, but Cassie was worried sick that they'd been stranded at sea, the result of an earthquake-related accident.

Cassie, Meztli, and I settled around the campfire. Some Aztec music consisting of flutes and drums played on a battery-operated tape deck. Meztli was dining on raw food, like our ancestors had. Paleo before it was trendy. I'd made some hash, smoked chicken, corn, and eggplant from his stock. I worried that Cassie would protest and refuse to eat the meat, but she must have known our bodies needed protein because she didn't complain.

She excused herself to try the satellite phone again to call her dad. "So," Meztli asked while he sipped his homemade blend of medicinal tea, "how long have you been together?"

"We're not together. She's my stepsister . . . well will be in a few days."

Meztli gave out a hearty laugh. "Stepsister? I see the way you look at her. Your heart has become white, her heart has become white."

I took a sip of the tea he'd made me. Tasted like licorice. "Well, it's complicated. We met before our parents did, but I don't need a girlfriend. She's cool, though."

Meztli slapped my leg. "Listen, *Huitzilopochtli,* you scratch the jade, you tear apart the quetzal feather. She is worthy of honor."

I finished my crappy tea. Needed a break from his new-age crap. "Thanks for dinner. I'm gonna check on Cass."

My job pressures were different than from other men's. It would never work with Cassie. I didn't even know how to be in a relationship, and I had no examples to emulate. Fuck 'em and leave them. On to the next. No worries about her cheating when I was thousands of miles away from her, unable to even call. No worries about not being around to protect her. Who would want to date me anyway? I was gone most of the year, and when I was home, I was training. Cassie deserved someone who could listen to her, share her interests, someone better than me.

Besides, she was about to be my stepsister. She'd claimed I was in denial about that, and maybe she was right. I sure didn't want to think about it. Or face it. It was too fucked up.

Now was not the time to worry about our future. I rummaged through Meztli's tools and started working on my bike.

CHAPTER 39

Cassie

A LITTLE LATER THAT EVENING, while Shane was tinkering with his motorcycle, I sat in Metzli's hut with him and chatted a bit. He seemed remarkably revived for someone who had been injured in the earthquake, especially considering how old he was. But I noticed that despite his age, he had strong ropey muscles, proving, I guess, that if you use it, you don't lose it.

Metzli spoke a combination of Nahuatl, Spanish and English. When he discovered how bad I was at his two primary languages, he lapsed into English for my sake. Shane was much better with Spanish than I was.

"Is it true, sir, that you are a whale-whisperer?" I couldn't resist asking.

His wise old eyes gazed deeply into mine. "What the whales say to each other is beyond my understanding. But sometimes they grace me with a song."

"What do they sing to you?"

"They sing of friendship and fellowship and long journeys through waters cold and warm, turbulent and still. They sing of love and sorrow, loss and joy. Their songs are much like the songs of men. They sing of fear, for they notice changes in the seas that they do not understand. They dream of refuge, but the race of man has taken over the seas and they know not what to do."

"Wow. That's so sad. I'm a marine biologist. I study the seas and the creatures that live within."

He smiled at me. "Perhaps you are a whale-whisperer, too. Do you ever hear them speak to you?"

"Not whales, but seals and sea lions, yes, sometimes. I can recognize some of their calls, but their world remains largely a mystery to me."

"Some things should stay mysteries," said Metzli. "The moon would not be the same moon, if one side did not remain in the dark."

Maybe he had a point. As a scientist, I believed in shining light upon mysteries. Explaining things. Learning, knowing. But Metzli had lived a great deal longer than I had, so I respected his wisdom.

Shane called me over and handed me one of the now-empty water canteens. "Can you fill this for me? His well's out back. I'll need it boiled up for the next time I change our bandages."

"Sure thing. I saw the well. I'll take another container and fill them both."

"Thanks."

I didn't tell him that I had never operated a real well before. I doubted it was powered by electricity. But I knew the basic idea from watching frontier movies and stuff. Amazing how an earthquake could send us all back into our more primitive past. Then I reminded myself that our host lived this way all the time and, from the looks of his neat and well organized camp, he was happy with his simple lifestyle. He had a well for his water, the sea for his fish, the grains for his chickens and his plants and vegetables to supplement his meals. He had his old gods and goddesses to listen to his prayers. He had the sun and the moon and the brilliant panoply of stars. What more did he need?

I figured out the well. It worked just the way you'd expect. Bucket down, wind the crank, and bring the much heavier bucket back up. I was surprised at the strain it put on my arms and shoulders. No wonder Metzli had such powerful muscles at his age—living in a simple, primitive manner was hard work!

It had been something to watch Shane go into full EMT mode when we'd first arrived. I knew he was a corpsman, and I'd watched him check me out in the desert and tend to his own lacerations, but the old man had clearly been in bad shape after being stuck under that heavy ice chest ever since the earthquake, if that was how long he'd been there.

I was amazed at how tenderly Shane had treated Metzli. He'd spoken gently to him, words of encouragement and praise, and the old man seemed to draw strength and hope from his touch.

I'd felt a twinge of envy. Why didn't he show that kind of tenderness to me? But I was ashamed as soon as I thought it. My feelings about Shane were starting to tumble about wildly. I didn't understand myself, and I didn't really want to.

This would all be over soon. Somehow we'd make it to Cabo, find our parents, do the wedding thing, and then play the roles that we'd be stuck with for the rest of our lives.

Assuming Dad was really okay. Now that we had found some sort of shelter, and the promise of food and water and maybe a way to fix Shane's Harley, my own single-mindedness about surviving had begun to give way to other thoughts. We were going to be fine, but what about Dad and Molly? Until I heard Dad's voice again, I wasn't going to be able to relax.

We set up our tents as soon as the sun went down. Two tents again. I was getting so sick of that. Now that we were relatively safe, with food and water, my nerves seemed more frayed than ever. I wanted Shane to hold me, comfort me. I think I wanted it even more than I wanted sex. But I guess the food and all the excitement made us sleepy, because he didn't stay in my tent for long before crawling out and going to his. I couldn't even resent it, because I quickly fell into a deep sleep.

I woke up in the middle of the night, uncertain of what had awakened me. All was quiet. Perhaps another aftershock? I realized, though, that I had to pee. Metzli had a comfortable hut that he used as an outhouse, and it was not far away. So I grabbed my flashlight and left my tent.

On other nights when we'd camped, Shane had told me to wake him if I needed to relieve myself. When I'd objected that I could pee all by myself, thank you, he'd explained that he didn't want me leaving camp without his knowing about it.

It hadn't come up, though. Peeing hadn't been a big problem when we were low on water.

I didn't have to leave camp now, though. The outhouse was right in the camp. It was dark, yes, but the stars were bright. Shane was exhausted, and it seemed silly to wake him.

I finished in the outhouse and went quietly back toward the tents, stopping at the well for the luxury of a cool drink of water. The crank made a loud squeaking noise, which might have been why I didn't hear anything odd. Or realize that something was amiss. I didn't even have that creepy feeling on the back of my neck that was supposed to warn of danger.

So I was both startled and horrified when I felt the air shift behind me as I was struggling to scoop some water from the bucket. A heavy hand gripped my shoulder and a low voice at my ear said, "Well now, girly-girl. Who'd a thought we'd be meeting your fine ass again so soon?"

CHAPTER 40

Cassie

I KNEW THE VOICE, ALTHOUGH I'd only heard it once before. The sour smell of body odor was recognizable, too. As Big Biceps biker said the words "your fine ass," his other hand grabbed my buttocks and squeezed painfully, telling me, just in case I had any doubt, that this was not going to be a friendly encounter.

I didn't hesitate. I was still gripping the metal water bucket in one hand; it was half full of water and attached to its thick chain. I whirled around, pulled with all my strength on the chain so the bucket flew around in a half circle and struck Biceps squarely in his left side. Too bad I hadn't hit his head, but he was too tall for that. "Get your fucking hands off me," I yelled, hoping Shane would wake up and hear me.

Biker guy swore loudly and grabbed me by the hair. I must have hurt him, but the pain just seemed to fire him up. He dragged me away from the well and clamped a hand over my mouth as I drew breath to scream.

"Bitch likes it rough, does she? Hey Cub, get over here. We

got us a fighter. Bring some of that rope and a rag or something to stuff in her gob. Her man's around here somewhere, but dude must have sent her out at night to fetch him water. The guy must be soft. Makes his old lady do the lifting n' carrying."

Shane soft? These guys would learn a thing or two about Shane if I could just get him to wake up. I was kicking and writhing and trying to bite the guy's filthy fingers, but he was huge and I wasn't having any success trying to squirm away from him. It only took him one hand to wrench both my arms behind my back, and then the other guy, the younger guy, was there and they were both on me.

Fuck, fuck, fuck! I was more angry than scared at first. Angry at myself for not sensing that I was being stalked. Angry at Shane for not instantly perceiving I was in trouble. And most of all angry at these two creeps for making it through the earthquake unhurt and getting themselves to the same camp that Shane and I had struggled so hard to reach.

As they dragged me around the old abandoned pick-up truck where all the herbs and flowers were growing, I saw their bikes, standing there with all their chrome looking in perfect working order. What had they done for water? How long had they been here? What the fuck were they planning here, skulking in the dark?

Nothing good.

I was beginning to realize how stupid I'd been. I should have followed Shane's directions and wakened him before going to the outhouse. But I'd been pissed off about his continuing refusal to relax and fall asleep with me. How long was he going to keep this shit up? We had been through so much together during the past few days and he still wouldn't let me close?

Dammit! Would he have woken me up if he'd had to go? No way.

My mind was distracted from these recriminations when the other guy shoved a foul-tasting rag in my mouth. I managed to get out a bit of a cry as they were switching from the first man's hand to the second man's rag, but it wasn't very loud. And it cost me a hard swat across the face that made my entire head ring.

When I felt the two of them pushing up my T shirt and tearing at the waist of my pants, I was forced to confront the reality of the situation. Two bikers were about to rape me. When they were done with that, they would probably kill me. Or kidnap me and force me to be their "old lady." Shane was exhausted, sleeping. No one was going to help me unless I figured out a way to help myself.

Through my panic, I tried to find out a way to give myself a chance. The big guy seemed to be all the more turned on by my struggles, so I let my muscles slacken a bit. Just like in the desert, I shouldn't waste my energy. I had to be smart.

"There now," Biceps crooned. "I think she likes you, Cub. I think she's gonna be a real good bitch for you. Help me lay her down, now."

The two of them lifted me off my feet and shoved me down on my ass in the dirt. Biceps took a piece of cord the kid gave him and bound my wrists painfully behind my back. Then he pushed me down so I was lying on my bound hands. It hurt. I was breathing hard, and my heart was thundering. They were so strong. How the hell could I get away from two big hulking bikers?

Biceps was clearly the one calling the shots. The other guy, Cub, as he called him, didn't look much older than eighteen or nineteen. He was skinny and ragged and his eyes looked a little bit scared. I probably wouldn't even have feared him if he hadn't been following his leader's commands with no hesitation. Maybe he didn't really want to do this? But he was afraid to go against the older guy's demands?

If there hadn't been a gag in my mouth, maybe I could have talked my way out of this. Or at least tried to set Cub against Biceps long enough so scramble away.

It wasn't like me to let something awful happen to me without any resistance. An earthquake was one thing—you couldn't fight that—but it burned me to see myself as a victim to these two pieces of shit.

"Pull those pants down over those shapely hips. Nice. No panties. Bet she's real soft and sweet up there. She'll be wet soon. Yeah, she likes you, kid. I might even let you go first so I can watch you stick it to her. If you rape the bitch real good, you might even earn your patch on this ride, boy."

Oh God, the kid was on some kind of initiation trip for the older guy's motorcycle club? That meant he would have to be cruel, scared or not, or risk losing the chance to join this charming fraternity.

"I'll give it to her good, don't you worry," Cub said. He made a show of jerking down his pants and stroking his dick. Not much of a dick, I thought absurdly, wondering if he was even hard. The first guy was, no doubt about that. I'd felt it as soon as he'd jerked me against him, and he was stroking himself now through the leather of his biker duds.

"Damn, I want that gag out of her mouth," the first guy said. "I wanna make her blow me while you fuck the shit out of her. Then we can trade places."

I began to fight again. No way this was happening to me! Goddammit! Where were Metzli's powerful gods when I needed them?

Biceps cut away the gag with a huge, ugly knife, making sure I could see it right against the side of my face. "You make one sound, bitch, and I'll slice your throat open and drink the blood. All I wanna hear is the sound of you sucking me nice and hard while Cub here drills you."

But what we all heard was a sound like a train roaring through as the earth rolled beneath us in a stronger aftershock than we'd had all day. Biceps, squatting beside my head now, lost his balance and fell sideways. And I screamed. Long and loud, despite the threat of the guy's blade.

Biceps cursed and fumbled for his knife, which he'd dropped. I rolled in the other direction. The kid was holding his cock and looking scared. I screamed again and threw myself forward so I could get to my feet. My hands were still tied behind me and my pants were around my ankles, but I managed to stand up. I nearly fell again, though, as pain radiated through my ass and back. It took me a second to realize the big guy had kicked me. "Shut the fuck up," he snarled.

"You guys better run because my boyfriend is a fucking US Navy SEAL and he is going to split you both open for this," I shrieked, trying to run, despite the pain that was rocketing along all my nerves.

The fear in Cub's face turned real. But Biceps just kicked me again. I stumbled and fell to my knees. He had his knife back, I saw.

And he was coming at me.

CHAPTER 41

Shane

A DISTANT SCREAM IN THE night roused me from my sleep. "Cass."

I scrambled out of my tent, taking my blades and my chemlights. I raced to hers but it was empty. What the fuck?

"Cass, where the fuck are you?"

Silence, complete silence. She would answer me. Something wasn't right.

I grabbed my fixed-blade from my pocket and tried to assess which direction the scream came from.

Another scream, desperate, haunting. Fuck, I'd left her alone in the tent, snuck out like a fucking coward in the middle of the night.

I ran toward the sound of her voice. The silhouette of Metzli's old rusted-away truck loomed in the distance. I flashed my chemlight and I saw Cassie pinned down by two bikers, one motherfucker undoing his belt, another holding his small dick.

Fuck no.

My adrenaline spiked. I was outnumbered, I had one weapon and it was a blade, not a gun. No backup.

I was trained for this, I was made for this moment. No one would touch my woman.

The older greasy biker held up a knife, a switchblade. "Some old man. She says you're one of them SEALs, eh? If she was my woman, I'd never let her out of my sight."

He let out a guttural laugh, motioning to the younger guy to stay near Cassie. I held my position, waited for him to come toward me.

"I've never killed a SEAL, that would definitely get me a new patch, what do you say Cub? You could come out with two patches tonight instead of one?"

Calm, steady, I'd done this before, but this time was the first that I was solo. The goal in a knife fight is to keep your distance, and try to disarm your attacker. But the younger guy had a knife too, and this was Cassie's life. I wasn't going to take any chances.

The jackass lunged toward me, I used my arm to deflect his attack. This fat-ass was at least two-hundred and fifty pounds. The carotid artery in his neck flared. As his hand jabbed toward me again, I used my free arm to hold him back and plunged the blade into his neck, immediately severing his artery. I brought my knife around his neck to the carotid on the other side, stopping blood to his brain. Thick blood squirted all over me, the rest gushing out onto the dirt. His eyes rolled back in his head, and within seconds, he fell to the ground.

The younger guy jumped up, releasing Cassie.

"No!"

He barreled toward me, clutching a knife, his arm unsteady. I had another blade in my pocket, but I didn't have a second to grab it. I cocked my arm back and struck him with my palm. I aimed upward at the front of his nose with my hand. The impact made a swift crack and he fell back, the blade flying out of his hand. I hesitated for a second.

He grasped an unmistakable gun grip, and I knew I didn't have a second to waste. My boot pressed into his face and a hard kick to the skull knocked the life out of him.

Did I have to kill him? The guilt washed over me; this kid was young, maybe he'd had a future in front of him outside of the club and the influence of this older guy.

Cassie sat in the dirt, silent. I squatted down beside her. "You okay?"

"No. I mean I will be, I don't know—everything happened so fast."

I couldn't read her, especially not now with the adrenaline pulsing through my veins. Was she in shock? Pissed?

I put my arm around her. "I'm sorry. I should've slept with you. This would've never happened."

She leaned into me. "You saved my life. You're incredible."

I kissed her on the forehead and we walked back to the tents. She allowed me to examine her. She had bruises on her wrists and across her face, and what looked like a boot print on her back. I checked her pulse for signs of shock. It was weak but steady. I pulled her to me so I could feel her heartbeat.

We didn't speak a word, didn't kiss, didn't even attempt to have sex. She crawled back into her tent, and zipped the flap up. I stood there, for a second, nervous for one of the few times in my life. I stuck my finger through the flap, unzipped it.

"Can I sleep here?" I didn't want to talk, tell her my fears of intimacy, my fear that she would be horrified to learn about the real me. But she had just witnessed me killing two men. In a way, it made me feel safe with her.

"Of course. I'd like that." I wrapped her in a blanket.

She snuggled up to me, and I held her. I didn't want to have sex with her, I just wanted to be close to her, listen to her breath, wake up with her in the morning, see her smile.

Cassie rolled over, her breath purring. Her body melted into mine. I wrapped my arms around her, inhaled her sweet scent, and drifted off to sleep.

CHAPTER 42

Cassie

I THINK I MUST HAVE been dazed by the attack, because I got all shivery. Shane wrapped me in a blanket and rubbed my arms and shoulders until my teeth stopped chattering. He came into my tent, lay down with me and held me.

I must have dozed off for a while, because I woke with a start, feeling scared. I jerked upright and realized Shane was lying next to me. We weren't in the middle of sex, but he was right here. Beside me.

His hands were gentle on me, soothing. He lifted his head with a sleepy look, proving he'd been asleep, too. Wow, that was a first.

"Cassie? It's okay. You're safe." He slung an arm around me and gently pulled me back down beside him. "I've got you, Cass."

I pressed my face into his shoulder. There was an odd, coppery smell about him that I dimly recognized as blood. The horror of what had happened was all rushing back at me. Those thugs grabbing me, hitting me, tying my hands. The filthy-tasting rag in my mouth. My clothes stripped from me. Their disgusting hands on my body.

I'd wondered where the old gods of Mexico were, and they had given me their answer. The earth had moved, granting me the chance to twist away and scream. Shane had come for me. He had come when I'd needed him most.

They would have killed me when they were done using me like a hole to be filled. At least, Biceps would have killed me. As for the other guy, Cub, he was young but I didn't feel sorry for him. He'd done what he was told without a single murmur of protest. All I'd been to him was a piece of meat to be consumed so he could enter some club full of creeps who treated women like toilet paper to be soiled and thrown away.

I hated them both. I was glad they were dead.

Still, I had a flash of the knives, the blood, the crunch of bone. Shane had killed them. He'd put them down without any hesitation at all.

Tears filled my eyes. I wasn't crying for the dead bikers, though. I was thinking of Shane when I'd asked him that night why he'd become a SEAL. "To kill people," he'd said in that dry mocking tone. That was what so many people believed about SEALs and other special forces—that they were trained to be killing machines. Warriors who killed when they had to— perfectly, precisely. Some of them might even enjoy the killing.

But Shane was not like that. He was a corpsman, an EMT, whose role was to keep his men alive. I'd seen him in action in the desert and here, in the camp when he'd saved Metzli. Saving lives was what he'd devoted himself to. Not taking them.

He was highly skilled at all the arts of war. But he was a healer, not an avenger. Could he be both? What did I know about these things? I'd never been in combat; I'd rarely even lived rough. I'd never lived my life as close to the edge as I had the past week.

Some things should stay mysteries, Metzli had said.

Shane moved and I realized he had woken up. "Shane," I whispered. "I'm so sorry. I had to pee. I shouldn't have gone alone. I don't know where those guys came from or why they were here."

"Looked like they were setting up to attack the camp. They had guns. Must have bought them here in Mexico. They had drugs, too." He spoke calmly. "They weren't just a couple of asshole bikers touring Baja. They were probably hooked up with some local crime ring. They would have killed us all. But they wanted to have a little fun with you first."

I shuddered again. "Thanks for stopping their fun. Bastards."

It seemed to me that he shuddered a little, too. "I can't even stand to think about it...God...if they had hurt you..."

"I'm okay," I assured him. "I mean, I'm shaken up but I'll be fine." I laughed a little. "This had been some week, hasn't it?"

He slid a hand into my hair and held my face still. "I love it that you can still smile even when all the shit in the world is going down."

Whoa. He had never said anything that sweet to me before. I pulled his face down to mine. We both went for the kiss, and it tasted just right. Desire flared in me, and I welcomed it. I pressed deeper into him.

"Is this okay?" he asked as he began touching me, courting me.

"Oh yes. Yes, please."

I was thankful for the way my body reacted. It could have been different. I had friends who had been assaulted or raped and for some, no matter how loving their boyfriends behaved afterwards, they just couldn't get back into sex.

For me, though, it was as if sex with Shane somehow washed all the filth of those two men away. His hands erased their touch, his mouth sent his warmth, his breath into me, his cock, when it finally slid inside me, was healing. As if he'd given me a lifeline. As if he'd revived me and held me back from the black precipice that had loomed before me.

I expected him to get up the way he always did after we finished having sex. I figured he'd come into my tent after the attack because he must have known how freaked out I'd been. But now that I was well enough to fuck, he'd leave me, right?

But he didn't. He turned me on my side and cuddled me close again. Maybe he was just trying to help me get to sleep again? As soon as I was still, he would creep away and return to his own territory, his own bed. After all, I wasn't allowed any kind of intimacy with him, any kind of closeness.

Okay. Okay, fine. I was too weary and confused to worry about that now. I had to live in the present, because in the future, Shane would be gone.

So I was amazed when I woke up in the morning light and found Shane asleep beside me, his arm still around me and one of his legs draped possessively over mine.

I felt something slide together in me, deep down in my chest, slide and click and take shape in a new and different way. With it came comfort and peace and happiness. He was with me. Beside me, holding me. Shane was part of me and he was still here.

I could feel my lips curve up in one of those smiles he'd talked about. It grew wider until I wanted to laugh out loud. But if I did that, I might wake him, and he needed to rest.

Carefully, so as not to disturb him, I pushed up on one elbow and looked at his body in the weak morning light. His high forehead, his strong jaw, his firm sensuous lips, the curve of his throat. His body and his muscles I already knew so well, but now I considered his face. It was a nice face. Strong, Dependable. Trustworthy. Honorable. It was a face I could look at for the rest of my life.

In that place deep inside me, something began to glow. Shane Tyler. I wanted him, but it was more than that. Somehow it had become so much more.

I was falling in love with him. With my future stepbrother.

How crazy was that? He was the one man I could never have...not for love. Not to keep.

He didn't love me. Why should he? I'd done nothing but challenge him and argue with him and cause trouble for him all week. He'd just had to kill two guys because of my stupidity. He wanted to get to Cabo, grit his teeth through the wedding, and say goodbye. He'd made that clear all along. He didn't have relationships. He just fucked.

As for spending the night in my bed, he'd been in a fight and killed a couple of bad guys. He was probably exhausted. It didn't change anything. He wanted me gone.

And that was fine, right? Because I didn't do relationships, either. The thought of being dependent on another person gave me the shudders. I'd needed my mom, and she'd died. Shane had a dangerous job. He could get killed anytime. Even if he'd wanted me, how could I ever have dealt with that?

I wouldn't allow myself to think crazy impossible thoughts. We'd taken this road trip to have some fun. We'd had it. We'd gone through a lot of other things, too, but that just proved you couldn't count on life working out the way you planned it. Being with Shane was one unplanned mess from beginning to end. Getting far, far away from him would be the smartest move I could ever make.

Resolved, I slid out from under his leg and away from his warm body. He'd been right—it had been a really bad idea to sleep in his arms.

CHAPTER 43

Shane

CASSIE WAS GONE FROM THE tent when I woke up.

I sat up with a jerk, feeling as if a fist was around my heart. It was morning. I couldn't believe I had slept right through to the dawn.

I stank. There was still blood on me from the two men I'd killed. I had fucked Cassie with their blood on me. No wonder she had fled from the tent.

I pulled on a shirt and hurried outside, looking for her. I felt intense relief when I saw her crouching at the entrance to Metzli's hut and heard her steady voice talking to him. They were both alive. They were okay. I checked around the camp, still feeling tense and edgy. There were no other bikers. Those two had been alone. But I shouldn't have let myself sleep. I should have stood guard. The fuckers might have friends in Mexico. Or other members of their club who might be looking for them.

I hadn't even gotten rid of the evidence. That was a task I was going to have to attend to right away.

I had to get into the water, first though. The smell of their blood was making my stomach queasy. Must be that. It wasn't like I'd never killed a man before. Hell, I was a SEAL, a fucking death-dealing machine, right?

I nodded to Cassie as I passed, indicating that I was going for a swim. From the looks of her wet hair, she had already done the same thing. Probably cleansing herself of the blood I'd transferred to her body from mine. "How's Metzli?" I grunted as I passed. I ought to check on him before going into the water. But I couldn't stand my own stench.

"He's good. Better."

It was enough. I passed the hut and flung my body into the sea.

I was shivering when I got out, despite a rough scrub down and a fast-paced swim. It was winter; the water was probably about 60 degrees. I could handle chilly swims, not a problem for a SEAL. No, the coldness came from somewhere deep inside.

Cassie was preparing breakfast when I walked back up the beach to the camp. Metzli had emerged from his hut and was crouching beside the fire with her. They were drinking some of his herbal tea or whatever that stuff was.

I checked him out. Vital signs were fine. He had more color in his cheeks today. In fact, he looked surprisingly good for a guy who'd seemed frail yesterday. When I asked him how his legs felt, he answered, "The gods provide." I guess that meant he felt better.

I wasn't sure about Cassie, though. She was uncharacteristically quiet and she looked pale. She passed me a wood bowl with some sort of hot mush in it. There were berries I couldn't identify on top of the mush. When I looked askance at the stuff, Metzli said,

"Eat. The fruits of the earth will sustain your flesh just as the sea washes clean your spirit."

Right. Whatever the fuck that meant.

The three of us ate in silence. I was thinking about the bodies. Cassie had her back to the place where she had been attacked. Where the dead guys lay. Just as well. I had to take care of that as soon I got the mush into me. They'd be attracting flies and I didn't even want to think about what else.

When we all finished eating, I looked at Cassie. There were things she didn't need to hear, didn't need to see. "I'd like you to go back in your tent now. Read your Kindle or something, if its battery is still alive. I'll tell you when you can come out."

Her face was expressionless. But she understood me. She said quietly, "I can help, Shane."

No way I was allowing that. "No you can't. Can't you just follow instructions for once?"

She colored slightly and I thought she was going to argue. I wasn't even playing fair with her. I knew that. She had followed my orders surprisingly well the whole trip.

She just nodded. Then she rose and walked slowly to the tent, bent down, and crawled inside.

"That is well done," Metzli said in his hollow voice. "That one, she bends like the grasses with the wind. But the iron devils tried to crush her."

"Yeah, well, I crushed them instead."

"Take care you do not crush your own heart."

I stiffened. What the fuck? "I did what I had to do," I said, rising.

"The hand of the god was upon you," he agreed, making some sort of strange gesture with his fingers. "He sent you to me as defender. And to her," he nodded toward the tent. "But his can be a terrible hold. No man can endure his touch too often in his life."

Truth, I thought, thinking of some of my fellow SEALs. I could kill when I had to. Obviously. But it always scared me how easy it was. They said it got even easier, the more you did it. I didn't like that idea. I didn't like how easy it had been to stop that young kid last night from firing his gun. To stop his heart, his breath, his future all in a split second. He couldn't have been more then 18 or 19. A lawless thug and fuck-up, but I'd been something of a fuck-up myself when I was young. This kid had never had a chance.

Don't fucking think about that.

"Have you got a shovel?"

Metzli pointed to the smaller hut where he kept a variety of strange things. Junk mostly, it looked like. Scavenged perhaps. "You will find the tools you seek there." He stood, leaning on his cane. "Come. I will show you a place where they will lie undisturbed."

I assured him that was unnecessary, but he insisted on walking a distance that I would have thought was too far for a wounded old man. He seemed spry, though, and calm. He led me to a place where the soil was soft but not too wet, behind some rocks, under some trees. "The gods alone will know their resting place," he told me solemnly.

I guess that meant he wouldn't be telling anybody that I'd killed two men last night. I wouldn't be telling anyone, either.

I worked hard and fast and got the messy task done before the sun got too hot. Metzli squatted in the shade and offered suggestions, most of which I followed. Cassie stayed in her tent.

"Your woman has a full heart," Metzli commented as I stamped down the last of the dirt covering the two graves.

"I told you. She's not my woman."

He looked at me skeptically. He was right to. She *is* my woman, a voice inside me said. But what I said aloud was, "It's just a temporary thing."

Metzli's old face crinkled in a smile. "You are like beans and corn. Different, but together you are stronger."

"I don't need a woman to make me strong."

"She will nourish your spirit."

I liked the old guy, but his claptrap was beginning to irritate me. My spirit, if I had one, didn't need any fucking nourishing.

"She has not seen men die in violence before. Not as you have. She will need tenderness." His voice was sharper as he said this, as if he needed to be sure I heard him. He was probably right, but I wondered how he knew what Cassie had or hadn't seen before. Or what I had, for that matter.

Tenderness. That wasn't a quality I was well acquainted with. Well. Soon we would be in Cabo, I hoped. She could get all the tenderness she needed at the wedding. I was pretty sure her dad and even my Mom would have plenty of that shit to offer her. Good. She couldn't expect tenderness from a killer.

I planned to strip the dead guys' motorcycles for parts so I could get my own fixed up and running again. That was my task for the afternoon. With any luck at all, we could get back on our way tomorrow.

I helped the old man back to his hut and called out to Cassie that she could come out now if she wanted. She didn't answer me. When I went to check on her, I found her sleeping, her red hair wild around her face and her breath coming fast, as if she were having a vivid dream.

Something inside me clenched at the thought that she'd have been dead if I hadn't made it to her in time last night. I felt a moment of vertigo at the thought. What if it had been Cassie going into the ground, her bright hair, her laughing eyes and her quick smile extinguished forever?

No. I couldn't think about that. I wouldn't.

I slammed back out of the tent and sprinted down to the water. I needed another hard swim.

CHAPTER 44

Cassie

THERE WAS SOMETHING DIFFERENT ABOUT Shane when he came over to me after working on his Harley. His face looked grim, his eyes worried.

"What's the matter? Can't you fix it?"

"No, I got it working. Engine sounds good now. We should be fine the rest of the way to Cabo. Assuming the main road, once we get back on it, hasn't been too torn up by the quake."

I knew him a lot better now. We had been together 24/7, and we'd been through a lot. I could tell he was edgy about something. "So we're leaving? How is Metzli? Can he stay here alone?"

"He is better, and he insists he can manage. He says fate is whistling for us up the road and that we must heed its call." He said this with that sarcastic smirk that I had grown to know well by now.

"I hope he'll be okay." I was worried about Metzli. He was so old. But this was the life he had chosen, and he loved it here.

"Me, too," said Shane. "Cassie—" he hesitated.

"What are you not telling me?"

He nodded, as if he'd knew I'd call him out on this. "I'll tell you. I just don't want you to freak out, okay?"

I immediately started to freak out, but I kept it inside. "What? Is it my father? Did you find out something about my— our parents from your military contacts?"

"I asked one of my friends to check on your father's boat. There's a lot of craziness down here in Mexico right now, so it's not easy to find out anything, but with military connections and all—"

"What did they find out? Where are our parents?"

"No one is sure. Hopefully they are fine. But there was a call after the earthquake. Your dad was having some trouble with his communications equipment. Not a shock because everyone was. We think that's all he was reporting and that it wasn't a distress call, but there were heavy seas, so the authorities are checking it out. They haven't heard from him again, you see. They're looking for the boat now."

My belly had dropped out of me. For a moment I felt as if I was going to throw up. My dad had to be okay. He *had* to be.

"So no one has been able to contact my father's boat since the earthquake?"

"Cassie, no one has been able to contact anyone since the earthquake. It took down the internet, the cell towers and most other forms of communications for the entire Baja peninsula."

"He has a satellite phone."

"So did we. They've made the damn things a lot smaller and they're easier to break. And if they get wet—forget it—they can't be fixed. Water destroys the inside, salt water especially."

I could hear the stress in his voice. It wasn't just my father we were talking about, but his mother as well. I reached for him, gripping his hand hard. He squeezed my fingers back, and then he pulled me into his arms. As I pressed against his chest, I could feel his heart beating faster than usual. He was always so calm, so cool, so good in an emergency. But he must be feeling just as frantic with worry as I was.

"We have to get on the road. Get to Cabo. Maybe they're already there. Dad's a really good sailor, and he knows that boat. He's like you, Shane. He can handle things."

It was true. The only thing he hadn't been able to handle had been my mother's death, but I'd been there for him then. I'd be there for him now. And for Shane.

"I hope so," Shane muttered. He didn't sound confident. He probably didn't trust anybody except himself and the men he worked with. The badass SEALs who could do anything. Naturally he wouldn't believe an ordinary non-military man like my father—a professor of all things!—could take care of his mother in a crisis.

I thought he could. I just hoped the sea, like the earth that had nearly done Shane and me in, hadn't been too much for our parents.

We said goodbye to Metzli and were packed and ready to leave within an hour. We had plenty of water and fresh fruits, nuts and vegetables from Metzli's gardens. The bike worked fine. We got on the road, and we flew toward Cabo.

PART THREE

CHAPTER 45

Shane

I PULLED UP TO THE lobby in Cabo. There was definitely damage to the resort, broken columns, rubble in the street, but nothing as extensive as we saw deep in Baja.

Cassie's hair was staticky and wild, dirt smeared on her face, scratches on her arms. But I still thought she looked hot.

We checked in, and asked if our parents had arrived. Cassie's face fell when the concierge told us that our parents hadn't arrived. But I assured Cassie that they were probably still safely at sea, even though I had my own doubts.

Though we had been booked separate rooms, there was nothing that could stop me from staying with Cassie, which wasn't even a concern at this point since our parents hadn't arrived. For appearances, I took what was left of my stuff up to my room, and then met Cassie in her room, which was on a separate floor under mine. We each took a quick shower, scrubbed the dirt off our bodies, and collapsed onto her bed. I'd never been more grateful to be in a cool air-conditioned room. I'd rather be stuck in Afghanistan again than in Baja.

Cassie crawled on top of me, kissed me deeply. "Do you think they're okay?"

"I'm sure they will show up soon." Though I had no official word about our parents' safety, my soul told me that she was fine. My mom and I had always been strongly connected—she told me that she felt a sharp pang in her core when I'd blown my eardrums out during skydiving training.

Cassie seemed satisfied with my response. She traced my beard with her fingers, sending a shock to my core.

I stroked her hair; she smelled so sweet. This night felt different than the other nights we'd spent together, and it wasn't just because I would be sleeping with her.

She leaned toward me and kissed me, her warm tongue lovingly caressing mine. I'd never felt anything like this kiss. There was a lack of urgency between us, like neither of us cared about immediately proceeding to the next base. We kissed for what seemed like hours, her hands lightly massaging my body. Did she love me? Did I love her? All I knew was that I needed her, I never wanted to be away from her again. But none of my feelings mattered—this road trip was over, we'd arrived safely at our destination.

The sun beamed through our hotel window. I stood out on the balcony, gazing at the ocean. I hadn't been on a vacation in years. I was either training my ass off or deployed. The little leave I took, I'd either headed back to Montana to visit with my mom, or spent it hung over in San Diego.

The waiter had brought us fresh squeezed orange juice, tropical fruit, yogurt, and omelets. Cassie and I sat down at the little table on the balcony. I squeezed her tanned thigh.

"Babe, I called the Coast Guard again. No word on our parents but they are still looking. There's nothing we can do but wait. What do you want to do today? The concierge said they are still running whale and dolphin boats."

It seemed inappropriate to me to be acting like a goddam tourist with all the devastation around us. But I wanted to make Cassie happy. She'd been through enough bullshit on this road trip from hell with me—first with my attitude, then with the earthquake; she had been nearly raped, and now her dad was missing. If she needed some fun to take her mind off this mind-fuck, I'd be happy to help.

She took a sip of her juice. "Thanks. I'd love to, but I think we should go help out in town. The waiter said that a local church had collapsed. I think it's the church the wedding was going to be in. They're organizing a cleanup. Let's go."

Most girls I had dated would be booking a massage now, feeling entitled and selfish. But no, not Cassie. She was hurting, physically and emotionally. I could still see the gash on her leg, the scar on her forehead. Her dad could be dead. But instead of dwelling on her pain, she wanted to help others.

I leaned in and gave her a kiss. "You're fucking incredible. Let's do this."

Had I met my match? This girl didn't mind getting dirty, in or out of the bedroom. She was passionate, humble, smart as fuck, and strong. I didn't want this trip to end.

CHAPTER 46

Cassie

I WANTED TO HELP WITH the relief effort because I needed to work. Physical labor. I couldn't just go lie on a beach somewhere, not while my dad was missing. And Shane's mom. No matter how hard I tried to be cheerful and optimistic, not only for my sake, but for his, I knew I wouldn't be able to keep it together if I didn't have something constructive to do with my hands and with my mind.

Cabo had not been devastated by the earthquake. Because the epicenter had been so close to the barren land where we'd been traveling, no large population centers had taken a direct hit, but the whole southern half of the Baja peninsula had suffered from collapsed structures, downed power lines, road and bridge damage, many injuries and a few deaths. Hospitals were full, communications were slowly coming back, and there was a lot of damage to old historical buildings.

Including the small church where our parents had planned to be married. Its bell tower had collapsed and one of its walls had crumbled in places, but thankfully there had been no injuries. It was near our hotel, and the parishioners were eager to get the rubble cleared away so they could rebuild. Shane and I went to help with that effort.

I didn't mind the hard work in the heat or even the stone dust that was kicked up every time we tried to move a chunk of rubble. I was soon sweating and aching all over, but I welcomed it. Anything to make me focus on the work instead of worrying about my dad and re-experiencing the grief of losing my mom.

Shane worked by my side, solid and strong and just as into the job as I was. Maybe it helped him, too, to pour his energy into physical labor. As a team, we operated really well together. We always had—from the moment he had showed up in the water to help me escape the wrath of the sea lion who had not understood that I had just saved her pup from a slow and horrible death. We had dived for lobsters together. Camped in the desert and survived the aftermath of an earthquake. Ridden a thousand miles on a Harley, our bodies pressed together as one. Made love with such mutual ease and delight.

Or fucked, as he preferred to call it. But to me, now, after everything, I would always remember it as making love. Even if I could never tell him how I felt about him. How I trusted him. How I had learned to depend upon him. How I craved his body and wanted to learn him, all of him, all about him. All the things he could not share.

How I would miss him.

But I couldn't think about that. It wasn't fair to him to think it. He had never been mine and never could be. You couldn't lose what you had never had.

"Cassie," he said to me after we had moved a particularly large stone together. "You're exhausted. You need to sit down in the shade and take a rest for a while. Here," he handed me a water bottle. Precious water—we didn't have to hunt for it anymore. "Drink. I don't want you getting dehydrated in the middle of a city."

I laughed a little and accepted the water. True. It would be stupid to pass out from dehydration now.

"We've done enough here, I think," he said. "Let's go back to the hotel."

On the way, a couple blocks from the church, I realized we were passing through one of the more devastated areas. There were collapsed buildings and lots of rubble in the streets. Rescue workers and firefighters everywhere, including a couple of military guys with dogs on leashes, obviously searching for bodies.

I hesitated, memories swamping me what had happened at Metzli's camp. The assault and near rape. Shane's miraculous appearance. The blood. Crouching in my tent the next morning, knowing he was burying the corpses. My dad, missing at sea. My mom, gone for nearly five years.

I didn't think I could face seeing the earthquake relief squads pull corpses from the wreckage. I tried to steady myself. I didn't want Shane to see my weakness. I didn't even want to admit it to myself.

There was an excited shout from the building where some of the workers were now concentrated. One of the dogs barked and started wagging his tail. Then more shouts. In Spanish, of course.

"What are they saying?" I asked Shane.

"I think they've found someone alive under the rubble. Yeah. They're hearing sounds, cries. Shit. I think it's a baby."

He went rushing forward and I tore after him. I hoped it wasn't a false alarm. A baby was alive, after so many hours? The earthquake had been three days ago. Or was it four? Time had run together in my mind. Could a baby survive for that long?

People were moving wood and metal and passing pieces along a line that had spontaneously formed. The situation was too delicate for machinery. Shane plunged right into the action, speaking rapid Spanish with the workers and helping to move rubble. The dogs kept barking and the cries of everyone around grew more excited.

At last a joyful shout went up as a grimy rescue worker rose to his feet with a squirming toddler in his arms. Shane must have explained that he was a medic, because they handed the child to him to examine. He did it quickly but efficiently, then smiled and gave the crowd a thumbs-up signal. The kid was not only alive, but conscious. Covered with grime, he was screaming for his mother.

And the mother came. More screaming and crying and shouts of happiness and relief as a young woman limped forward with an older man and woman at her side. She was weeping, but when she saw the child, she smiled through her tears. When Shane placed him in her arms, the kid smiled, too, through all the grime that covered him.

And I burst into tears.

I didn't even know why I was crying, there in the middle of a narrow Mexican street, but I couldn't seem to stop. Shane came back to me, pulled me against his strong chest and stroked my hair.

"It's okay, babe," he said gently. "They're saying that building collapsed not in the original tremor but in an aftershock two days later. That's probably why the kid survived. He's not even in too bad shape, although the firefighters are taking mother and child to the hospital now."

"I'm so happy for them," I blurted, still sobbing against his chest.

I felt Shane chuckle.

"I am!" I insisted. "It's life. Life when there's been so much death and destruction. Look. Even the rescue dogs are smiling their big, slobbery grins."

Shane brushed tears off my cheeks. His touch was gentle, and I leaned into his hand. I wanted to say, "I love you, Shane," but I couldn't do that. I could never do that. So I pressed my face against his neck and cried some more.

My cell phone rang. Since it hadn't made a sound for four whole days, I jumped when it chimed. It was in the back pocket of my pants, and I fumbled as I tried to find it. Shane reached his own hand down along my ass and pulled the phone out of my pocket. I grabbed it from him, squinting through my tears at the screen. Oh my God! My dad's number was lit up there.

"Hello? Dad? Dad is that you?" I practically screamed into the phone.

When his own dear voice filled my ear, I started bawling again.

"Cassie? Are you okay? Cassie!"

"Dad!" I croaked. "Thank God!"

Shane took the phone from my trembling hand. "Mr. Bennings? This is Shane. Cassie's fine. Where are you? The Coast Guard got a distress call. Is my mom all right? Are you both safe?"

I leaned my cheek against Shane's chin so I could hear. "Yes, we are okay," Dad said. "We just moored in the harbor. Molly is fine. She sprained her ankle when things got rough, but she's all bandaged up and the swelling is going down. Is everything good with the two of you? We've been frantic with worry."

"So have we," I said, taking the phone back. "Shane has been worried about his mom and I've been so worried about you. About both of you."

"I'm sorry about that, Cassie. We had some electronic problems during the storm. We had rough seas for a while. My sat phone and some other equipment got wet. GPS still worked, though, we were able to set a course to Cabo. How much damage is there? That felt like a huge earthquake."

"Yeah, it's bad. Your church? The one where the wedding was supposed to be? It's a mess. We were just over there helping with the clean-up. I'm afraid you'll have to hold the ceremony somewhere else."

"Well, that's a shame, but what about the people? Are there

many dead and injured?"

"They just saved a little boy. A baby, Dad. They pulled a baby out of a collapsed building. He's alive. He's alive and Shane examined him and then they gave him to his mother and—"

I started to cry again. I hadn't cried so much since Mom had died, and I wasn't even sad. What the fuck was wrong with me?

"That's great, sweetheart," Dad said. "Are you sure you're okay?"

"Yes, Dad, I'm just so happy to hear your voice."

"Me, too, Cassie, me too. I'm going to give the phone to Molly. She wants to speak to her son."

I handed the phone back to Shane. The look on his face when he heard his mother's voice was pure relief and delight.

I cried all the way back to the hotel. I'm sure Shane thought I had lost all my marbles, but he was wonderfully patient and tender with me. Which only made me cry even more.

CHAPTER 47

Cassie

IT WAS A STRANGE EVENING.

Awesome to see my dad again when the four of us met for dinner. And I was also happy to see Shane's mom, who was on crutches, but didn't seem to be slowed down very much. In many ways, she was as tough as her son.

We hugged and kissed and made a big fuss over each other. Over dinner, Dad and Molly were full of stories about their adventures at sea. Shane and I were a good deal quieter.

"Your dad is such a skilled sailor that we were never in any danger," Molly insisted. "I was the fool who dropped the sat phone in the water as we were trying to pull the sail down. I tried to dry the damn thing, but it was too late."

"My bike rolled over and killed our sat phone, too," said Shane.

"*Our* sat phone?" my father repeated, eyebrows raised. "So you and Cassie ended up traveling together, after all?"

Uh-oh. My heart sank to the floor. I'd told Dad I was driving here separately. That hadn't been too well thought out, I realized now.

"Yeah, Cassie's car was having some engine trouble so we took my Harley," Shane said smoothly.

"You were out in an earthquake on a Harley?" my dad growled.

"Yeah, it was a wild ride. But we made it, safe and sound." I decided not to mention the nearly dying of thirst, the trek over the ridge toward the sea, the attempted rape, or the two dead guys.

"Where did you sleep?" Dad shot a withering look in Shane's direction. Molly reached over and patted him on the arm, as if to say, "Calm down, dear."

Shane glowered right back at my father. "We camped out."

"We each had our own tent," I said quickly. I was glad, for once, that this was the truth.

They both looked from me to Shane and back again. Dammit! Was I blushing? Of course I was. I could feel the heat in my neck and face. It was one of the worst things about having red hair—I blush far too easily.

My father's eyes had narrowed and he looked as if he needed to pop a blood pressure pill. I abruptly remembered how hostile I'd been to Shane before the trip. I probably wasn't acting hostile now. Was it obvious that I had gone from "I can't stand this guy" to "oh my God, I'm so in love"? Was I behaving like some sort of infatuated idiot?

I didn't think I was, but I realized I probably couldn't trust my own perceptions on this. I was never going to win an Academy Award for my acting.

I cast a panicky glance at Shane. His expression betrayed nothing.

"Once the earthquake hit, we had bigger things to worry about than the sleeping arrangements," he said. "We were out in the desert very close to the epicenter. We had to find water and shelter. Fortunately, we came upon an old man's camp. We helped him and he returned the favor."

"He was injured," I put in, eager to distract Dad and Molly from any suspicions they might have about Shane and me. "Shane treated him. His corpsman skills proved super useful, especially when the earthquake hit and he picked up two nasty lacerations. Which reminds me," I added, turning to Shane and trying to sound cool and distant, "you should see a doctor about those cuts now that we're back in civilization. Just to make sure they're healing properly."

Shane scowled at me as his mother started fussing over him, asking where he was hurt and how badly. This gave me a few moments to collect myself.

"Sounds like you two had even more of an adventure than we did," said Molly, after Shane had reassured her. She smiled at me. "I'm so glad you had my son to take care of you and vice versa, from the sound of things. Just as I was lucky enough to have your dad taking care of me." She gave me a mischievous look that I suspected meant, "not that either of us really needs a man, but hey, they like to hear it."

"Yes," said my father. He still looked suspicious. "I'm grateful Cassie had her stepbrother the SEAL with her during this disaster. There are times when it's good to have a family member to rely on." Dad's eyes drilled me the same way they used to when I was a teenager who'd been up to some sort of mischief. "When you were little, you used to say you wished you had a brother. Now you do."

Oh God. Did he know what I'd done? Slept with my stepbrother? The shame. I wanted to slide under the table and die.

Shane didn't say anything. I couldn't tell what he was thinking. He was probably wishing he were a hundred miles away. A thousand.

"I'm so happy we all made it here safely," Molly said. "I don't know what we are going to do about the wedding, though, given the sad condition of that lovely little church. Maybe the priest can marry us outside, or even on the beach? What do you think, Henry?"

"I think we should get married in some other church. Or in a damn registry office. They have those here, right?"

"The priest is an old friend," Molly reminded him. "I'll have a chat with him tomorrow. I suggest we follow Cassie and Shane's excellent example and go over there to help him and his parishioners clean up. We can arrange something then, and in the meantime, I'd like to do some good here, if we can."

"Okay," Dad said, giving her a warm smile. "I like that idea."

I liked Molly more and more. She would be good for my father. She was an upbeat, sensible woman. And I could see that he loved her. The way he looked at her—I wished Shane would look at me that way.

Just once.

But Shane was looking at his plate and shoveling food into his mouth as if he hadn't eaten for weeks.

My heart ached. I hoped we wouldn't have to stay too long in Cabo, waiting for our parents to figure out where and when to get married. Shane and I couldn't be together now, even if we still wanted to—which I of course did.

Last night, upon arriving at the hotel, we had crashed in the same bed. But now that our parents were here we had to take our previously-reserved rooms. Which were on separate floors.

CHAPTER 48

Shane

I WAITED UNTIL THE SUNSET to make my move. Our parents were surely asleep by now, especially since my mom's ankle was sprained.

Cassie on the other hand was in the room under me. Maybe she was naked, lying in her bed pleasuring herself thinking about me.

Only one way to find out. Now I could've just taken the normal path, use the stairs. Knock on Cassie's door, risk waking our parents in the adjacent room. Henry was probably a light sleeper, his ears listening for a noise to confirm his suspicions that I was fucking his daughter.

Can't blame the guy—I'd do the same thing if I had a daughter as hot as Cassie.

But I wasn't just fucking her, I was obsessed with her, even though we had no future together. But she wasn't my stepsister yet. I was gonna fuck her senseless until my mom said "I do."

I tied a bed sheet to the steel balcony and slid down it. Once on Cassie's balcony I simply opened the sliding glass door.

Gaining entry to her room was so easy it was almost laughable.

She wasn't in her bed. I crept up to the bathroom, and found my girl naked, bubbles covering her nipples, water beads glistening on her neck. With her long red hair draped against the back of the tub, she almost looked like a goddess. My own personal mermaid.

She didn't notice me at first, but once she caught a glimpse of me in the mirror her face went white. I covered her mouth with my hand before she could let out a scream.

CHAPTER 49

Cassie

WHEN I SAW MOVEMENT OUT of the corner of my eye, I freaked. In an instant I realized it was Shane, but my heart was gunning enough to rattle my entire chest. I guess the attack by those two vicious bikers was going to haunt me for a while.

"What are you doing in here? The door was locked."

He looked gorgeous—all six-foot-two of his sculpted hard-ass body—but I couldn't let him get to me. Not again. The road trip had come to an end and we were both going to have to accept it, and not just for our parents' sake. I couldn't go on like this anymore, hiding what I really felt for him. It was too damn hard.

I could see from his body language and the look in his eyes what he had in mind. Another mind-bending fuck. He was primed and ready for it and it didn't take anything more than seeing him, hearing his voice, remembering how it felt to be together to make me wet. Well, wetter. I could invite him into the tub—we'd done it in the shower, but never in the bathtub, and this one even had Jacuzzi jets.

"Shane, we can't. Our parents are right next door, and they are already suspicious. We agreed—it was only for the road trip. And our road trip is over."

"So it's forbidden now, huh?"

"It was forbidden as soon as we found out about them."

"Yeah? We met first. How come it's not forbidden for them?"

I didn't have a good answer for that.

"Anyway," he said, caressing me gently, "I like forbidden. It's hot."

The weirdest feeling ripped through me—I wanted to do it even more. Now that Dad and Molly were here, safe and sound and so obviously together, the thing between Shane and me seemed even more forbidden. And he was right: it was hot.

Goddammit. I was in love with Shane, but I wanted to bone my stepbrother. Was I some kind of deviant?

"We'll be quiet," he said, starting to pull off his clothes. "You'll have to keep your mouth shut and not scream as loudly as you usually do." He ripped his shirt off, balled it up, and shook it threateningly at me. "Or I'll have to gag you."

Oh God. I was such a loser. I'd fallen for him, but he, badass that he was, was into me just for the hot sex. That had been all I'd wanted at the start, too, but I at some point I had let my defenses down.

All it had taken was a little crack, and in he had slipped. Into the fortress of my heart.

I stood up with a jerk, feeling the water spill down my body. I stepped out of the tub and grabbed a towel from the rack. "No." I tossed my wet hair out of my eyes, took another towel for my head, and stormed out of the bathroom. I think I scratched myself with the towels, so hard did I rub my wet skin, but I couldn't do anything to appease the ache inside.

He followed me as I started toward the bed. I was about to sit down on it when I thought twice and circled it instead, putting the queen-sized bed between us. Shane was naked now, too, and his cock—his lovely thick delicious cock—was jutting.

"Shane, please."

"I love it when you say please." He stroked his own cock, rather absently. "Please fuck me, Shane. Please go down on me, Shane. Please let me come, Shane."

Each word of his caused a throb deep inside me. I squeezed my eyes closed for a moment. This was just too difficult!

"Please let me go, Shane," I whispered. "I can't do this anymore."

His face screwed up as he stared at me. I could feel him probing. They probably taught him shit like that in the military— how to tell if your adversary is telling the truth or lying. How to read their body language. I was dead sure that mine was revealing every tiny bit of how much I was yearning to be with him. What he didn't know was that I yearned for it to be something more than just another casual fuck.

When he spoke again, his voice was gentler: "Cassie, it's our last chance. I was hoping maybe they wouldn't get married when the church walls caved in, but they're gonna do it on the beach or something. We have one more night. Let's not waste it."

When he put it that way, I was lost. I *wanted* one more night. But I was terrified that I would give myself away. I didn't think I could bear to see him withdraw from me if I foolishly lost control and screamed out "I love you." I wasn't sure I could keep it inside.

So I pointed rather shakily toward the door. "I'm sorry. Just go, okay? Please."

He put one knee on the bed and reached over it for me. I backed away, but the windows were behind me—curtains closed, thank goodness—so I couldn't retreat far. He fisted a hunk of my wet hair with one hand and pulled. Not too hard. He didn't hurt me, but he was firm and unyielding and he knew me well enough by now to push my most erotic buttons.

I submitted, just as he had known I would. The bastard gave me a wicked grin and used his other arm to drag me onto the bed. What could I do, I asked myself. He was a SEAL with a dominant streak. I couldn't fight him, even if I'd wanted to.

Good excuse, right?

"I'm not leaving without one last kiss."

"We're naked on my bed and you're talking about one last kiss?"

He laughed softly and pulled me against him so we were kneeling on the mattress, pressed together face to face. His chest, his hard belly, his urgent cock, his firm ass that my fingers couldn't resist stroking. When he tilted his head and gave me that kiss, I felt myself go all loose and soft and mushy. I couldn't resist him. I must have been crazy to even think resisting was possible.

I started stroking his body because I had to. He was so perfect. So beautiful. And I wanted him so much.

One of his hands coasted gently over my breast. His fingers teased my nipple, which was already popping out, full and erect. "One last everything, Cass. I know it's fucked up. I feel weird about it, too. But I couldn't stay up there alone. Not while there was any chance to be inside you again." His mouth moved down my throat, and one of his hands somehow got between us to press and rub against my clit. "I fucking *need* you, Cass."

And over the edge I went. Need wasn't love. But it was something. And I was so hungry for him that those words were all it took. I gave in to the tumult inside me. If this was the last time, then we had to make it count.

We kissed deep and long and I tried to hold on to every moment. See and feel every moment. Because once our parents were married, we could never be together again. Not like this.

So I touched him as if I had never touched him before. Discovered him. The way his hair felt springy under my palms. The surprising gentleness of his lips as they settled over mine. The sensitivity of his tongue. The strong tendons in his neck as I moved my fingertips over them. The firmness of his shoulders and the way the muscles flexed and played under his skin when I caressed him.

As I moved my fingers and my mouth over his body, I kept finding things I hadn't really noticed before—the intricate designs of his tattoos, which I traced slowly, both with my fingers and my tongue. The tiny crinkles of hair on his chest. The hills and valleys of his amazing six-pack of abs. The impudent way his cock twitched every time I brushed my fingers there, the way it thickened when I thought it couldn't get any larger.

If Shane had been a sea creature, I'd have certified him as a perfect specimen. But even though I adored and enjoyed the beauty of his body, it wasn't what was primary in my thoughts that night. I was seeing him in a different way—not just as the super sexy hot fuck I'd planned on taking for my own on our out-of time, out-of-mind fantasy road trip. But as the real man I'd slowly come to know as we had traveled together and challenged each other.

I couldn't claim to understand him very well yet, despite all the time we had spent together. He was a complicated man, and he hid his real feelings behind a wall of attitude and toughness. His whole "I sleep alone" thing proved how unwilling he was to let anybody in. That along with the "I don't have lovers; I fuck."

I couldn't fault him for those things because I was kinda the same way. Too busy for boyfriends. Too hard at work for a social life. Intimacy was scary because if I gave my heart to someone, he'd probably just stomp on it. Or leave me the way my mother had.

So it was a good thing, I told myself, that Shane had his own intimacy problems. We were alike in that way. We knew where the boundaries were. We knew how to keep ourselves safe.

It had taken an earthquake and a near rape to break through my walls. To make me want something more with this man who had pestered me, annoyed me, made me laugh, made me cry, and made my body sing. I had no idea what it would take to smash down his walls, but I wasn't going to try to find out.

Even if it had only been the two of us, and nobody else involved, I wouldn't have wished to destroy the equilibrium that Shane, a man with a difficult and dangerous job, had created for himself. I didn't want him to ache the way I was now aching. I didn't want him to feel the pain of loving when love was not allowed.

But if it was forbidden to speak my love, I could show it. That could not be denied me.

Shane lay back on the bed while I kissed and caressed him all over. While I learned him and tried to memorize every bump and curve of his body. While I worshipped him. It was long and slow and loving. When I had explored every inch of him, he pulled me down and did the same to me. His lips, his tongue, the sweet, sharp pleasure of his hands touching me, arousing, me, driving me into never-ending spirals of delight.

I don't know how we found the patience to draw it out. Usually we couldn't wait to smash our bodies together—fingers and tongues and pelvises jerking into wild, crazy action. Not this time. This time we treated our passion like a slow fire to be coaxed and nurtured into a deeper, steadier flame.

When at last he loomed over me, his cock poised at my entrance, his eyes smiling down at me in the sweetest look I had ever seen on his face, I reached up and cupped his cheek, which was rough and unshaven. "You're such a badass," I said with a smile. But what I was really saying was, *I love you.*

He grinned right back at me, and then he bowed his hips and pushed into me, hard. I arched, my entire body aching with my need for him. It felt *so* good. "And you're such a kickass." His eyes were twinkling. "Kickass Cass."

Then his rhythm picked up, and soon neither of us was capable of rational thought or speech.

CHAPTER 50

Shane

I HELD HER CLOSE FOR a while after our first round. If this was our last night together, I'd make sure neither of us got any sleep.

She looked up at me and I pressed my body against hers, hovering on top of her tits, I kissed her.

Cassie pushed me off her.

"What's wrong, babe?"

"It's nothing."

But she didn't have to tell me what was bothering her. I knew already. It was making me crazy too. It, us, whatever this had been, was done. I doubt she understood what she was feeling. I didn't understand what I was feeling either. But I wasn't ready to even try to talk about it with her. If we didn't have a future together, what was the point of expressing my feelings?

"Let's just enjoy the time we have left," I started kissing down her body.

She opened her mouth, probably to protest, but I stopped her with a kiss. I took her mouth, my lips covering hers. We fell into each other like we were the newlyweds and this was our honeymoon. Our kisses were sweet and loving, and I stared into her eyes. Slow, I wanted to go so slow that it hurt, savor every kiss, every breath, every touch. I moved my hand over her warm flesh, kneading her thighs, urging her closer to me. I caressed her nipples, licking the buds, swirling my tongue around them, savoring her scent. My tongue lapped at her right nipple, sucking it until she moaned, and my fingers squeezed her left nipple. I moved my mouth off her nipple and switched to the other one.

She became alive under me, her breath hitched. Her hands grasped my back, tracing my muscles, pulling me into her. I reached my hand down to her pussy and parted her lips. She was warm, wet. And I couldn't wait to taste her.

"Open your legs, babe. I want you to come all over my face."

My finger found her clit and I rubbed it, as she spread her legs wider for me. I pressed her tight thighs back. I slipped my tongue inside of her and explored her with my fingers. She moaned and grabbed my hair and pressed me deeper into her pussy.

I was fucking addicted to her. I licked and licked and licked, sending her into a frenzy. Her back arched and her breath quickened. Her pussy clenched and she came, my mouth soaked in her sweet juices.

After a few adorable giggles, she knelt on the bed, stroking my cock. She reached for a condom, but I grabbed her hand.

I wanted to be inside her, without any barrier between us. "Cassie, the Navy tests us every month. And I give you my word you're the only woman I've been with since the night at the cove. I'm clean."

Her brow furrowed for a few seconds, then she nodded her head. "Okay, I'm on the pill. I want to feel all of you."

I'd never had sex without a condom before, never wanting to risk becoming a father to some kid I'd never see or getting some disease. But I trusted Cassie.

I slid my length into her hot sheath, feeling her all along my length. Every nerve ending on my cock awoke. That sweet silky feel of my flesh pressed against hers. We couldn't be any fucking closer. We'd become one.

She gasped, and pulled me deeper. "Make love to me."

And that's exactly what I did. Something I'd never done. I made love to her all night long. We didn't fuck, no raw and dirty sex. I showed Cassie with my love and my touch what I could never express to her through words.

She was riding me, thrashing around in the covers, my mouth sucking on her nipples. I pulled her hair back and made strong eye contact. "Say my name, baby."

Her eyes focused on me, penetrating my soul. "Shane, I love you Shane."

Love. No girl had ever told me that she loved me. Her words put me over the edge, and we came together, her screaming my name over and over.

After she fell asleep in my arms, I escaped from her embrace. I sat on the chair across from the bed and watched her sleep. I grabbed my sketchpad and drew her for a final time, her soft curves, her wild hair, her beautiful face. When I finished the picture, I placed it on the nightstand under her phone. On second thought, I left her several of my sketches from the past few nights. They would tell her better than I ever could how I felt about her.

Did she really love me? I'd never been in love, but often heard some of my married buddies talking incessantly about their wives. They'd carry their wives' pictures in their packs, sneaking a glimpse when they had a chance. But I'd never wanted that, to be dependent on another person. I placed my hand on her naked thigh and she rolled over in her sleep. This could never work. Never. Even without our parents getting married, we weren't right for each other. Cassie deserved to be with some guy who had fancy degrees and could make small talk at her university receptions. I was not that man. I could hear it now. "What does your boyfriend do? Oh, he's a killer."

My gut wrenched. There, my Achilles heel. I was proud of who I was, what I had accomplished. But Cassie was out of my league. I may be a cocky SEAL, but she was a Ph.D. student. I'd been a fuckup in school. She may enjoy me for now, but when she became bored, she'd trade up and I'd be forced to see her a few Christmases from now, newly engaged to her preppy asshat boyfriend. My dad had been a professor and left my mom, Cassie would do the same to me one day. One thing I learned in the SEALs is history will repeat itself, unless you change course.

Daylight would break soon. Fuck my promise to Cassie—I absolutely refused to go to our parents' wedding. I would be unable to hold back my anger. Their relationship was destroying what I could've had with Cassie.

I leaned over to Cassie, gave her a final kiss goodbye. I savored the softness of her lips, inhaled her scent for one last time. We knew all along this day would come. Even after this trip, no matter what happened between us, for the rest of her life, if she ever needed something, anything, and I was stateside, I'd drop anything to race to her side to protect her. But for now—I had to escape.

I snuck out of our hotel room and never looked back.

CHAPTER 51

Shane

I SAT IN THE LOBBY, waiting for my mom to come down after I'd texted her. I had to at least say goodbye to her before leaving.

A young couple kissed by the lobby counter. Maybe they were here on their honeymoon. For a second, I imagined that Cassie and I were here, not on a honeymoon, but on a romantic vacation.

My mom limped toward me, dressed in a long sundress. "Shane, what is it? We're planning to go to the church to help with the clean up."

"I've got to go. This trip was already extended by the earthquake; my leave is up. A taxi is coming for me now. I wanted to say goodbye."

My mom's brow furrowed. "This is about Cassie, isn't it? I see the way you look at each other. What's going on, Shane? The truth, please."

I sighed. My mom and I were close, it had been only us for so long. "Cassie and I had met in La Jolla a year ago, the night before I deployed. We hooked up, and I left the country without telling her. Next time I saw her was when you introduced us in Coronado. She didn't even know I was a SEAL."

My mom's lips parted and she held up her hand to her mouth. "Wow. What a small world. I'm sorry we put you both in such an awkward position. We had no idea. I had my suspicions, but Henry kept saying he knew his daughter and she wasn't interested in dating anyone."

I cringed remembering my words to Cassie. "I don't have lovers, I fuck." God, was I really that much of an asshole? Maybe last night was a fluke, she'd only said she'd loved me in the heat of the moment. How could she ever love a man who had been such a prick to her?

My mom's voice was a pleasant break from my guilty thoughts about Cassie. "Do you love her?"

Did I love her? I'd never been in love so I couldn't even begin to answer that question. I loved having sex with her; I loved the way she'd never said no to me, in or out of the bedroom. She was adventurous. She'd caught lobsters with me. I'm sure she'd be up for rappelling, spear fishing, or cave diving. She was everything I could ever want in a woman.

I looked at the ground. "Maybe."

My mom gasped her hands. "Have you told her that?"

"What's the point, Mom? She's about to be my stepsister? If not today, then next week. We're young; if it doesn't work out, I'm going to have to see her for the rest of my life. This was all a big fucking mistake."

There was an awkward silence between us. I'd said too much—I was already bailing on my mom's wedding day, I didn't want to make her even more upset.

I glanced at my watch. "I have to go. Can you arrange to ship my bike back? I'll pay for it."

My mom hugged me goodbye. "Of course, Shane. Don't worry about it. I love you. As for my marriage, nothing is decided yet. I know you have to go back to work."

"Love you, too." I grabbed my seabag, and loaded it into the taxi in front of the hotel.

As the taxi drove away from Cabo, from Cassie, there was heaviness in my chest. As a SEAL, I'd been taught to work through the pain, focus on the goal, ignore any distractions. But most importantly to never quit. Yet I had just rung that bell three times when I'd said goodbye to Cassie.

CHAPTER 52

Cassie

HE HAD LEFT WHILE I'D been asleep.

Again.

This time he didn't just leave me in the bed or in the tent. He left Cabo. Left Mexico. He'd even abandoned his Harley. As Molly told me at breakfast the next morning, looking embarrassed and perhaps a little thoughtful as she watched my reaction, "I promised I'd arrange to have his bike shipped back to San Diego."

I don't think I was capable of doing more than gaping at her for a moment. Long enough for her to add,

"You didn't know?' she asked gently.

I made a supreme effort to control myself. If he had left to make sure our parents never found out about our illicit relationship, I'd better not screw that up, no matter how angry and bewildered I was feeling. "Um, no. Why should he tell me? We're not that close."

She looked flustered. "His leave was up. He had to get back immediately or he'd have been in a lot of trouble."

"Gotcha. That makes sense." I had to turn away and escape back to my room, because there was no way I could keep up the front. Not until I beat my emotions back into submission somehow.

"Cassie?" she called after me as I walked quickly toward the elevator.

I pretended not to hear. Fortunately, an elevator car was just about to go up. I darted inside and sank back against the wall of the car as the doors slid shut.

I spent the morning in my room, curled up in the bed where we had made love, still smelling his scent on the sheets. I couldn't believe it had been the last time for us. How can it be that you can find someone, and feel so good with him, so happy, so sexy, and then just when everything is coming together and you truly feel you fit with that man—that he's, like, your other half or something—it just ends? You can look your whole life for that person. Many people never find their soulmate.

Shane and I were different in certain ways and we'd started out a bit rocky, but at some point along our journey everything had changed. I'd seen him as he truly was, not just as the badass SEAL persona he'd cultivated over the years.

And then he was the one. For me, at least. I saw his heart and I gave him mine.

But falling in love didn't give me any right to expect anything back. Just because he fit me, it didn't mean I fit him. He didn't want me. Or he didn't want love. It happened all the time.

And even if he did—I don't know why I kept forgetting this—there were our parents to think about. Loving Shane was a dead end and always had been.

He had left some of his sketches for me, though. I paged through them in wonder. He was so talented. Did he even know how smart and talented he was? He was good at so many things.

He had drawn several pictures of me sleeping. I tried to get my wits around it—did this mean that he'd waited until after I was asleep to draw me? Apparently so. He'd left me alone in my tent, but not before sketching me in what must have been very dim light. Was it my imagination or was the last one, the one done last night in this room, even more lovely than all the others? There was something soft and dreamy about it. Something tender.

I wasn't sure what to make of the drawings, but they did boost my spirits a bit. Surely a man who could draw me so lovingly must have feelings for me? What was he trying to tell me with his sketches?

I puzzled over this all morning. I didn't shake myself out of it until the maids knocked on the door, wanting to clean the room.

I had agreed last night to go with my Dad and Molly to the church again and help out some more. That would be good for me. It had distracted me yesterday when I'd still been so frantic about whether they had been drowned at sea. Their lives had been spared and I needed to set aside my gloom over my doomed love affair and focus on how thankful I was that my father was safe and alive.

Dad and I did most of the work at the church. Molly wanted to do more, but being on crutches made it difficult. She laughed and said, "Okay, I'll supervise. There's some more rubble over here. Think you two can move it or shall I rope in some of the other volunteers?"

She was a great organizer and she made both Dad and me laugh as we worked. Again, I thought how much I liked Shane's mother. Whatever resentment I might have had at the beginning about her taking my own mother's place had faded away.

At one point, when I had gone to wash the sweat off my face and the stone dust off my hands with the hose that was bringing us water outside the church, I passed near where Molly was talking to my dad. They were up near the altar, where there hadn't been much damage. She hadn't seen me, not because I was trying to be elusive, but because that part of the church was dimly lit.

"Wait. Are you telling me that my daughter and your son are—"his voice faltered for a moment "—involved?"

"Yes." Her voice contained a small chuckle. "Intimately involved."

Oh no! How did she know? Had I totally given us both away last night at dinner, or had she seen something? Heard something? Had we been too noisy last night, in my hotel room right next to Dad's?

I looked a little desperately toward the old-fashioned confession booth that this ancient little church still maintained. I wasn't even particularly religious, but I had this crazy thought maybe I should go to the priest and beg forgiveness.

But didn't you have to be sorry if you sought forgiveness? I wasn't sorry about anything except possibly getting caught!

"I knew it," my father said angrily. I could hear him clearly because his voice was very loud. I ducked behind a marble pillar and scurried away down the side aisle. But I could still hear them. Their voices carried in the quiet nave.

"I knew there was something odd about the way Cassie was blushing and stammering at dinner last night. Damn it. Ever since I caught them kissing under the mistletoe, I've been afraid this might happen." He paused for breath and added, "How could they do such a thing? And on the way to our wedding? If your son—"

I waited in dread for him to blame Shane. If he did, I was going to go back there and defend him. Nothing had happened between us that I hadn't wanted. But Dad must have thought better of accusing Molly's son of seducing me or leading me astray or whatever he secretly thought had happened.

To my relief, Dad didn't complete the sentence and Molly took no offense at his implication. "It's not surprising," she said in her usual no-nonsense voice. "They're both young and attractive, and they have just spent several days alone together in dire circumstances. What would you expect to happen? Two people, their lives in danger, with no one to depend on but each other—"

"Stop. I get it," my father said.

"What's more, I think it might be serious. I know my son. He's been casual about these things in the past, the way young men often are. But with Cassie, it's different. Do you remember the first time we got them together? The day we told them that we were planning on getting married? I had the strangest feeling, even back then, that something was going to happen between them."

"Shit," snarled my father.

"The atmosphere was charged. There was something brewing already, Henry. And in a lot of ways, Cassie is perfect for Shane. She's her own woman and she won't put up with his shit."

By now I had fled to the other end of the nave. They couldn't see me and I couldn't see them—but the acoustics of the little church were so good that I could still hear their voices. No wonder—they were standing at the front near the pulpit. Clearly this was a building where the priest's sermons could be heard all the way to the back row.

"I adore Cassie," Molly said. "I would love to have her as a daughter-in-law."

"You can't have her as a daughter-in-law. She's going to be your *stepdaughter*, remember? She and Shane can't have a relationship. That would be, I don't know, incestuous or something. Wouldn't it?"

"Of course not. They aren't related. They didn't grow up together, either. And we've already decided to postpone the wedding, so where's the harm?"

"We're only postponing it because of the damage to this church! Weren't you going to talk to your friend the priest about marrying us on the beach or somewhere?"

"I was going to yes, but honestly Henry, the poor man is so overwhelmed at the moment that I feel it's really not the time. Besides, wouldn't it be insensitive to hold a celebration in a town that has taken so much damage?" Molly sounded matter-of-fact about this. As in, of *course* we're postponing the wedding. "Now I'm thinking maybe it is a good thing."

"What's so good about it?" my father growled.

"What I mean is, do we really need to get married at all?"

"Molly, what are you saying? Don't you love me? Don't you want to be with me?"

"Of course I do, you dear man. I love you very much. But you know how agonized I've been for the past few days. Worrying about Shane and about Cassie. It's bad enough that I have to stress over him when he's deployed, but an earthquake? And it never stops. The worry, I mean. Not just that I might lose him because of his military duty, but my fears that he'll never have a normal relationship. That he'll always be alone. I don't want him to copy his old Ma and be solitary for most of his life. He needs a wife, a family."

"I want my daughter to be happy, too. But she's only known Shane for a brief time and—"

"Sometimes it happens like that."

"So what are you saying? I don't understand, Molly."

"I'm saying that if our kids are in love, we should give them a chance. I'm willing to make that sacrifice for their sake, aren't you?"

"What sacrifice?" My father's voice sounded anguished and confused.

I was utterly confused myself. She thought we were in love? My legs were shaking and my heart wouldn't stop hammering. Not only did Molly know, but she approved. She seemed to think, in fact, that Shane and I had a future together. Why did she think that? Did she know something I didn't know? Had Shane told her about us?

"Well, the whole marriage thing. I mean, do we really care? It's not as if we're going to have more children. We're both too old for that. If they want to be together, let them. I don't need a formal marriage to know you're my man."

"But, the wedding. It was all planned. I thought you *wanted* to get married."

"What I really want is to sail the seas with you on your boat and fish the rivers and lakes with you in Montana. Yes, I want us to be together. But I've never been married and the only thing I've missed about my situation is the regular sex. If we were young, it would be a different story. But the world has changed since we were their age, Henry. Marriage is no longer required for a couple like us. For the younger generation, though, who have children to raise, marriage is still important."

"I'm dumbfounded," my father said.

He wasn't the only one.

"You're already marrying our kids off and giving them children, just because you suspect them of having sex on the road to Cabo?"

Molly must have shrugged or something because I didn't hear her speak. But I had to slam my hand over my mouth to stop myself from laughing out loud. This was *insane*.

"This isn't a crazy way of breaking up with me, is it?"

"Henry, really. You have the oddest notions at times. Of course not!" There was a pause and then the distinct sound of a kiss. Damn, they were kissing in public, right up near the altar where they were supposed to have been married today.

I had to talk to Shane. Right now. I had to find out what, if anything, he had said to his mother. I had to tell him that our parents were actually considering *not getting married*. Or at least, Molly was.

I called him. It felt strange because I had never called him before. I wouldn't have even known his number if I hadn't tried so many times after the earthquake to get both of our cell phones working.

The call went through. I waited, my heart fluttering. But he neither picked up nor called me back.

CHAPTER 53

Cassie

THE NEXT MORNING MY DAD presented me with a plane ticket home. He didn't say a single word about what Molly had told him about Shane and me. "I know you have to get back, Cassie. Your classes will be starting. Molly and I are going to sail back, and we've decided to leave immediately because the weather's good now."

My heart was beating erratically as I asked, "But, Dad, what about the wedding?"

"We're going to postpone it for a while." He said this tightly, as if he hated the idea.

"Is everything all right?" I was torn between guilt and hope. But every time hope soared, I had to beat it down. I had to remind myself that I was the one with the lovesick heart. Not Shane. His heart was still free.

He still hadn't returned my call.

"The earthquake messed with everyone's schedules. You and I both have to get back to the university. And her son, as you know, had to return to duty. We'll figure out what to do about the wedding later. There's no rush."

I could tell by the way he almost sneered the words, "her son," that he was angry at Shane, no doubt because of what Molly had told him in the church. And suddenly I couldn't stand it anymore. I had never been good with secrets, and Dad and I had always been close.

"Dad." I heard the tremulous sound of my own voice and stiffened my shoulders. I could do this. It was partly my fault that Dad didn't like Shane, and it wasn't fair to him at all. It wasn't fair to either of them. But I had made it worse by acting as if I couldn't stand him, either. All to cover up my increasing feelings for Shane. "I guess you know that I lied to you. About Shane, I mean. I'm sorry for that. I hope it isn't, um, causing trouble between you and his mom. Because it shouldn't. It was just a—I mean—" I trailed off, not wanting to lie any further. But from what I'd over heard in the church, Molly had implied that Shane and I were serious, which wasn't true, at least not on Shane's side.

I couldn't tell what Dad was thinking. But after a long minute of silence, he spoke, "She thinks we should call off the wedding."

"No, Dad. You don't have to do that. It's not as if I have any future with him. But you and his mother seem really happy."

He grabbed me by the arm, startling me. "What did that bastard do? I knew he couldn't be trusted. Those Special Forces guys—I know about them. I had friends in the military, years ago. I know how they act. I've seen the guys drilling out on the beach at Coronado, and I've also seen them hanging out in the bars, with women falling all over them. What they do for our country, that's all fine and good, but I would never want a man like that hanging out with my daughter. Much less—" now it was his turn to falter.

"Shane's not like that."

"Yeah? Then where the fuck is he? He abandoned both you

and his mother at the slightest hint of conflict. He took off and left everything. He asked Molly to take care of his fucking motorcycle and ship it home. With all his stuff. What kind of an asshole does that? What kind of an asshole fucks my daughter when she's about to become his sister and then leaves her crying?"

Wow, I had rarely heard my dad use that kind of language with me. He was really upset. But he was wrong about Shane. I thought of our last night together—how strangely tender Shane had been. So different from our previous nights together. Did he have feelings for me, after all?

"Dad, you don't understand. Shane and I met a long time ago. Almost a year ago. We first got together before you even knew Molly. Then he was deployed for nine months. He had just returned home when you and Molly invited us to dinner that night. Neither one of us had any idea that we were about to encounter a stepsibling. We were both horrified."

Dad was blinking at me in astonishment.

"We knew it couldn't go on as soon as we saw that you and Molly were serious about each other. The road trip to Cabo was just a last minute fling. To get it out of our systems. It ended when we got here. We knew it had to end. It's over. Done."

He didn't say anything. He still looked stunned. Whatever Molly had told him—whatever she knew or had guessed—I guess she hadn't told him that Shane and I had met last year.

"He saved my life. First during the earthquake when he kept us from wrecking ourselves in the rift in the earth that opened right ahead of us. And then again when he found us water in the desert. And got us to safety. And finally…" My voice was shaking by now. "Dad, I was attacked by two vicious bikers, who were going to rape and murder me. Shane saved me from them, even though he'd been hurt in the earthquake. If it hadn't been for him, I wouldn't be here to tell you any of this. I'd be dead now, if not for Shane."

I was gulping for breath as it all came back. I felt my dad's hands on my shoulders, steadying me. "Please don't distrust him or accuse him of anything, because he is a wonderful man who put himself at risk to protect me."

I could have gone on to spill my praises for the man I'd fallen in love with, but I'd already said enough. Dad pulled me close and held me, but not before I caught a glimpse of the stricken expression on his face. "I didn't know any of that, Cassie. Hush, sweetie. I've got you. It's okay."

"Nothing that happened was Shane's fault. I wanted it too. I wanted everything and I took it. That's how we got into this mess, and, God, Dad, I'm so sorry! I mean, I'm not sorry for anything that happened with Shane and me, but I'm really sorry for hurting you or disappointing you or making you angry or unhappy or—"

"Cassie," he said, patting my back in a way that reminded me of my childhood. "I could never be disappointed in you. I love you and that's all that matters."

"But you love Molly, too," I blubbered.

"There's always room enough for love," my father said.

I took the airplane ticket Dad offered me and left Mexico a few hours later. There was no point in staying there now that the wedding seemed to be on hold. With Shane gone, I just wanted to get out of Mexico. Everything about the place reminded me of him.

The sooner I got back to my research on marine animals, the sooner I could lose myself in my work. And Dad and Molly would probably be much better off figuring out what they were going to do next if I wasn't around to remind them of their wayward children.

Shane still hadn't called or texted me. I needed to put him behind me and get on with my life.

Somehow.

A few hours later, as my plane flew north over the Baja Peninsula where my world had been forever changed by a gorgeous, irritating jerk with wicked blue eyes and a body that could fuck me a hundred ways and make me scream in joy, I pressed my face against the cold airplane window and fought to hide my tears.

CHAPTER 54

Shane

Two weeks later

WE ARRIVED BACK FROM OUR latest training by helicopter. It had been a quick trip, dare I say relaxing, teaching the candidates to skydive. My buddy Grant gave me a ride to my place. After I took a quick shower, I hopped into my truck, and rolled down the windows. I was grateful to the cool breeze from the ocean welcoming me back to San Diego.

I got a shock when I got home, though. My mom called me and told me that she and Henry had decided that they weren't getting married, after all.

At first, I was angry for my mom's sake, jumping to the conclusion that Henry must have dumped her just like various guys had done in the past. Including my biological father.

But Mom reassured me, explaining that she didn't want to leave our home in Montana, at least not full time, although she was happy to stay with Henry during her off seasons. "I told him there was no way I'd give up the business I've built in Billings for the past twenty years. Besides, there isn't any serious trout fishing in the San Diego area."

As for Henry, he didn't want to leave his tenured full professorship at USD to move to Montana. Apparently he'd been assuming that Mom would move down here when they got married. When she'd made him understand that wouldn't be happening, they'd agreed to be life partners without bothering with the technicality of marriage.

"It's not like I'm ever going to have any more kids," she said. "Henry and I are hoping for grandchildren."

That was about as broad a hint as I'd ever heard from my mother. I was still trying to process it when she asked me to come over and pick up my bike.

I believed that she was happy and at peace with her decision. So I let go any remaining anger and guilt that I'd felt about the wedding.

Cassie was not going to be my stepsister. My heart raced, there was no external barrier keeping us apart. We had a chance. I missed everything about her, her smile, her laugh, her wit, her body. But I still wasn't sure if I could make her happy. She said she loved me, but it was in a moment of passion. Did she really want to be with me?

I drove down to Henry's house. But before I could ring the doorbell, I saw it. There, sitting in the driveway. A Harley. My Harley. It looked brand new.

My hands glided over the custom paint job, the new leather scent filled my nostrils. My mom didn't have the money for this. I studied it closer—completely rebuilt, new parts, and even a custom-painted trident on the fuel cover.

"You like it?" I tore my eyes away from the bike for a second to see Henry standing by the door, a smile on his face.

"Yes, sir. But I can't accept this. I do appreciate it. Please, let me know how much I owe you."

He took a few steps forward. "Son, you don't owe me anything. Cassie told me how you saved her life."

I looked him in the eyes. "I'm sorry, sir. I never meant to ruin your wedding. You make my mom happy and I'm glad you're there for her. As for Cassie—" I hesitated, "—she deserves someone better than me, someone more refined, educated. Someone more like you."

Henry put his arm around my shoulder, and this time, I resisted the urge to shrug him off. "I'm not so refined. Look, son. You remind me a bit of myself when I was your age. I also had a bike, loved that thing. It was a classic." He paused for a moment, and then added with a grin, "Your mom mentioned that maybe I should get another one. You and I could ride together. Nothing like driving on the open road. What do you think?"

Whoa. Henry was blowing my mind. "I'd like that, sir."

"Cassie would be lucky to have a man like you. That's what I think. Now come inside and visit with your mother."

And that was it. He turned and walked back into the door. No lecture, no stay the fuck away from my daughter, no I know about you SEALs.

He approved of me. He approved of *us*. He thought I was good for her.

Was I so completely fucked up that I'd convinced myself that our relationship was impossible, even though our parents were no longer getting married?

I greeted my mom but excused myself the first second I had a chance.

I felt as though an enormous load had just been lifted off my back.

I grabbed my phone to call Cassie. But there was already a text blinking from her.

"Meet me. Down by the sea lions."

CHAPTER 55

Cassie

I WAS AT THE LA JOLLA cove again.

I came sometimes to watch the sea lions. And the sea. To listen to the comforting sounds of the waves splashing against the rocks in their never-ending rhythms. Sometimes I sat under the awning where I had sat on the night I'd met Shane. I liked to meditate there, with the sounds of the sea in my ears and the breeze in my hair. But I kept getting distracted by thoughts of my crazy road trip with Shane.

I hadn't heard a word from him.

It still hurt.

I knew he cared about me. He might pretend that he had no feelings for me, but his hands when he caressed my body and his fingers when held a sketching pencil told me a different story.

I wasn't sure what good it would do, though, if he couldn't cope with his feelings. I couldn't force him back into my arms.

He might be a kickass SEAL who could take all kinds of physical torture and be lethal in a fight and an ace survivalist and all those things, but perhaps dealing with a real-life woman was too much for him.

My mind got into such tangles whenever I thought about Shane. I usually moved from blaming him to blaming myself—believing that he couldn't really love me enough because I just wasn't that lovable. I'd argued with him and defied him and challenged him right from the start. Maybe he'd been glad to get rid of me.

I had to know for certain, though. Especially since the wedding between our parents was now off. Not that they weren't still together. They were. Very much so. But both of them had told me that they were no longer so inclined to formalize their relationship with, as Molly put it, "the outdated ritual of marriage."

But I knew they must have changed their plans because they'd found out about Shane and me.

If so, it was a damn shame, since Shane had been incommunicado ever since he'd left me alone in Cabo.

I was going to give it one last try.

This evening I had finally decided to confront him. Once and for all.

I'd sent him a text and asked him to meet me here. But he hadn't answered and it was beginning to look as though he wasn't going to show up.

I walked down to the water line and let the waves break over my bare feet. There were no sea lions close to shore where I was standing. I could see some lights on buoys out in the water near the reef, though. Night divers, marking their dive spot. I'd never dived at night here. I'd like to some time, but not without a partner, of course. Shane had been such a great diver. A SEAL would be, I guess. The water was their thing, after all.

We'd only dived that one time together. Lobster hunting—something I'd resented hugely at the time, although I'd done it. I'd dive for lobsters again with him, and even eat the damn things afterward, if I could just have Shane back for one more night.

"Hey," a voice said from just behind me.

Oh my God. Magic? Wish upon a lobster and it comes true? I turned slowly, afraid that it had been some kind of hallucination. I knew his voice, of course. I was sure I would hear it in my head for my whole life.

He was there, tall and beautiful, his hair a little longer and his beard grown in a little rougher. I wanted to grab him or do one of those leaps where the girl hurls herself at the guy pelvis first and scissors her thighs around him and he supports her back and—

"Cassie? Are you okay?"

I obviously had frozen-face or something. "Um, hiya. I'm fine. Just surprised. I didn't hear you coming. I didn't know if you'd gotten my text."

"Just got it about thirty minutes ago."

I couldn't seem to gauge his mood. I felt awkward. The little speech I'd prepared went completely out of my head. "Molly told me you've been away on some kind of training thing?"

"Yup. I was doing a BUD/s rotation. Teaching the candidates to skydive. Just got back to town."

My body was reacting to his in the old instant-attraction way. Heat and chills both at once. Heart pounding, Breasts tingling. Belly convulsing with sexual tension. Desire flooding every cell. Why didn't this happen with any other good-looking man? It was so unfair that he was the only guy who could unleash this wild response in me.

I stepped back a pace and tried to glare at him. I don't think it came out as a glare, though. Just seeing him made me want to smile, to grin, to laugh out loud. I hated him for making me so unhappy, but I loved him anyway, damn the man!

"Thank you for coming," I said, gathering my tattered courage. "I need to talk to you. Actually, I need to ask you about these."

I opened the Manila envelope I'd kept folded to my chest

and pulled out the sketches he'd left for me.

He looked surprised. "You kept them? I thought you might toss them in the wastebasket."

"Why would I do that? They're wonderful. You have a real talent. You're good at so many things." I stopped, hesitated, and then plunged on, "Why did you draw me so lovingly? You made me far prettier than I am, and yet the sketches don't feel like flattery. I mean, they aren't idealized. They're accurate, real. They show my flaws. And still they somehow make me look beautiful. Why is that, Shane? What does it mean?"

He stared at the drawings and then he smiled at me. "They're the way I see you, Cass. You're beautiful to me."

I swallowed hard. That was lovely to hear, but where did it leave me? Where did it leave us?

I had told him I loved him that night in Cabo. If he didn't have the guts to say the same to me, I wasn't going to repeat it.

"Did you hear about our parents? It seems we're not gonna be stepsiblings, after all."

"I just heard. My mom told me a little while ago when I got back to town."

Silence fell between us. I heard a sea lion bark nearby and I was grateful for the distraction. I half turned away and look down toward the water. I didn't know what else to say to Shane.

Then he spoke: "I need to talk to you, Cass. I've been doing some thinking. I've been trying to process everything. You know?"

I refused to nurse the spark of hope that flared in me then. "Last time we were together you didn't want to talk about anything. And then you left me. You told your mother you were leaving Mexico, but you didn't tell me!"

The accusation burst out of me. Not good. But I couldn't hold it back. Part of me wanted to beat with my fists upon his chest and scream, "Why don't you love me? Why don't you? Why, why, why?"

"I'm sorry," he said. Which amazed me. Shane didn't seem like the type of guy who apologized too often. "I haven't had any real girlfriends before. I mean, women that I cared about. Real relationships. I just, you know, fucked. My mom has always said I was relationship-handicapped. But now I think she believes there might be hope for me."

"There's hope for you?" I was confused. I wasn't sure what he was saying and I didn't dare believe there was hope for me. For us. "What do you mean? Did you tell her about us? When we were in Cabo? Because somehow or the other, she knew."

He looked away for a moment, and then back at me. "My mother's the only woman I've ever really been close to. Before you came along, I mean. So, yeah. I may have told her that I was in love with you."

Were my ears ringing or had he just said he was in love with me? "You told her what?"

He caught one of my wrists and pulled me close. "I love you, Cassie. Don't make me say it again. Once a day is probably all you're gonna get."

Joy was running through my veins instead of the blood that had been there a couple moments ago. But there was no way he was getting away with this! "You leave me alone in Mexico and disappear for a couple more weeks and you don't even call me or text me or anything and now all of a sudden you're in love with me?"

"Shut up," he said. His arms came around me and his mouth came down on mine. After we had both kissed so hard we nearly fell over, he raised his lips to say, "You talk too much. You always did."

I laughed again, hearing my own voice ringing out. But after another long kiss, I said, "Sometimes a couple has to talk. I mean, I love you, you love me...now what?"

He grinned. "Now we fuck?"

I poked him in his rock-hard shoulder. "Shane, you have to

give me something. Some tiny hope that you're not going to keep disappearing on me and leaving me to wake up alone!"

"Shit, Cassie, I don't even know if I can ever make you happy. You don't know what you are getting into dating a Team guy."

"So tell me."

"I get deployed a lot. It's a dangerous job. You will go months without knowing if I'm alive or dead. It's not fair to ask you to put up with that. You might end up hating me and wishing you'd never met me."

Did he think I'd never considered that? It would be difficult, I knew. Worrying about him and missing him would be the worst. I hated to even think about how hard it would be. But other women did it when they loved their man.

"I hear what you're saying, but I have plenty going on in my life to keep me busy while you're away. I'm in grad school, I work, I do research projects. Hell, I do yoga. I don't need you to hold my hand every day to make me happy. Have I ever seemed to you like a woman who couldn't get along without a guy?"

"Well, no," he admitted. He paused for a bit, and then added, "But you know what I do, right? I kill people. You've seen that first hand."

"You defend people. You protected me. Shane, you saved my life." Was he worried that I'd reject him because I'd seen him kill those two motorcycle thugs? I knew what SEALs did. I knew that those creeps weren't the first men he'd killed, nor would they be the last. But if I hadn't accepted that side of him long ago, I never would have let myself fall in love. "I don't see you as a killer. The way you were with Meztli, with me, with that baby you helped pull out of the rubble. I see you as a healer and a protector, Shane."

He still looked a little dubious.

"Look, you're passionate, smart, and incredible in bed. You're principled, honorable and artistic. Shane, you're everything I want, everything I need." I kissed him again, hard. "I fucking love you."

As his arms enfolded me tightly, I noticed a sea lion staring up at us. The scarring around his neck suggested that he was the one I'd saved. The now almost full-grown pup who had brought us together. Was he rooting for us from his home in the sea?

Perhaps you are a whale-whisperer too, Metzli had said.

When Shane finished kissing me thoroughly, he lifted his head and gave me that old familiar leer. "I think you're a little crazy if you can love a guy like me, but you're my kind of crazy. Crazy beautiful. You're coming home with me, babe. Right now."

"Oh yeah? What for?"

"I'm gonna fuck you silly, that's what for." With one arm firmly around my waist he dragged me up the path to the parking lot. Okay, he didn't have to drag. I was jogging along beside him, as eager to get to a bed as he was to take me to one.

"Look what your dad did," he said, taking me to...wow... the Harley. All bright and shiny and repaired and looking as good as new. "He had the whole thing refurbished for me after shipping it back up here. Nice, huh? I wouldn't have thought a prof like him even knew anything about bikes, but I guess he's not as much of a stick in the mud as I thought. He confessed he'd had a Harley of his own when he was young."

"My father did that?" I'd had no idea Dad was fixing Shane's bike.

"He didn't tell you?"

"Nobody tells me anything!"

He grinned at me. "I love you."

"Well, I love you, too, you big jerk!"

"Then get on the bike. Because I'm gonna make you prove it tonight in about a hundred ways."

I laughed and hugged him hard. Then he mounted his shiny Harley, the one that had borne us a thousand miles into the wilderness and been a cold metal witness to our love, and I climbed on behind him, pressed myself against his ass, and hung on tight.

This was where I belonged, and this was where I was gonna stay, no matter where the next road trip took us. This badass was mine and I was his.

Forever.

FROM THE AUTHORS

If you enjoyed this book, we have more!

LINDA

If you love bad boys, check out Cassie's hometown friends:

Stephen: I want it all: whips and chains. Hearts and kisses. *The Dangerous Hero.*

Nick: She thinks I'm dominating. Cruel. But I've got a dirty job to do. *Uncover Me.*

Daniel: She's a psychic? With a reincarnated cat? Don't make me laugh. *Blazing Nights.*

Connor: She accepted a ride with me? Her troubles are just beginning. *Color Me Blue* (novella).

If you love alpha male shifters, check out *The Zrakon's Bride* and *The Zrakon's Curse.*

For the latest updates, release, and giveaways,
Subscribe to Linda's newsletter [http://eepurl.com/yB2x5].

For all her available books,
Check out Linda's website [http://www.lindabarlow.com/]
or Facebook page
[https://www.facebook.com/LindaBarlowAuthor].

BONUS CONTENT

**For the first chapter of Linda's *The Dangerous Hero*,
continue reading!**

ALANA

Want to meet Shane's SEAL buddies?

Meet Pat! I had one chance to put on the cape and be her hero. *Invincible.*

Meet Grant! She wants to get wild? I will fulfill her every fantasy. *Conceit.*

Like Marines?

Meet Bret! The thought of being with a real man, muscles sculpted from carrying weapons, not practicing pilates made her quiver. *Love Waltzes In.*

Like Rockstars?

Meet Tony! This Greek God of a man is six feet five inches of perfection. *Waltz on the Wild Side.*

For the latest updates, release, and giveaways,
Subscribe to Alana's newsletter
[http://www.alanaalbertson.com/newsletter/].

For all her available books,
Check out Alana's website [http://www.alanaalbertson.com/]
or Facebook page
[https://www.facebook.com/AuthorAlanaAlbertson].

BONUS CONTENT

**For the first chapter of Alana's *Invincible*,
continue reading!**

The Dangerous Hero

by Linda Barlow

Blurb

I want it all. Whips and chains. Hearts and kisses.
Viola was the first woman I ever tied up. We had one of those
brief but intense summer romances.

OK, so I screwed that up. But now, years later, I've got a second
chance.

The thing is, she doesn't trust me. I write novels about a brutal
spymaster whose craving for blood and torture is insatiable. Hidden in my home is an authentic medieval dungeon. I'm a connoisseur of finely-wrought leather floggers, silken ropes, the restrictive corset, the binding cuff.

I don't mean to frighten her. But hey, I want it all. Whips and
chains. Hearts and kisses. Domination and submission, pleasure
and pain. I'm looking for that special partner—somebody to torment, somebody to love.

The door to my playroom is open. It is up to her to walk in.

Chapter One

She recognized him instantly. It had been nine years since she had last seen the tall man with curly dark hair who was striding toward the table where she was seated. He was Stephen Silkwood, the mystery writer, and he was famous, at least among detective fiction buffs. But as he moved to the empty chair beside her, looking too damn hot for words, Viola forgot about his novels, which she loathed. Stephen had been the first man she had ever loved.

He was also the first to break her heart. The pain of that experience rushed back with surprising intensity. Shit. She thought she'd recovered from that melodrama years ago.

She wanted to jump up and flee the small Massachusetts college where she and her old flame were about to meet. But she couldn't do that.

Calm down, heart. Stop thumping. It happened eons ago.

She shot a pained glance at Jeff Slayton, a professor in the Whittacre College history department, who had told her that Silkwood had declined the invitation to participate in tonight's panel discussion. She'd mentioned to Jeff that she didn't want to be grouped with this author.

Slayton had grinned at her and said, "Are you afraid he'll reproach you for that scathing review you wrote when his latest book came out?"

The review *had* been scathing. Viola had argued that Silkwood's popular historical mysteries pandered to the public's lowest taste for brutality and violence. She objected to Silkwood's hero Bartholomew Giles, intelligence agent for Queen Elizabeth's spymaster Walsingham. Giles had a nasty predilection for torture, and he seemed particularly fond of torturing women. Viola's review had suggested that Silkwood should depend less on blood and guts and more on realistic character development and plot.

She knew that Silkwood had seen her review—which had appeared in both print and digital forms—because she had heard him interviewed on a popular podcast. "V. J. Bennett, whoever he—or more likely *she*—is, sounds like a malicious idiot," he'd said. "Maybe she should stick to reading cozy mysteries and romances."

He didn't know, apparently, that V. J. Bennett was Viola Quentin, his brief summer love of nine years ago, whom he had lied to and abandoned.

Viola pretended to be clicking through the notes on her tablet as Stephen coiled his long-limbed body into the chair beside her, accidentally bumping against one of her legs. The brief contact electrified her, transmitting a jolt that sizzled all the way down to her toes. Jeez! Didn't sexual chemistry have an expiration date?

Any hope that, up close, his once-gorgeous features would have aged into something ordinary vanished. The years barely seemed to have touched him. He'd been a sex god nine years ago, and he still was. It wasn't classical beauty that he possessed—his features were a bit too honed and edgy for that—rather it was that smoky impression of something dark and dangerous lurking beneath the surface. He'd always had that bad boy thing going for him.

His green eyes met and held hers. Hot, shared connection. She saw curiosity in those eyes, and a trace of amusement, but no hint of recognition.

"Am I late?" he asked, glancing around at the other seated participants. "I had a bit of car trouble."

He spoke with the impersonality of a stranger. The years that had passed since their final encounter must have erased her image from his mind.

"You're fine. We haven't started yet."

So. He didn't know who she was. Good. Much easier that way. There wouldn't be any awkwardness. She could pretend not to remember him, either.

As he surveyed the audience and the other panelists, she gave in to the temptation to check him out a bit more. His wavy dark hair was longer than was fashionable, its silky ends brushing the back of collar. Those expressive green eyes were distanced by a pair of dark-rimmed glasses, the angular cheekbones and sensuous mouth were just as she remembered them. A tingle went through her as she recalled some the wicked things he could do with that mouth.

Stop that, hormones! Behave yourselves.

His gaze shifted, and he caught her staring. He smiled as she hurriedly glanced away. It was a friendly smile, and it reminded her that he used to smile a lot. He had been an outgoing, genial sort of guy. "I'm Stephen. Who are you?"

Pinned to her jacket was a tag that identified her simply as Prof. Bennett. He stared at it for such a long moment that she thought he'd identified her as the hostile book reviewer. But then she realized he was focusing on the open neckline of her blouse. That wretched tingle ran through her again, moving lower this time. Grrr! Surely that was nothing more than old memories churning. He was hot, yes, but so what?

"So, Professor," said Silkwood. "What do you profess?"

Something about the way he pronounced the word made it sound as though he regarded teaching as an activity that got you all slick and sweaty. "English lit." She nodded at Slayton, who had risen to make the introductions. "I think we're about to begin."

Silkwood politely turned his attention to Slayton, who got the panel rolling.

He didn't remember her. She could hardly believe it. His face and form were branded on her memory, but he had obviously forgotten the many hours they'd spent together back when he'd been a student of her father, Percy Quentin, also a novelist. Viola had been a teenager, just graduating from high school. Stephen had been a charming and talented writer who had not yet published his first book.

In those days, her father and Stephen had been close. Because her parents were divorced and Viola spent most of her time with her mother in San Francisco, she didn't meet Stephen until she spent that lazy summer before college on Cape Cod.

Stephen came down several times to visit her dad and talk about writing. He'd made friends with the cheerful teenager who was his mentor's only daughter. When he wasn't busy workshopping the latest chapters of his novel with her father, they'd hung out. One balmy weekend in August, she tried to teach him how to windsurf. Although Stephen was fit and athletic—he had been a track star in college—he couldn't quite get the hang of windsurfing.

Her lesson had caused them both to collapse with laughter as he kept toppling over into the waves. They'd spent several hours in close physical contact, hauling each other up onto the board while she demonstrated the positioning and tried to help him stand and remain upright. He was determined to learn, and took his setbacks with good grace. She'd liked that about him. He had a calm, lighthearted attitude, and he didn't seem to mind that she, a teenager, was far more adept at the sport than he was.

Although she'd thought of Stephen as her father's friend, and much too old for her, on this afternoon the knowledge penetrated her brain that he wasn't *that* old. He had a beautiful body, long and lean, subtly muscled, with an ass to die for. At some point, as they bumped up against one another in the water, a spark caught. Stephen shoved the windsurf rig toward the shore, swam up against her slick body, fondled her long hair, and kissed her salt-sprayed lips.

She had fallen for him on the spot. She hadn't found out until later that he was engaged to be married.

Her father had broken the news to her at the end of that weekend, not long after Stephen had left. Percy Quentin must have noticed the change that had come over both of them after the windsurfing lesson. "He's got a girlfriend," he'd told her gently. "They're getting married. He's an unprincipled rascal. Forget him, child."

Forget him? She had tried. But she'd fallen hard. Even though he never wrote her any of the emails he promised, never texted, never called, it had taken a long time for the magic of that weekend to recede from her mind. Now here he was again, unearthing all those painful memories.

"What are we supposed to be discussing, anyway?" he asked under his breath. "Tell me, Professor, so I don't make an ass of myself."

"I think you'll mostly be taking questions from the audience." Mischievously she added, "I see several other members of the English department present, so you'd better be prepared to discuss stuff like post-colonial metaphor and allusion."

"Ouch. Wake me up when we get to the symbolism of murder or something equally literary."

"If you don't care for academic discussions, why are you here?"

"Jeff's an old friend. He talked me into it. Besides, my publisher likes it when I do these things." He grinned at her. "Gotta try to sell a few books." There was a cheerful note of self-mockery in his tone.

Once again, his deep green gaze flickered over her without a trace of recognition. His eyes were the same shade as the sea. The damn water where he had first kissed her...touched her...given her pleasure.

But he didn't remember. Well, shit. She didn't want to remember either.

She knew she must look different now. In those days, she

still had the short, spiky black hair she'd adopted for her senior year of high school. It had been summer vacation, so she'd run around with no make-up, dressed casually in shorts and bikini tops, spending so many hours in the sun that her fair skin must have been dotted with freckles. Today she was clad in a well-tailored suit. Her hair, long restored to its natural auburn, was loose on her shoulders. Her freckles, mercifully, had faded. She was more mature than she'd been that summer, more self-assured, and, she hoped, more resistant to the man's deadly charm.

"Relax," she said, tossing him a grin. "Think of the royalties."

He smiled back, sipped water from the bottle someone had left for him, and fielded a question from the audience. He answered with wit and self-deprecation, and after a couple of brief exchanges, he said, "I think you ought to ask this lovely lady beside me a question or two." He glanced once again at Viola's nametag. "Professor, uh, Bennett is undoubtedly an expert on Umberto Eco or Ellis Peters or—"

"Or you," David Newstead interrupted. David, another member of the English department, was seated on the other side of Viola, and he leaned eagerly across her as he spoke. "She's quite an expert on you, Mr. Silkwood, even if she's not one of your most ardent admirers."

Viola shot her colleague a quelling look, but it was too late. Behind his wire-rimmed glasses, Stephen's eyes narrowed as he stared harder at Viola's uninformative nametag. He raised his glance and looked at her as if they were alone in the room. "Not the immortal V. J. Bennett?"

"I'm afraid so."

A broad smile transformed his features, but the glint that flashed in his eyes was both a challenge and a goad. "My interest in this discussion has suddenly increased," he said.

Someone from the audience asked why the professor was

not one of Silkwood's admirers. Since she hadn't expected him to show up, Viola hadn't come prepared to discuss his novels. Besides, although she disliked his work, she felt a bit guilty about writing such a negative review.

Oh well. She couldn't back down now. "Your sadistic hero, Bartholomew Giles, has either raped, tortured, or brutally killed a woman in each of his last three adventures. Don't you think it's time he got over his blatant misogyny?"

Since the audience was packed with female students, several shouts of approval greeted her comment. Heartened, she went on, "After all, books like yours have a certain influence on the people who read them. It seems ethically questionable to me to suggest it's okay for a man to treat women the way Giles does."

"Bart Giles is the product of my imagination. I try to make him behave in a manner consistent with the times. Misogyny was not something folks gave much thought to in the 16th century."

"I don't find woman-haters appealing, no matter what century they appear in."

"Fair enough," said Stephen. "Neither do I, in the real world. But this is fiction. I'm not suggesting people go out and imitate my protagonist's actions." He grinned at the audience. "Not that it would be too easy to do. I don't think most people have a rack in their basement. Or thumbscrews."

This got a laugh, and Viola smiled, too. It wasn't easy to resist his charm. *Focus.*

"Besides," he added, still flirting with the audience, "I get fan mail from a lot of women who like Bart. The dangerous hero has always had a certain appeal."

Some members of the audience nodded, laughed and clapped. It wasn't easy to debate a dude who knew all there was to know about getting females to pant over him.

"Suppose somebody was inspired to attack a woman after reading one of your torture scenes?" she tried. "Would you feel morally responsible?"

"If a man murders his brother and marries his sister-in-law after a performance of Hamlet, does that make Shakespeare morally responsible?"

"Are you comparing yourself to Shakespeare, Mr. Silkwood?"

He grinned. "I hope I'm not that arrogant." He paused, taking off his glasses and cleaning them off with a handkerchief he pulled from his pants' pocket. "Tell me, Ms. Bennett, why do academics criticize living writers so harshly? You wait until we're dead before giving us any credit for artistry. Yet without us, where would literature professors be? You need me, Professor Bennett. You really ought to support my work."

He got another round of applause for this, but something about the way he said, "You need me," and the mischievous gleam in his eyes as he said it, sent another flash of awareness through her. Jeez, not again!

"Plenty of critics love your work," she said, meeting his smile and raising him a wink. "I doubt you're injured by the criticism of one insignificant reviewer."

"Just because Bart's a hard-ass doesn't mean I am. I could be a shy man who reveres women, abhors violence, and spills copious tears over bad reviews."

But his words mocked her gently, and she knew he wasn't shy. "It's also possible the author and hero *are* alike. Maybe in more ways than the author is willing to admit?"

Stephen's eyebrows rose extravagantly, but before he could respond to this salvo, Jeff Slayton, grinning, cut in and raised a different question altogether.

"What are you doing when this is over?" Stephen whispered.

Viola's heart just about leapt out of her ribcage. "What? Why?"

"I like a spirited debate." He shot her a smile. "Come somewhere with me and have a coffee?"

"You're married," she objected.

He looked faintly puzzled. "No, I'm not." He pointed his thumb at his chest. "Single. Very much so."

Uh-oh. Headrush. He must have gotten divorced. This was so not good. She needed him to be unavailable. Off limits. Well and truly unfuckable. She did not need him suggesting they hang out.

It was still there, that magnetic pull. She knew it, and he was giving off the kind of vibes that meant he felt it, too.

"There's a reception when this is over," she reminded him. "You have to be there to sign your books and meet your fans."

"After that?" he said, keeping his voice low as the literary discussion continued around them. "Bart and I would like to get to know you better. But don't worry, there's nary a dungeon in sight."

She smiled, in spite of herself. But she wasn't going to accept his invitation. No way.

Continue reading *The Dangerous Hero*
Available now at your favorite online retailer

INVINCIBLE

I'LL BE HONEST WITH YOU—I'm no hero. Sure, the media tries to brand every Navy SEAL as some kind of Batman dressed in cammies. There's even a line in one of our cadences: Superman is the man of steel, he ain't no match for Navy SEAL. You've seen the movies—we're infallible, invaluable, invincible. But that night, the one you read about in the papers … all I really wanted to do was get laid.

One harmless fuck with an Aruban whore, no strings attached. I picked her out of a lineup—wild, dark hair, long legs and a crooked smile. After she sucked me off, I relaxed back onto the creaky, cum-stained cot, thankful for the blissful moments she gave me when I actually forgot for a second the faces of my buddies who died because I made the wrong call, the tears of the children I couldn't save, and the eyes of the enemies I slaughtered during their last seconds of life.

But before I left, her hazel eyes peered into my soul. She whispered in a distinct Californian accent, "My name is Annie Hamilton. I'm an American citizen. I was kidnapped on spring break five years ago. You're my last hope. Please save me."

One desperate plea. This wasn't a Hollywood blockbuster or a New York Times best-selling thriller. I knew this time there was no room for excuses, no margin for errors. I had one chance to put on the cape and be her hero.

1

PATRICK

LIBERTY. FINALLY, A NIGHT OFF. Fuck yeah!

Petty Officer 2nd Class Victor Gonzales slicked some gel into his dark brown hair and slathered on some after-shave. "Hey, Walsh—you wanna go to that club tonight? Near the plaza?"

Another tourist hotspot in picturesque Aruba—drunken college girls on spring break, wayward daughters escaping their parents on family vacations. I had no desire to spend my first night on land in six months making small talk, hoping to get lucky. I wanted a sure thing, with no strings.

"No thanks, man. I'm just going to head on into town and get a bite to eat."

Lieutenant Commander Kyle Lawson trimmed his short black beard and nodded toward me. "You sure? You're my wingman, bro. Vic over here can never close the deal."

Vic threw the bottle of hair gel at Kyle. "Fuck you, Kyle. I have standards—I don't just sleep with every girl who says hi to me."

Yeah, I definitely needed to go solo tonight, even though the three of us always made our mark when we hit the town. Three United States Navy SEALs didn't exactly blend in with the local tourists. We were all ripped, especially since on deployment we spent all our free time in the ship's gym. Vic's huge arms were decorated with tattoos. Stupid motherfucker, identifying markers weren't a plus in the Teams. He'd never make SEAL Team Six. And at six feet five inches tall, former NFL linebacker Kyle towered over Vic and me, though we could hardly be considered short since we both measured in at over six feet. People would stop Kyle all the time and ask him for an autograph, confusing him with a Hollywood movie star or a rapper. Not to mention, the two of them looked like a walking Navy SEAL diversity outreach recruitment poster, with me standing out as the blond-haired, blue-eyed boy.

"I'll meet up with you two fools later." For the past six months, I'd spent every waking minute with my Team—SEAL Team Seven to be precise. We'd been circling the Caribbean Islands, working our asses off, patrolling and hunting "go-fast" boats run by South American drug cartels. Tomorrow, I planned to snorkel, relax on the beach, and rest before we returned home from deployment. And later tonight I'd meet up with Kyle and Vic and get hammered.

But first things first—I needed some pussy.

I pulled on my civilian clothes, which felt foreign to my body. Sandals and shorts instead of boots and "utes." I glanced in the mirror and debated whether to shave off my full beard. No point. One benefit of being a SEAL was our relaxed grooming standards. The Marines on our carrier still had to shave daily and cut their hair within regulation. We SEALs could grow full beards and keep our hair longer, to blend in undercover. I certainly wasn't trying to impress anyone tonight, so I grabbed my wallet and headed out.

Where the fuck was that brothel again? I'd visited it last time we were here. Some of the Team guys refused to pay for sex—they'd rather cheat on their wives or girlfriends with unsuspecting coeds or stay on ship all night reading the Bible. Fuck that. I didn't have a wife, or a girlfriend. Some woman back home to screw around on me while I was off training or deployed nine months out of the year? No thanks. I'd tried that once—our ship hadn't even left the dock before she had another guy's cock in her mouth. Never again. At least I wasn't one of those guys slipping in and out of women's lives, filling them with empty promises. I'd seen enough of those men growing up—assholes taking me to baseball games, vowing to be my new dad, fucking my mom and then vanishing. I never made any commitments—except to my country and to my men. Sleeping with a prostitute was the definition of safe sex to me.

Neon-colored buildings lined the streets, some marked with graffiti. A dark-skinned man with an AK-47 slung across his body approached me. "Hey, Sailor, looking for a good time?"

Damn straight. I hadn't laid eyes on a woman in six months. I said no words, just nodded and followed him into an alley, where he frisked me for a weapon. I was all clear. The sun beat down on the broken pavement, and I realized what a dumbass I was for going to a brothel in daylight. But I didn't give a fuck.

The multi-colored beaded curtain crashed in the wind, and I heard some Caribbean music in the background. The man rang a bell, and at least a dozen women ran from the back of the ramshackle house. They were dressed in cheap heels and trashy nighties; this wasn't some high-class joint. But that was fine with me.

One brunette caught my eye. Her black thong was hiked high up on her hips, like she was stuck in some eighties music video. Light-skinned, long legs, small breasts. She seemed older and more withdrawn than the others—and she was the only one who didn't make eye contact with me.

I pointed. "Her."

The pimp let out a deep laugh. "Star? Good choice."

The other girls dispersed, probably grateful to get a small break from being forced to fuck a stranger.

But I didn't want to think about their pathetic lives. There was nothing I could do to improve their existences. My conscience was already filled with guilt—I didn't need to add their sob stories to my burden.

The whore led me down a hallway into a tiny room. The place reeked of cum and sweat, covered by some sort of coconut spritz. What did I expect for twenty dollars?

A tiny cot was pushed up to the left side of the room, a tattered teddy bear sat on the floor, and a plastic end table filled the other corner. Was this where she lived? There were a few needles lying haphazardly in the trashcan. Of course she was a heroin addict—how else could she live this life? I was a SEAL—I knew that these women were probably all forced into prostitution at a young age. They had once been little girls playing make believe, dreaming of princes and castles. But I was no prince. I'd done enough lifesaving in my time and I'd learned the hard way that I couldn't save them all.

"Star? What's your real name?" I didn't really care, but I felt that since she'd be sucking my dick, I should at least know her name.

She pursed her lips as if she was trying to say something but couldn't get the words out. Her face looked vaguely familiar, but I was certain I hadn't fucked her before. My last whore was Dominican: dark, curvy, black eyes. This chick seemed different, more tragic.

"Fine, we don't have to talk. Blow me." I took twenty dollars out of my pocket. If she did a good job, I'd give her a tip.

Over the years, I'd learned blowjobs were the best way to go with a whore. They always gave amazing ones, and I never felt guilty like I did when I took extra-long to come as I had with my ex-fiancée. I couldn't risk getting a nameless hooker pregnant and leaving a kid fatherless and growing up in this hellhole. Plus, there was less chance for a disease, especially since I always wore a condom. The Navy tested me every month so I figured there was minimal risk.

"Take your panties off."

Her panties dropped to the floor, revealing a nicely trimmed triangle. I loved it. Why did all those American bitches wax everything off? I was a man; I didn't want a little girl.

I sat on the edge of the cot. She knelt in front of me, unbuckled my belt, and glanced up at me, taking a moment to stare. She wore a rusty necklace with a small key charm. There were drug tracks on her forearms and a deep scar on her right shoulder. Her eyes were hazel, deep set, and disturbed. I closed mine; I couldn't deal with her pain.

She rolled on the condom I'd handed her and took my cock in her mouth, slowly. I felt her warm tongue dance around me. Flicking, teasing, sucking. Damn, this bitch was good. Sometimes while getting a blowjob I couldn't help but imagine the whore was my girlfriend, or even my wife. That she loved me, was faithful to me, lived for pleasing me, and that having me take care of her even for just a few months out of the year was worth enduring the loneliness when I was gone. That she respected how I saw being a SEAL as more than a job—it was my calling.

I opened my eyes and placed my hand on the back of her head, her dark, wiry hair bobbing up and down. She stopped for a second, looked me dead in the eyes, and shifted from kneeling to sitting on her left side, exposing her right ankle. It had a tattoo of a surfboard painted with the American flag—why would a woman in the Caribbean have an American tattoo. Weird.

She got back down to business.

I didn't want to come, didn't want this moment to be over. But fuck, it had been so damn long. I mean, I barely even jerked off in my rack because my buddies were in the ones right next to mine.

Her mouth sucked on me hard, pulling and pushing. Man, why did this feel so good even with the latex barrier between us?

I couldn't hold back any longer—I exploded into the condom.

She handed me a towel. I took off the condom, threw it in the trash, cleaned myself up and then pulled on my shorts. This part was awkward, always was. At least she hadn't spoken, so her voice wouldn't haunt my dreams or my conscience.

Her lashes blinked twice, as if she was deep in thought and wanted to tell me something. I didn't want to know her problems—I just wanted to get the fuck out of there.

I threw down five twenties and pushed myself off the cot. She stood up on her tiptoes, took my hand, and her lips grazed my ear, making sure to shield her hair over her mouth.

"My name is Annie Hamilton. I'm an American citizen. I was kidnapped on spring break five years ago. You're my last hope. Please save me."

What the fuck? This bitch wanted me to believe she was a sex-trafficked American? What kind of con was this heroin-addicted whore trying to pull on me?

"I gotta go." I shoved her off me. This was not my problem. She was not my problem. I walked out of that smelly room and didn't look back.

The streets of Aruba were bustling now in the early evening; tourists strolling through this idyllic Caribbean island, unaware that around the corner from where they were buying shot glasses and sundries, women were turning tricks for less than the price of their margaritas. The view of the beach was blocked by the endless taxicabs and the cobblestone streets were littered with cigarette butts.

Dammit. Of all the brothels, all the whores, why did I go there? Why did I choose her? I didn't need this shit. I headed to the closest bar to get drunk. Not one of those pretty tourist joints which served up fruity drinks. A seedy local dive, which offered nothing but hard liquor. No pictures of palm trees and beaches. The walls were barren, the air was thick with tobacco, and the bar stools had been cut with blades.

I should've listened to Kyle and fucked some college girl.

"Tequila, straight."

The bartender poured me a drink, then another. Smooth, sweet, salty, tart.

The more the liquor flowed, the more I tried to push her out of my mind. I thought about my dog back home, my mother, my ex-fiancée, my truck. I made small talk with the bartender; lied about my job, told him I was a tourist on a business retreat.

By the end of the night, I was blazed senseless. I stumbled back to the USS Ronald Reagan, our huge, naval nuclear-powered super carrier, and collapsed onto my rack.

There was one problem. Her voice. She had spoken with a perfect American accent; sounded like she was from California. And her vaguely familiar face now made me think I had seen her picture once in a magazine.

Christ. One fucking blowjob and now the whore was a constant presence in my brain. Maybe Kyle was right—I did need to get laid more often.

I closed my eyes and tried to sleep, praying to erase her from my memory.

Continue reading *Invincible*
Available now at your favorite online retailer.

Linda's Bio

LINDA BARLOW IS THE AUTHOR of 25 novels, with more on the way. She lives in New England with her spouse (who sleeps during the day, which has often made her wonder if he's a vampire) and their equally enigmatic and nocturnal cat.

Linda has written in various genres, including historical and contemporary romance, romantic suspense, paranormal romance, New Adult romance, family sagas, and general mainstream fiction. Publishers have included Doubleday, Dell, Penguin, Warner Books, Hachette, New American Library/Signet, Berkley/Putnam, Silhouette and Harlequin.

Linda is a *New York Times* and a *USA Today* bestselling author. She's proud to have earned a few awards over the years, including the Rita from Romance Writers of America for *Leaves of Fortune*; New Historical Novelist of the year from *Romantic Times* for *Fires of Destiny*; and a Career Achievement award from *RT*.

Alana's Bio

ALANA ALBERTSON IS THE PRESIDENT of Romance Writers of America's Contemporary Romance chapter and former President of RWA's Young Adult and Chick Lit chapters. Alana Albertson holds a Masters of Education from Harvard University and a Bachelor of Arts in English from Stanford University.

A recovering professional ballroom dancer, Alana currently writes new adult, romantic suspense, contemporary romance and paranormal young adult romance. She lives in San Diego, California, with her husband, two young sons, and four dogs. When she's not spending her time needlepointing, dancing, or saving dogs from high kill shelters through Pugs N Roses, the rescue she founded, she can be found watching episodes of House Hunters, Homeland, or Dallas Cowboys Cheerleaders: Making the Team.

49103379R00182

Made in the USA
Lexington, KY
25 January 2016